Down the Figure 7

the

Figure

A FICTIONAL
MEMOIR

TREVOR HOYLE

To Glyn & Liz (May 2010)

POMONA

Trevor Hoyle

A Pomona Book

P - 0 1 9

Published by Pomona Books 2009
PO Box 50, Hebden Bridge, West Yorkshire HX7 8WA, England, UK
Telephone 01422 846900 · e-mail admin@pomonauk.co.uk

www.pomonauk.co.uk

1

A CIP catalogue record for this book
is available from the British Library

ISBN 978-1-904590-25-5

Every effort has been made to trace and give credit to the copyright holders
of the images in this book. Anyone not traced should contact the
publishers to be credited in any future editions.

Cover photo: Mary Evans Picture Library / Roger Mayne

Set in Monotype Perpetua
Typeset by Christian Brett

Printed and bound in England by
CPI Cox & Wyman, Reading, RG1 8EX

This book, which is dedicated to the Denby gang,
is a work of fiction. While some of the streets and places
are real, the characters and situations are imaginary
and exist only in the mind of the author.

*

Also dedicated to the memory of my friend,
another Rochdale lad and a fine writer:

Mike Stott
1944 − 2009

†

Parts of this fictional memoir have been published in magazines, broadcast on BBC Radio 4, and dramatised by the author in the BBC radio play "Conflagration".

The chapter "Down the Figure 7" was the winning British entry in the *Transatlantic Review* short story competition.

The book won the Ray Mort Northern Novel prize.

*

I should like to thank the following people
for their generous help and advice in locating
and supplying photographs and images for this book:
Julian Jefferson, Arts & Heritage Manager,
David Pugh, Museum Officer,
Andrew Moore, Collections Manager,
Joan Hinds and Lorraine Ashworth,
Arts & Heritage Service, Rochdale.
Chris Lloyd, Assistant Editor, and Katie Fitzpatrick
of the *Rochdale Observer*.
And Julie Stevens-Smith.

CONTENTS

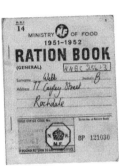

R.B.1
14

MINISTRY OF FOOD
1951-1952

RATION BOOK

(GENERAL)

WNBC 254:3

Surname *Webb*   Initials *B*

Address *77 Cayley Street*

Rochdale

FOOD OFFICE CODE No.   SERIAL No. of RATION BOOK

N M R
M.F.   BP 121030

IF FOUND RETURN TO ANY FOOD OFFICE

Part 1

The Denby Gang

*

WHEN THE MISTY BLUE NOVEMBER NIGHTS came on there was always that extra-special magic in the air because the weeks of collecting bommie wood now seemed worthwhile, what with the 5th only days away.

The Gang had been scrounging for wood since the first week in October, storing it in backyards next to outside lavatories and in the damp gloomy interiors of concrete air-raid shelters. The shelters had never served their true purpose, even at the height of the bombing, because the town was some distance from the nearest prime target, the Old Trafford docks; only a single stick had fallen in the vicinity, obliterating two houses in Sudden, when the raiders had been seeking the Dunlop Tyre factory and over-shot by a couple of miles. Now the shelters were used as military headquarters when the gang played at war, the British *v.* the Jerries – or, if they got bored with that, the Yanks *v.* the Nips.

This small area of sooty terraced houses, streets, alleyways, pens and allotments known as Denby (though no one knew why) comprised the battleground, with each army leaving two men on guard at HQ and stalking the enemy in raiding parties of three or four, lurking in shadowed doorways, signalling with candles in jam-jars, planning top secret rendezvous on corners where the gaslamps fluffed and stuttered.

During the hours of daylight the streets belonged to grown-ups: workers on their way to the Clover and Croft mills; delivery vans bringing supplies of Brasso and Ovaltine, Fynon's Liver

Salts and Reckitt's Dolly Blue to Wellens's corner shop; housewives with their hair in curlers over which they wore lumpy printed scarves knotted under their chins, setting out for the evening shift, 7 – 9.30, at Oswald & Duncan's. But afterwards (when the mist curled from the river and hung in streamers above the slate rooftops and the stone setts gleamed under the lamps) Denby became a deadly battlefield whose silence and darkness were rent by bursts of adenoidal machine-gun fire and the blood-curdling shriek of yet another adolescent Hun on his way to the Fatherland in the sky. No quarter was sought, none given; few prisoners were taken; bloody annihilation was preferred to a mere flesh wound, spectacular instant death to tame surrender.

This world was circumscribed by the geography of streets, alleys and ginnels, by the joys of unbounded imagination when an old worn cotton bobbin became, in the right hands, a polished high-precision weapon capable of wiping out an entire platoon, and the Bottom Track after dark the haunt of the undead where at any moment Frankenstein's monster might stumble mechanically from the shadows or Count Dracula rise up like an undertaker's shroud from the long grass, eyes bloodshot, fangs all agleam, nails curved into talons and twitching with lust for warm human flesh. Phantoms of the night were as palpable as the woman who kept the corner shop or the coalman humping bags of nutty slack from the horse and cart to the cellar grate outside the front door. You believed, at ten years old, that the world was infinitely beautiful, mysterious, terrifying; a place of dark wonder, cruelty, and boredom.

By nine o'clock most of the gang had decided it was time to go in or were being called by their mothers from the back step. They departed reluctantly, dawdling for a moment under the gaslamps, until the group had dwindled to the usual hardcore who huddled against the corroding wall of the Good Shepherd Church telling ghost stories or loitered in the doorway of the empty shop on the corner of Hovingham Street, swapping dirty jokes and speculating in random fashion on the procreation of the species. Being older, Dave Spencer, who everybody called Spenner, seemed to know a lot about the subject, and Terry Webb and Alec Bland wanted to stay and learn more. But already they'd heard the call: they would have to contain their curiosity and wait for another night to discover whether babies appeared from the navel or by way of some other orifice.

Terry's mam was baking, leaning over the scrubbed kitchen table with flour up to her elbows, kneading and twisting the dough; the covering of flour camouflaged her red veined hands. His father was asleep in the rocking-chair in front of the black-leaded grate, bare feet stuck into worn slippers, stomach rising and falling, soft grunted snores making his lower lip shudder. Terry prised off his boots and threw them under the square pot sink with the curly cast-iron legs. His mother said, 'Don't wake your father, you know what he's like.' Her mousy brown hair was piled on top of her head, wisps of it trailing on her neck.

'Anything to eat?' Terry said. He was a good-looking lad, and well aware of the fact, though not too big for his age.

'What do you want?'

'What have we got?'

'Shredded Wheat,' his mother said, opening the cupboard door with her elbow and reaching down the packet. Terry took his bowl to the stool in the corner by the sink, avoiding leaning against the bare plaster wall which was wet with condensation. He scooped up the Shredded Wheat and milk, being careful to leave the dissolved sugar in the bottom of the bowl till last. His large brown eyes stared unseeingly into the glowing coals, the spoon moving from bowl to mouth. He was thinking about the discussion they had been having in the shop doorway. Of course he knew (though found it hard to credit) how women got babies, but somebody had said that to get the baby out they had to ... no, he couldn't believe it. How could you cut someone with a knife from their belly-button to their bottom, extract an awkward thing like a baby and sew the split up again?

He glanced covertly at his mother's pelvic region, slightly distended beneath the faded cotton pinny, and knew that it couldn't be so. For one thing, what stopped all their insides falling out?

The galvanised bath on the wall in the small backyard clanked against the brickwork as the wind swooped low over the grey slate roofs: some kind of bird squawked in the distance as it circled the ash-tips across the black river: a spatter of rain hit the window pane like bits of gravel.

'It's half-past nine,' his mother said without looking up, trimming a frayed circle of pastry from the edge of the dish.

'I want to read.'

'You know what your father will say, Terry.'

She was a small, round-shouldered, frail-looking woman with the eyes, nose and chin that Terry had inherited, though her frailness was deceiving. She had borne almost four children, one of which, the first, had died of diptheria at the age of eighteen months, and one that didn't count: a miscarriage at five months. She had once been pretty, with sharp striking features, but now at the age of thirty-seven the daily grind of work and bringing up kids and making ends meet had begun to show on her face: the sparkle still twinkled occasionally in her eyes but the face was now tired, dispirited, dimmed by the kind of life that washed the best out of you before you were forty. Why, there had been times in her twenties when Barbara Webb had danced all night at the Carlton – she had been a good dancer too, and so had Joe, before his stomach sagged and his young man's muscles ran to fat. You had your young fun and spent the rest of your life paying for it.

'Where's our kid?'

'Where do you think; in bed.'

'Can I read for a bit?'

4

'Go on then.' His mother was stacking the baking utensils in the sink. 'Ten minutes. You know your father gets aeriated if you stay up late.' She wiped her hands on the towel hanging on the wooden rail behind the back door, then ruffled his hair. 'Do you want a drink, love?'

Terry said, 'Give over, mam,' hunching his shoulders to avoid her hand. He rummaged under the cushion looking for the *Rover*; he was halfway through reading a 'Tough of the Track' story, with Terry's favourite hero, Alf Tupper.

'Too big for a bit of love and affection, are we?'

'I don't like to be marded.'

'Go on, our Terry. I can remember when you used to sit on me knee for hours at a time. "In't he lovely, Mrs Webb. What big brown eyes! He'll break a few hearts when he grows up."' She laughed at the expression on his face and set the kettle on the gas-ring.

Joe Webb grumbled a little in his sleep and came slowly awake, his belly heaving underneath his pants and vest. He was a year younger than Barbara but already his hair was receding and there were flecks of grey at the temples. He was a taciturn man, not given much to jollity, and in his younger days had knocked about the local amateur boxing rings. His arms were huge, running to flab, and there was a pale scar on his right bicep where the ropes had burned it. The first thing he said was:

'You still up?'

'I'm just making him a drink, Joe.'

Terry's head was buried in the *Rover*. His father had nothing more to say to him and he had nothing to say to his father. The nearest they ever came to communication was when his dad helped Terry with his pigeons: he had lifted the makeshift pigeon cote (two bobbin crates nailed together) onto the roof of the lavatory single-handed and held it in position while Terry nailed it to the battens. And before he went to work in the mornings he let the half-dozen birds out and fed them: from the back bedroom window Terry had actually seen him holding out his heavy blunt hands filled with corn and black peas and calling softly to the dark fluttering shapes in the grey morning air.

'Right then,' Joe said, leaning back and scratching under his arms, 'don't be all night.' The rocking-chair creaked with his weight.

Terry sipped his cocoa and didn't look up. He wouldn't meet his father's eyes.

His mother said, 'I saw Mrs Pickup in Wellens's today; she says their Roy's doing really well at the High School. He does look smart in his uniform.'

'What did that lot cost?' Joe said. 'Not a farthing under ten quid I bet. Course, they can afford it, they've only got the one lad.'

'He's got his chance, though, hasn't he?' Barbara said, picking up her knitting. She put her hand to the back of her neck. 'There in't half a draught from that cellar door, Joe. Can't you nail a bit of sacking round it or something?'

'He's got a real leather satchel,' Terry said.

'Another three quids' worth,' his father said, firmly entrenched in his favourite topic. 'I hope you don't pass for yon bloody place, otherwise we won't have two ha'pennies to rub together.'

'Joe, what a thing to say to the lad.' Barbara Webb's expression was hurt, resentful. She wanted the best for their Terry, even if it did mean sacrifices. When Sylvia was old enough she intended getting a part-time job at Cowling's, the confectioner's on Entwisle Road, or going along with Bessie Smith to the house-wives' shift at Oswald & Duncan's. If you couldn't give your kids a proper start in life what was the point of anything – all this scratching and scrimping and making every penny stretch that little bit farther? But Joe didn't see it that way. He was like a man floundering in a quicksand: the harder he struggled the deeper he sank. His life was oppressed as if by a great weight – a millstone – gradually forcing him down, down; and all his vast strength

6

seemed powerless to prevent it; it was wasted strength, futile, impotent.

The wind rattled the window frame and the bath clanked in the backyard. Terry folded his comic and put his empty beaker in the sink. He opened the stairs door and was about to say goodnight when Joe said:

'Aren't you having a wash?'

'I'll have one in the morning.'

'Not much good in the morning, is it, when you've been sleeping in your muck all night.'

'Leave him be, Joe, leave him,' his mother said. She looked tired and rather old, the mousy hair held up by pins with strands of it falling across her forehead. The day was long enough without bickering.

Terry went up the narrow dark stairs, feeling his way round the bend, and tiptoed across the lino into the back bedroom in his stocking feet. The room was cold. He daren't switch the light on in case it woke Sylvia (then his mother would be onto him too) but undressed quickly in the dark, down to his vest, and laid himself flat on the square of carpet in a prone position. With his hands spreadeagled under his chest he straightened his arms and did twenty press-ups, feeling the muscles tensing and slackening in his shoulders and stomach. He had started with ten, increased it to fifteen, and was now up to twenty; next week twenty-five.

Panting very slightly Terry got into the single bed between the freezing sheets and curled up into a ball. He remembered something: got out of bed and as slowly and quietly as he could removed the top right-hand drawer from the dresser. His fingers moved along the dusty ledge until, right at the back, they encountered a small packet. He took it to the window, opened the curtains a crack, and counted the four-and-a-half Woodbines. He thought for a moment of smoking the dimp but then decided it was too risky, and besides, he hadn't any matches. Back in bed, the covers pulled over his head, he snuggled himself into the smallest possible area and waited for the slow warmth of sleep to take the numbness from his bones. On the other side of the room Sylvia's breathing came in short wheezing gasps: she had trouble with her adenoids and slept with her mouth open. He hoped she wasn't going to start grinding her teeth. The wheezing he could put up with but the grinding got on his nerves.

Tiredness began to press down on him. He could hear the dim murmur of voices from the kitchen below. The same bird cried out across the dirty, slow-moving stream of the river, rolling onwards past the ash-tips and the paint depot and the Yelloway coach station until it disappeared into the tunnel under the town centre. In his dwindling mind's eye he saw Spenner's face with its ragged fringe of red hair and row of yellow teeth. Spenner was two and a bit years older than Terry and if anybody knew how babies were born it was surely him. He remembered when Syl had been born, in the front bedroom, and a vision of his mother's pale damp face came to his mind: she had looked sapped of all strength, washed out, and he recalled thinking at the time how glad he was not to be a woman and have to go through all that.

Terry fell asleep, his breath steaming gently in the cold air, his last conscious image of babies popping out from everywhere: navels, arseholes, ears, mouths ...

Simple Annie

*

TERRY HAD GONE THROUGH A 'RELIGIOUS' PHASE the year before, going to church three times on a Sunday. This was for two reasons: first, he was a member of the Church Lads' Brigade, and in order to qualify for your cap, tunic and belt you had to have a good record of church attendance; second, there were a couple of girls Terry fancied – Jean Ashmore and Betty Wheatcroft – who sat together like two sweet-smelling primroses on the third pew from the front, left-hand aisle. They were both in his class at school, and twice he had been dinner monitor with Betty but hadn't had the nerve to ask her to go with him. Jean was the better looking of the two, with a round face, dark sparkling eyes and a delicate bloom in her cheeks. He had tried to kiss her once in the schoolyard, missed her mouth completely and smeared her chin instead with spit. He hadn't been able to look at her for three days after that without going red.

Terry liked going to Heybrook. He enjoyed most of the lessons and was usually in the first half-dozen when they had exams. Mrs Butterworth, his teacher, had told him he could be top of the class if he concentrated more. 'Why you and Alec Bland have to be so silly, Terry, I don't know.'

The pair of them were sometimes silly, it was true, passing notes back and forth with rude words and drawings on them, and dipping Brenda Harrison's pigtails in the inkwell. But she was toffee-nosed, Brenda Harrison, and nobody like her.

Coming home from school one day (it was the first week in November), Terry, Alec Bland and Malc Smith were crossing Yorkshire Street and about to turn down Oswald Street when they heard a muffled shout. Terry glanced up at the iron railway bridge almost directly above them and saw a grimy hand sticking out from between the riveted stanchions giving them the vee-sign. It was followed by a mop of red hair, and underneath that, Spenner's grinning mug. The three lads scrambled up the embankment and shinned over the wooden fence that was made out of old railway sleepers, their tops cut into points.

'I've found a stack of wood.' Spenner was excited. 'You know Wardleworth Station? The one they've shut down? Loads of it: doors, benches, tables, window-frames, the lot.'

'How we going to get it all the way back to Denby?' Malc Smith said. 'It's miles.'

'Is it buggery; a mile at most,' said Spenner, who was twelve-and-three quarters and therefore had a better conception of distance.

Alec Bland looked dubious. 'Still too far to carry all that bommie.'

Spenner curled his lip and said scathingly, '*Bogies*, you pie-can. Wait till tonight and take the bogies along th'Arches and load 'em up. Us lot and some more of the lads could shift tons of stuff. Dead easy!'

Something had occurred to Terry. He said, 'We'll have to pass South Street.'

There were two rival gangs in the area, Gowers Street and South Street, and of the two the South Street mob was the worst.

'Who's chicken-shit scared of South Street?' Spenner said jeeringly; he slouched with his hands in his pockets and kicked at one of the rusting stanchions. The three smaller boys watched him, unsure and a bit fearful, uncertain what went on in a big lad's head. 'Not scared of Brian Creegan, are you?'

No one said anything because this was precisely who they were scared of. South Street were mostly big lads, and Brian Creegan's reputation as a sadistic nutcase struck terror into younger kids.

'I don't think me mam'll let me stay out that late,' Malc said, chewing his thumbnail. He was a full half-inch smaller than Terry and Alec and this always seemed to put him at a disadvantage, or he thought it did.

'Mard bugger,' Spenner snarled, and gave Malc a push in the chest. 'His mam won't let him stay out that late,' he taunted in a jeering whine.

Terry was glad it was Malc and not him that Spenner was getting at; all the same he didn't feel too comfortable about it either. Malc sat next to him in 4A, they were good pals, and Terry liked him.

The four of them walked down Oswald Street, crossed Entwisle Road near the UCP tripe shop and went behind the hoardings which advertised Rinso 'for Whites that are Whiter than New!'and Mansion Polish and Dinneford's Pure Fluid Magnesia.

This was the Common: a rough square of dirt and cinders enclosed on all four sides by the hoardings, the Arches, a foul trickling stream called the Hey, and the bare brick ends of two rows of houses. The Common was the Gang's cricket pitch in summer, its football field in winter, and it was here they built their bonfire. And behind the hoardings on most dark nights you could find one or two of the older lads groping the girls.

A low stone wall bordered the brook, the water sluggish and sulphurous with swirling patterns of brown and purple and dirty white. A grey viscous tidemark of chemical scum clung to the far bank: the residue of the Eclipse, Rydings and Buckley mills upstream. At this time of year the brook was fairly innocuous, but in the heat of summer the smell rose in dense torpid waves, sickly and slightly sweetish, like rotting meat, infiltrating through open back doors into the kitchens of houses even as far as Hovingham Street.

Spenner issued final instructions. 'You tell Mitch and Danny, Terry. Alec can tell Roy Pickup and I'll see the others.' He was exultant. 'It'll be bloody great' – he hunched his body low down – 'ten of us creeping along th'Arches with our bogies, sneaking in under Creegan's nose and raiding Wardleworth Station! Eh, Terry?'

Terry nodded. He could feel the tension rising in his chest. Scrounging for bommie in the South Street gang's territory. Bloody Nora. It was exciting all right, but he was scared and wasn't sure he really wanted to go. He said calmly, 'About eight?'

Spenner nodded. He was picking his nose and examining the results on his fingers. 'Yeh, we'll all meet up here, on't Common. Tell 'em to bring as many bogies as they can. We're going to need six or seven at least —'

He jerked his head up. He said softly, 'Look who's coming. Owd Riggy.'

Through the iron railings the lads could see old Ma Rigall tottering slowly down Cayley Street in her worn pointed shoes and wrinkled black woollen stockings. She lived next door to Terry at number seventy-nine, alone in filth and squalor. The house was a tip and stank of cat pee, and once when Terry had gone down her cellar-grate because she'd locked herself out he had to hold his breath while he stumbled to unlock the front door and rushed out gasping into the fresh air. She had given him an apple for his trouble, which Terry, having seen *Snow White and the Seven Dwarfs*, had chucked into the brook.

The lads crouched behind the low brick wall, just their heads showing, their noses poking through the railings, and chanted:

'Rigall is a Witch, Rigall is a Witch . . . Ee-Aye-Addio, Rigall is a Witch.'

Ma Rigall perked her head up inside her shawl, the face like an ancient yellow prune with dirt etched into the cracks as into a scrap of soiled parchment. She carried a string shopping bag of indeterminate colour and her hands were like claws, with black curved nails.

'Dirty Old Witch, Dirty Old Witch!'

Ma Rigall crossed the muddy street, avoiding the puddles. She had to bear these taunts, as well as having bangers pushed through her letterbox and dead cats thrown over her backyard gate. Partial deafness and near blindness meant that she was isolated in a dim private world, lost in her own loneliness, but even so she heard the taunts.

'Terry Webb! Alec Bland! David Spencer!'

It was Bessie Smith, Malcolm's mam, poking her fat red face into things as usual. She was a large woman, broad-shouldered and big-bosomed, and carried her ample body like a sergeant-major on parade. At the moment she was leaning out of her front bedroom window, pointing a finger at them as steady as a Colt 45.

'I can see you, don't think I can't! I'll tell your mothers. Get off home, the lot of you.'

Spenner was staring up at her with a perfectly bland, innocent expression on his face, while below the level of the wall both hands were giving her vigorous vee-signs. Terry's face cracked in a smile and Mrs Smith shouted, 'Right, Terry Webb. Just wait till I see your mother!'

Bessie Smith's face disappeared and the window slammed shut.

Spenner jumped onto the low wall bordering the brook, pretending to lose his balance and teetering on the balls of his feet, arms circling backwards like the sails of a windmill.

Terry said, 'I'll have to go in for me tea.'

Spenner said, 'What you having, bread and spit?'

'No,' Terry said. 'Shit with sugar on.'

Joe came into the small, steamy, overheated kitchen in his greasy raincoat and heavy boots, smelling of metal turnings and machine-oil. He pulled a wadded bundle from his pocket, grimy in the folds from spending all day in the locker of an engineering works. Tuesdays he brought home the *Adventure* and the *Wizard,* Thursdays the *Rover* and the *Hotspur.* The *Rover* was Terry's favourite because it had the best stories: 'The Tough of the Track', 'Morgyn the Mighty', and Nick Smith, the football hero of 'It's Goals That Count'.

Sometimes Joe would relax enough to wrestle Terry to the floor in a claustrophobic bear-hug, rubbing his sandpaper chin against Terry's cheeks until they were inflamed and burning. Barbara would say: 'You're far too rough with him, Joe, you'll hurt him.'

'You mard him too much,' Joe replied. 'You'll have the lad growing up a cissy.'

Terry still had a vivid memory of that time last summer when he lifted half-a-dozen flags in the backyard, intending to make a vegetable garden between Ma Rigall's wall and the outside lavatory. Joe came home from work and the first thing he did, even before sitting down to his tea, was to march straight outside and lay them all down again. Barabra had to physically restrain him from taking extreme retribution; as it was, Terry got a crack that sent him reeling across the kitchen and head-first into the back door, which made him literally see stars.

There had been another incident last summer that Terry found himself smiling at every time he recalled it, involving Simple Annie, who was the younger sister of Mad Johnnie Johnson.

Annie was eight or thereabouts: a dirty, bedraggled girl with matted hair and dark staring eyes, always in the same torn frock and wearing clogs on her bare feet, the ankles caked with dirt. As usual he had been out playing with Alec and Malc, the three of them messing about (which they shouldn't have been) in Sam Clegg's coalyard at the back of Terry's house.

It was mid-summer, the day baking hot, the tar melting and bubbling in-between the stone setts and seeping sluggishly into the drainage grids. The three of them were mixing mud, dropping a tin can on the end of a piece of string into the brook and using the discoloured water to shape mud pies, which were then lined up on a stone slab to dry in the sun. Alec and Malc mixed while Terry decorated the pies with dandelions and dock leaves. They looked appetizing on the slab, and when Simple Annie drifted by they called her over and told her how tasty they were, and which flavour did she prefer, and would she like to try one?

Simple Annie sat down cross-legged, her bony knees sticking out, and picked up a pie in her grimy little paws. Then Terry had a fiendish idea. He said that before she could eat it she had to play Truth, Dare, Force or Promise. Simple Annie gazed at him incomprehendingly out of a blank face and vacant eyes, and Terry said quickly, while he had the nerve, almost stammering it: 'I dare you to show us your bum.' (It was a well-known fact that Simple Annie never wore any knickers.) She stood up at once, lifted her ragged dress, and the three of them sat in a circle, leaning forward for a better view. There wasn't much to see, and what there was was mostly covered in dirt.

When their curiosity had been satisfied and they reckoned the forfeit had been paid, Terry said, 'All right, Annie, you can have the pie now,' and Simple Annie crammed it into her mouth and wolfed it down.

The three of them looked at one another, shocked and amazed, and a bit frightened. They hoped that mud wasn't poisonous or that the stinking water of the brook wouldn't give her a disease.

'Do you really like them?' Terry asked her.

'Mmm,' Simple Annie said. Her little pink pointed tongue came out and licked a few crumbs of mud from the sides of her mouth. 'Can I have 'nother please?'

If Simple Annie was a harmless simpleton, her brother was a raving nutter.

Mad Johnnie Johnson didn't belong to any gang (it's doubtful whether any gang would have tolerated him): he was a loner who came and went mysteriously. You might see him chasing rabbits across the ash-tips, firing at them with his Diana air pistol, or building a fire for himself dangerously close to the wooden garages under the Arches. The truth was, the other lads were scared of him because his behaviour was completely unpredictable – such as the time he tied an old car inner-tube to a length of rope, which he fixed to a telegraph pole, and performed a wild yelling Tarzan act over the brook, skimming the rusted bedsteads and slimy green house bricks and whirlpools of scum. Sometimes his feet struck the water but Johhnie didn't care. Then one of his shoes came off and sailed away, without him bothering to retrieve it.

A little crowd gathered. It was good spectator sport, and besides, everyone knew what was bound to happen sooner or later, and of course it did: the inner-tube snapped and Johnnie fell into the brook. It wasn't more than two feet deep but he went completely under and emerged with the foul liquid dripping from his hair and a gaping stupid grin on his face. There was an appreciative spatter of applause as he crawled up the bank, barefoot, with his trousers stuck to his legs.

Terry recalled, with a sense of disbelief even now, what Mad Johnnie Johnson did next: how he built a fire against one of the brick archways, stripped down to just his yellowing shrunken vest that finished at the navel, and sat drying his clothing while a semi-circle of nine- and ten-year old girls gazed wide-eyed at the willy of this fifteen-year old youth. Dusk came on and the group huddled closer as he told them ghost stories in the cosy fireglow and held up his trousers to dry.

Across the brook, Terry and the other members of the Gang lounged on the wall, lobbing stones into the water and making crude, sarcastic remarks, loud enough for Mad Johnnie Johnson to hear; still, they kept their distance.

Scrounging for Bommie

*

T HE GANG ASSEMBLED AT EIGHT O'CLOCK: THERE were nine of them altogether, with five bogies and an old pram with buckled wheels. Malc Smith wanted to bring his kid brother but the others wouldn't let him.

'Suppose we have to run for it,' Kevin Hartley said, 'he wouldn't stand a chance. And we couldn't wait for him.' Malc Smith's kid brother went home scriking his eyes out.

They wheeled their bogies across the wooden footbridge at the end of Gowers Street and climbed the embankment: the Arches loomed above them in the darkness, the huge semi-circular archways of Victorian brick rising out of the mist that drifted like steam from the river. There was a nip of frost in the air, the grass on the embankment a ghostly frozen white crackling underfoot like splintered glass. Terry looked over the mill-stone parapet and saw, far below, the gaslamps of Denby gleaming faintly, dim glow-worms all in a row. He felt suddenly afraid and wished the scrounging expedition was over and done with. Why did they have to go to Wardleworth Station anyway? There was tons of wood to be had without traipsing miles to get it – and without running the risk of a gang fight with the South Street mob. Some of them carried half house-bricks and Tizer bottles broken off at the neck.

In single file, Spenner leading the way, they crossed over Entwisle Road, then Yorkshire Street, cars speeding underneath with their yellow lights fanning out, and were soon approaching the deserted station. With the closure of the Rugby Road LMS Cotton Warehouse the station was no longer used: a cluster of abandoned buildings with rusted tracks disappearing into an overgrowth of stunted grass and dandelion leaves. So far nobody had dared speak, until Malc said in a hoarse whisper: 'I can see a light.'

Everybody froze. Then Dougie Milne said, 'It is nowt.'

'It's miles away,' Spenner said. 'Up Syke somewhere. Come on, don't be yeller.'

They crept up onto the platforms and started tearing doors off their hinges, gently at first, with consideration and the minimum of noise, and then with increasing force as the thrill of destruction overcame them. Kevin Hartley swung a bucket of sand through a window and wrenched out the frame, scattering glass everywhere, and Roy Pickup set to work with a hacksaw blade, cutting an LMS bench into manageable portions.

'Give us a hand with this,' Spenner said to Terry, and together they hung onto the guttering and brought it crashing down, almost crowning Danny Travis in the process. The station was filled with the clamour of banging, hammering, smashing and sawing as the gang tore the buildings to pieces – haphazardly and yet with great efficiency – as a group of lads can do when toiling earnestly as if to some methodical, carefully-worked-out plan. They were adept at destruction and went about their task joyfully.

After twenty minutes the bogies were loaded to the gunnels and they took a break, sitting amidst the wreckage and passing Woodbine dimps from hand to hand. Terry had forgotten his fear. He dragged on the dimp and felt the satisfying contentment of comradeship and of a job well done. He still wasn't completely sure about being accepted as one of the older members of the gang and not just a snivelling mard-arse kid. He thought back to the time when he'd been a scrotty eight-year-old, when he, Alec Bland and Malc Smith had been on the fringe of things and never

been allowed to go on raiding parties, always being told by the big lads to stand guard over the bommie and keep a look-out for Mad Johnnie Johnson and stop him crapping on the roof of the air-raid shelter, which he was wont to do.

Spenner started to sing softly, and it was taken up by the others:

'Don't eat Brierley's bread
It makes your shit like lead
No bloody wonder
You fart like thunder
Don't eat Brierley's bread.'

It was getting late; Terry would get murdered if he wasn't in by half-past nine. At the same time he couldn't suggest moving till one of the older lads did, or he'd be branded a soft cock.

'Anybody fancy the flicks this week?' Dougie asked, the glow of the dimp lighting up his squarish chin with the faint white scar across it.

'Ceylon Saturday afternoon?' somebody suggested.

Roy Pickup said shortly, 'Don't be stupid. If we're having the bommie Saturday night we'll have to stack the wood Saturday afternoon.' Roy was in the second year at High School and already had come to regard himself as a cut above the rest. When you took the eleven-plus one of three things happened: either you were one of the bright boys and joined the elite ten per cent at the High School in their smart green blazers and caps, or you passed for the Technical College, which was supposed to be for the joiners, plumbers and pattern-makers of the future, or failing these you stayed on at the Secondary Modern and simply moved up one floor; in other words you became one of the dregs. There was some prestige in passing for the High School, but of even greater merit was to have won a scholarship to De La Salle College in Middleton, which was what Phil Kershaw had done.

'We'll miss Part Ten of *Flash Gordon Conquers the Universe*.' Alec Bland said.

'You go if you want to,' Kevin Hartley said. 'But don't expect to come to the bommie Saturday night. Anybody who doesn't help stack the wood isn't coming to the bommie. That's the rule.'

'Me mam's making some black peas,' Alec said defensively.

'So what?'

'Mine's making some parkin.'

'Mine's making treacle toffee.'

'Well?' Alec said uncertainly.

'*Well?*' several voices said together.

Spenner flicked his fag-end into the darkness and it exploded in a shower of sparks amongst the rusted tracks. Billy Mitchell, known as Mitch, said: 'We'll have to be quiet going back and keep our heads down.'

'Single file, no talking, keep low,' Spenner said, grabbing hold of the rope of his bogie.

'All right, all right,' Kevin Hartley said. 'We know you fancy

20

yourself as bleeding Rommel. We're not thick, you know. Some of us can even read and write.'

'Who's Rommel?' Alec Bland asked Terry in an undertone.

'A German General,' Terry said, not absolutely sure. He remembered vaguely that his Uncle Jack (who he was proud to boast had been one of the real Desert Rats) had mentioned the name a few times.

The bogies rattled and bumped over the sleepers until, clear of the station, they came to the narrow beaten path that ran alongside the track. They had to cross the iron bridge over Yorkshire Street and travel quite some distance along open embankment before reaching the safety of the parapet that marked the beginning of the Arches. South Street butted onto the railway line at right-angles, a steep grassy bank sloping down to the backyards of a row of houses. The haze from the lads' breaths rose in clouds in the chill dark air.

As they were approaching the danger zone Spenner stopped abruptly and Alec Bland walked into the back of him.

'What's up?' several voices hissed.

Spenner got down on his knees and the others did the same. Ahead of them a short distance and to their right, on a piece of waste ground at the bottom of the banking, half a dozen lads were gathered round a small fire. Terry felt his stomach contract. He badly wanted to urinate. With tremendous caution the gang proceeded, crouched double; the bogies seemed to be making a hell of a racket and the pram's wheels were squeaking loud enough to wake the dead.

They passed by the firelit group, hardly daring to breathe, and were within yards of the millstone parapet when one of the front wheels of Danny Travis's bogie fell off, the bogie tipped, and the entire load of wood spilled down the embankment.

Somebody pushed Terry savagely in the back and shouted, 'Run!' and he was pulling hard on the rope and stumbling along, his heart hammering in his chest, the night suddenly transformed into dark running shapes and wild yells and squealing bogie wheels. The South Street gang came scrambling up the embankment, slipping on the frosty grass and uttering maniacal noises that made Terry's blood run cold. He wanted to leave go of the rope and forget the bogie and run for all he was worth but he couldn't until some of the others did. A clatter of sharp granite chippings landed all around and some of them bounced on the line making a series of hollow metallic clangs.

A voice cried out sharply and started yelling with real pain. A stone struck Terry on the shoulder and he nearly started scriking before he knew whether he was hurt or not. In an instant he recalled stories of what Creegan and his gang did to captured prisoners. They crammed them into dustbins, rammed the lid on tight and lit a fire underneath. Or tied them to a post, ripped their trousers open and covered their dicks with tar. There were other stories, even worse, though Terry didn't have the time or the inclination to bring them to mind.

He tripped over the protruding end of a sleeper, nearly fell, but the crawling panic in his bowels gave his legs the strength to carry on. The bogie was a dead, irksome weight, hampering him, holding him back. Leave it, he kept thinking, leave it, but couldn't, somehow he couldn't.

Spenner had stopped somewhere ahead; he was crouching behind his bogie and its load of wood, using it as a barricade, scooping up handfuls of white granite chips and flinging them at their pursuers. It was a holding operation, nothing more. The South Street gang came on – some of them, Terry noticed, *Bloody Nora*, carrying broken bottles. There was the flare of a match down the track and a fizzing banger curled gracefully through the air and went off three feet above Terry's head. He was struck deaf and blind, his eardrums reverberating with the shock, a blank brilliant globe of light where his vision should have been.

'Terry!'

His arm was nearly yanked out of its socket as someone pulled him along the track. He was still holding, unknowingly, the rope in his left hand, the laden bogie trundling after him like a punishment, an omen of ill-luck he couldn't shake off. Another banger fizzed through the air, then another and another, and there was the crack-crack-crack of three almost simultaneous explosions.

Some of the older lads – Spenner, Roy Pickup, Kevin Hartley – were mounting a counter-attack, using the granite chips as ammunition, and the other gang fell back a little way; by now the two rival forces were halfway across the Arches, directly above the Common, and it was Phil Kershaw's inspired idea to tip the wood over the parapet so that it landed inside their own territory. With the bogies empty and rattling lightly along the path by the side of the track it was fairly easy for Terry and the others to retreat out of harm's way. After a minute or two the older lads raced after them, shouting obscene abuse over their shoulders and laughing hysterically with fear, excitement and relief.

Apart from Dougie (always in the wars), who had sustained a nasty gash on the back of his leg, there were no serious casualties. Spenner leaned matily on Terry's shoulder and Terry felt great: he suddenly felt older and more important, one of the big lads.

One of the Denby gang.

Friday at the Flicks

*

O N FRIDAY NIGHT TERRY'S MAM TOOK HIM TO see *State Secret* at the Regal. The first call was always at Parkinson's on the bend near the Cloverdale public house where Barbara bought forty Woodbines and a big sixpenny bar of Needler's nut chocolate for Terry. The bus appeared out of the gloom, windows opaque with condensation, clear circular patches where people had rubbed peepholes with their gloves and elbows. They jolted into town past the Corporation Sanitary Depot and the Public Baths, down the gentle slope of Smith Street, the tyres making a peculiar sucking noise on the smooth black tarmacadam, got off outside the Electricity Showrooms and crossed over to the bright canopy of the cinema, an oasis of light with tinted photographs of Jack Hawkins, Glynis Johns and Douglas Fairbanks Jnr displayed in glass cases.

Terry loved going into town. There was always the feeling of something happening, of people going somewhere: the blue and cream buses lined up next to the glass shelters; the pubs buzzing and alive, a constant stream of people going in and spilling out; the faces under the yellow lights, smiling faces, freshly-washed, eager to celebrate the end of another working week and looking forward to the brief dizzy respite of this Friday night and the luxurious anticipation of Saturday and Sunday yet to come.

The Regal was his favourite cinema, and after that the Rialto (which had a posh cafe), Palace, Empire and Hippodrome. He wasn't all that keen on the Pavilion and Victory – they were

24

cheerless draughty places with worn carpets and hard seats with springs sticking up your behind and usually showed crackling old films made before the war. The Regal was warm and plush and sweet-smelling, and it was like going into a palace or a nob's house, the smooth marble foyer with its two semi-circular staircases leading up to the balcony, and everywhere thick red carpets, stretching from wall to wall.

They bought Butterkist at the kiosk and went through the swing doors into the thrilling darkness. Terry didn't mind what film he saw; some were better than others, of course, with adventure and fighting, but he relished them all.

During the interval he had a good look round and spotted several people he knew. There were two boys from his class sitting at the front in the ninepenny's; Betty Wheatcroft and her mother three rows from the back; and there was a pretty dark-eyed girl called Margaret Parry, the same age as Terry, who lived on Gowers Street. She messed around with Tony Shapcott's lot, so he didn't know her too well. All the same she recognised him

25

and smiled, and Terry leaned back in his seat, his heart skipping lightly and a small wicked smile on his lips.

They stood for the Anthem at the end and came out into the bright glare under the glass canopy, the cold night air striking through their clothing and raising goosepimples on Terry's bare legs. 'Shall we get the bus,' his mother said, 'or do you want some supper?'

Terry looked forward to his Friday night suppers, sitting up late with grown-up people at the tables with the big metal salt-cellar and vinegar bottle in the middle of the checked oilcloth: so they walked from the town centre along Smith Street and called in the chip shop, settling themselves in the high-backed wooden booths and waiting with relish for the large blue-patterned plates piled with chips, beef pudding done in a rag, and mushy peas, the whole mouth-watering concoction covered in thick brown gravy. A sprinkle of vinegar, a shake of the big salt pot, and to Terry it was the best food he had ever tasted.

There was a sailor sitting opposite and he said, 'It's Barbara, isn't it?'

Terry's mam said, 'Do I know you?'

The sailor tipped her a slow wink and mouthed elaborately so that the kid wouldn't catch on (except the kid did): 'Carlton. One afternoon. Two, three months ago?'

'Oh aye?' Barbara said, chewing and frowning slightly and half inclining her head towards Terry. The sailor got her point (and so did Terry) and said, 'Good-looking lad. He'll get the girls into trouble with eyes like that.' He addressed them both but he was looking at Barbara.

'You back on leave then?' Barbara asked.

'Till Wednesday. Still go to the Carlton?'

'Off and on.' She ate a forkful of chips and mushy peas with the utmost delicacy, as a lady should. 'Fred, isn't it?'

'You've a good memory,' the sailor said, 'for an attractive woman.'

Terry concentrated on his food, adopting the disguise of a ten-year-old boy and how he imagined one would behave under the circumstances. Inwardly he was somewhat perplexed at the way grown-up people treated kids: as though they were mindless imbeciles, without perceptions, eyes and brains. He looked up and smiled glassily at the sailor, all the guile of his ten years contained in that smile.

'What's your name, sonny?' The sailor had a thin pasty face and brilliant black hair cut very short. Something shiny – Brylcreem probably – gleamed on his neck.

'Terry,' Terry said.

'Which school do you go to?'

'Heybrook.'

'Do you like it then?'

'It's okay.'

The sailor nodded, at a loss as to how to prolong the conversation. His next question might have been to ask Terry what he wanted to be when he grew up, but instead Terry said:

'Were you in the War?'

The sailor, Fred, flushed slightly and shook his head. He opened a packet of Woodbines and offered one to Barbara, who said, 'They think you're ancient if you're over twenty-one. No conception of age.' Terry wanted to ask what conception meant.

'What football team do you support?' the sailor asked.

'I don't watch football,' Terry said. 'Are you on a ship?'

The sailor gave a weak grin, avoiding Barbara's eyes. 'No, I'm what they call shore-based.' Terry understood what this meant but even so Fred felt he ought to explain it, and did so.

Barbara took her purse from her handbag, saying, 'We'd better be off. Nice to have seen you again.' She seemed to spend a long time looking for change.

'Here, I'll get these,' Fred the sailor said.

'Are you sure? Oh I couldn't let you. Well thanks very much. Come on, our Terry.'

27

'Will you be going to the Carlton anytime?' Fred asked, his voice almost lost in the hiss from the tea-urn.

'Doubt it,' Barbara said, edging out of the booth.

'Well if you do ...' The sailor's face was already disappearing in the steam. Barbara waved vaguely in his direction and pushed Terry through the queue of customers at the high counter and down the steps into the street. For some reason she seemed annoyed; all along Smith Street and across the junction at Molesworth Street she kept muttering something under her breath.

As they were passing the Public Baths she said, 'I wonder who that fella was.'

'I thought you knew him,' Terry said, walking quickly beside her.

'Me? No,' his mother said scornfully. 'How'd I come to know a sailor?'

'At the Carlton,' Terry said, well aware that she was testing his discretion as much as his memory. He knew what was coming next, though they'd walked as far as Isaac Butterworth's fireplace showroom on the corner of Nile Street before she ventured to say:

'Don't tell – I mean, no need to mention owt to your father. We'll just say we had our suppers and walked home, eh?' She squeezed his hand in a gesture of impish conspiracy.

'Well, we did,' Terry said brightly, genuinely wishing to relieve her anxiety; really he wanted to tell her that he could be trusted but he knew it would be the wrong thing to say. She'd pretend not to understand, and it was easier and simpler to act out his part and set her mind at rest in that way. You couldn't have a proper adult conversation with a grown-up, he realised.

Mother and son turned from the sodium yellow brightness of Entwisle Road into the gaslit gloom of Hovingham Street. The lamps flickered on the corners, their reflections streaked faintly on the damp setts. There was a husk of cloud surrounding the moon so that it appeared like a pale watery balloon scudding through the overcast sky.

One or two of the gang were on the corner, leaning against the drainpipe, scuffing their shoes.

'Hi, Terry, where you bin?'

'Regal.'

'What was it?'

'State Secret.'

'Any good?'

'Not bad.'

'See you.'

'Ta-ra.'

Terry's mam fitted the key into the door of number seventy-seven and went through the cold and silent front room into the kitchen. The front room was only used at weekends, the rest of the time it mouldered in damp and decay: the polished walnut sideboard with brass handles and folding-leaf dining table bought from the Co-op, the three-piece suite in fake leather flaking and cracking on the arms, the upright radio console in the corner under the fringed standard lamp, the linoleum with its pattern of red and green squares surrounding the carpet that had been bought new from Webster's but was now frayed at the edges and worn into holes because the castors on the settee were always getting snagged in the weave.

Sometimes Terry's dad went in during the week to listen to a programme – a boxing commentary usually – and sat shivering in one of the cold armchairs with the light out. And when Terry listened each evening to *Dick Barton – Special Agent* he had to crouch in front of the receiver, hugging his knees for warmth and holding his breath so as not to miss a single word, gunshot or car crash as Dick, Snowy and Jock extricated themselves from one more impossible nailbiting situation.

Joe was dozing in the rocking-chair, his feet a nice shade of mottled pink. He never went to the pictures or out drinking, or anywhere, except to pay his union dues every third Thursday of the month and to a football match. Barbara filled the kettle and lit a ring on the gas stove, and Joe woke blearily, pushing his huge square hand through his receding hair and yawning enormously until his eyes disappeared. He smacked his chops.

'Was it any good, the film?'

'Not bad,' Barbara said. She got three beakers out of the cupboard.

'What you looking for?' Terry's dad asked him.

'The *Wizard*.'

'Too late now for reading.'

'I've got to have me drink. I can read while I'm drinking.'

'Joe, we've only just this minute walked in.'

'He won't be told; he has to defy me.'

'He only wants to read his comic.'

Terry sat down and stared into the fire.

'And don't bloody sigh at me,' Joe said.

'I wasn't sighing.'

'Go on, get off upstairs.'

'Let him have his drink first,' Barabara said. 'He won't be five minutes.' She sat down wearily in the chair. 'I don't know, you two never have a civil word to say to one another. Always on at each other. It's wearing.'

'I haven't said owt,' Terry said, which was quite true; but he knew that his mother never took account of what was said or who said it – only that the continual bickering got on her nerves and gave her a splitting headache.

Sylvia was making some horrible noises in her sleep: wheezing, slobbering and grinding her teeth. Terry did his press-ups, had a quick look at the river and the ash-tips in the weak shifting moonlight and climbed into bed, covering his ears with the pillow to shut out Syl's racket.

He was tired but he couldn't get to sleep. The house was full of creakings and the top window-pane kept rattling. He remembered sleeping with his mother in this bedroom before Sylvia was born: the two of them snuggled up together with his body curled to fit the shape of hers, like two coat-hangers side by side. His father was away in the Forces, somewhere in Egypt. One night in particular came back to him: they had been to the Ceylon to see *The Man in the Iron Mask*, and lying motionless in the dark, all alone together in the house, they kept imagining that the Man in the Iron Mask was creeping slowly up the stairs, coming to get them. They distinctly heard a creaking footfall on the stair, as though he were testing each tread before putting his weight on it, and Barbara, almost as petrified as Terry, murmured in his ear: 'There's nobody there really. Go to sleep. It's only the wind.' But if it was only the wind, why was she whispering?

Sylvia grunted and slobbered and turned onto her side and the vision was destroyed. He cast about for something else to think about, and thought of Margaret Parry. She was a nice girl, attractive, with lovely dark eyes and a slim figure. He wondered if she was the kind of girl who would be willing to go behind the garages; Dougie Milne said he'd taken Pat Sidebottom (Fat Pat) down the Figure 7 and put his hand up past the elastic in her blue knicker-legs, though Terry didn't believe him. Everybody knew Dougie Milne was a romancer and told outright fibs. He wondered if Margaret Parry had any hairs on her body. Laura Parfitt had a few: he had caught her peeing in the long grass on the Bottom Track and stopped himself giggling long enough to have a good look

Terry was restless. He was tired and yet couldn't sleep, which was odd. He knocked the pillow into shape with his fist and lay down on his stomach, pretending he was in a midget submarine, feeling itchy and uncomfortable between the legs.

Bonfire Night

*

ESSIE SMITH WAS LADLING BLACK PEAS INTO bowls and cups without handles, her big meaty arms glowing like cured hams in the light from the fire. The little squirts lined up in front of her, their faces grimy from the smoke, lips rosy red where they'd licked the soot away.

The fire was at its height, throwing gigantic shadows against the Arches and the back of the hoardings: a scene from a pagan ritual, a lunatic procession of prancing figures with wild eyes and tangled hair. There was a madness in it somewhere, a kind of imbecilic joy. Kevin Hartley screamed and hoisted a dead branch above his head and threw it into the flames, and the dry wood was instantly consumed, crackling angrily and wafting out fresh waves of heat.

The adults sat on a row of chairs with their backs to the blank end walls of the houses, looking on as fireworks exploded, rockets zoomed, Catherine Wheels whizzed. The old women were muffled in headscarves and heavy coats, their flowered pinnies underneath, some of them wearing clogs and sagging black woollen stockings; and the menfolk stood in small self-important groups, their faces serious and self-contained, trying to look as if they weren't enjoying it too much.

But Bonfire Night infected everybody: the fire was the centre of everything, to which all eyes were turned: petty jealousies and backyard intrigues were forgotten – or at least laid aside for the time being. Even Dolly Bland, Alec's mam, who everybody knew had a scandalous reputation, was forgiven her sins for the evening: she stood with Barbara Webb breaking trays of treacle toffee with a small hammer wrapped in cloth and then went along the line of chairs offering the sticky pieces to anybody with the jaws and teeth to withstand them. Sybil Travis and Ivy Kershaw were acting as supply team for big Bessie, ferrying pans of black peas from nearby kitchens, while Dot Hartley was slicing roasted spuds and inserting wedges of margarine; the little kids queued and took them away, juggling the hot charred jackets in their blackened paws; and they weren't even told to wash before eating!

To Terry, Bonfire Night was second only to Christmas. The smell of woodsmoke seemed to hang everywhere over the town and you only had to walk the length of Entwisle Road to see seven, eight, as many as ten bonfires crackling furiously down sidestreets and back entries and on pieces of waste ground, while in the distance you could hear faint bangs and wails and whoops as fireworks went off in a continuous barrage. As if in accordance with ratified treaty there was never any raiding on the night itself: in fact it was perfectly permissable to visit rival bonfires and throw a few friendly Mighty Atoms, just as the British and German troops had fraternised on that famous Christmas Day during the First World War.

Terry, Alec and Malc decided to cross the brook and pay a call on the Gowers Street Gang, whose bonfire they could see through the Arches, not too far away from Tony Shapcott's pigeon cote. They crept up behind the garages and watched the circle of bright faces, the tots sitting on their parents' laps, the older kids running in and out and bouncing on the old settees until the springs came through. Tony Shapcott (known as Shap) was setting off rockets, using milk bottles to hold them upright, and behind him, on the edge of the roaring glow where the shadows jumped and trembled, Terry caught sight of Margaret Parry, her face a pink oval blur in the firelight. His heart contracted and he felt a queer feverishness come over him. And when he fumbled for the box of matches in his pocket he discovered that his hands were shaking.

'Are you going to cob a banger?' Alec Bland asked.

Terry didn't answer. Instead he lit the dimp of a Woodbine and leaned against the creosoted timber wall of the garage, in full view. He wanted Margaret Parry to see him there, smoking, watching her; in his mind's eye he conjured up an image of himself: brown-eyed, sharp-featured, dark wavy hair, about average height for his age, fairly well built. It was a true portrait but slightly romanticised, similar to the one he had when he came out of the pictures and imagined he bore more than a passing resemblance to the hero in the film (Alan Ladd, say), even copying his walk and the way he held his cigarette.

'It's some of Denby's lot,' said a kid nearby.

Terry appraised him coolly, slouching a little as though wearing a white belted trenchcoat with the collar turned up and a soft fedora hat with a wide brim. He could visualise himself and the effect looked good. He said, 'Watch yer mouth, young 'un,' drawling the words and dragging deeply on the dimp. It stuck to his lip and he inadvertantly wrenched it away, drawing blood. The lighted end got caught between his fingers, stinging like buggery, bringing up a couple of blisters.

'Shap's seen us,' Alec said. 'He's coming over . . .'

Terry threw the shredded remains of the dimp away and sucked his fingers.

Shap was a tall firm-shouldered boy with a gleaming quiff of fair hair hanging over his eyes; it was dead obvious he fancied himself as somebody special: a natural leader and a bobby-dazzler with the girls. He came and stood a few feet away, legs braced apart, and regarded them insolently. After all, it was his turf.

'Come to see a real bommie, Webb?'

'We might have,' Terry said. 'When do you light it?'

'Bloody sharp, in't he?' Shap said to his circle of cronies.

'Swallowed a bread-knife,' said one of them.

'How much wood you got?' Alec Bland said placatingly. His dreamy brown eyes shifted hesitantly from face to face, a confused mixture of trepidation and mild appeasement.

Beyond Shap's broad shoulders Terry could see Margaret Parry and her three friends looking his way. The pattern of the flames flickered on her face, the dark eyes glistening inky-black. He wondered if Shap was after plonking it: he wouldn't mind betting he'd had a grope at least, taking her behind the garages one dark and moonless night and feeling the gentle sprouting of new breasts under the school blouse.

'Where's the rest of your mob?' Shap asked.

Terry jerked his head to indicate the Common across the brook; faint gleams from their bonfire reflected on the undersides of the Arches.

'Brave, aren't you, coming over here on your own?'

'The season of peace and goodwill towards all men,' Terry said.

'He's a poet and don't know it,' said one of the cronies.

'Go and fetch ten pounds of potatoes in your cap,' Terry said glibly, hoping he'd got it right. It was one of his father's few and far-between jokes, one he trotted out without fail whenever he was in a jovial mood. Terry let his eyes drift about; he felt quite reckless. Margaret Parry was watching and he couldn't betray any signs of weakness.

'Hey, tell you what,' Alec said, 'why don't you come and have a sken at our fire,' smiling vaguely at everybody.

Shap laughed, once. He said: 'You'd only have to piss on that to put it out.'

'It'd take more piss than you've got,' Terry said.

'Yeh?'

'Yeh.'

'Oh yeh?'

'Yeh.'

Alec Bland said, 'How many piddies have you got now, Shap?'

which was so feeble an attempt at a diversionary tactic that Shap came back without hesitation: 'What's it to you, fart-face?'

'We should be getting back,' Malc said. 'They'll be wondering where we've got to.' He said this carefully, as though it had been rehearsed.

One of the cronies jeered, 'Chicken?'

Shap said, 'They're not so tough now, are they, Denby lot, without the big lads to back 'em up.' He swayed on his heels and grinned with his large yellow teeth, overflowing with confidence.

'Which big lads would them be?' a voice said, and it was Spenner, bang on cue like the cavalry, sitting on the roof of the garage with his legs dangling down. Terry looked into Shap's eyes, fighting to check a smile; it was like a scene in a film, the big dramatic climax when the tables are turned and the baddies have the sneers wiped off their snivelling mugs. The best part was he didn't need to look at Spenner or even acknowledge his presence, but was strong inside with the warmth of comradeship. It was a good moment.

Kevin Hartley's uncle, Mr Heap, as self-appointed Master of Ceremonies, made periodic inspections of the store of wood, instructing the Gang what to burn and when, and what to save till later. The lads looked at him in mild astonishment: for 364 days a year he never spoke a word (except to move them on when they were kicking a ball outside his house), and here he was issuing orders as if he'd helped collect the bloody stuff.

Several supporting timbers collapsed inwards and a cloud of sparks erupted from the fiery depths and was borne aloft by the cool night breeze. Smoke hung like a menacing wraith over the garages, the cinder track, the scrub of dead vegetation, drifting under the brick archways and across the black sliding river to lose itself somewhere over the ash-tips.

A Roman Candle ejected three blobs of colour into the sky:

red, blue, green, and they faded away inconsequentially in sooty wisps.

Terry's dad never came to the bonfire, just as he never went anywhere else. He might lean on the railings at the end of Cayley Street for half an hour but he wasn't a mixer and found it difficult to sustain a conversation beyond the most trivial social pleasantries. Terry spotted him leaning there and ran across.

'Did you see that Roman Candle go off, dad?' He couldn't contain his excitement: it made his eyes round and shiny and his voice squeaked half an octave up the register.

Joe said, 'Where are your fireworks?'

'I've set 'em off.'

'A full five bob box?' His father's heavy pallid face showed a measure of disapprobation – but only for a moment – because tonight was Bonfire Night, time out of time, immune to the everyday pressures of scrimping and saving, turning off the light, raking out the ashes for bits of coal, using torn-up strips of the *Radio Times* in the outside lavatory.

'Mr Webb, do you want a roasted spud?' Malc Smith asked.

Joe said, 'No thanks,' and looked as if he wanted to go. You could get so close to people but get too close and sooner or later you had to respond, open yourself to them.

Phil Kershaw shouted: 'Hey, Terry, give us a hand,' and Terry ran off to drag some wood from behind the hoardings and chuck it on the fire.

'You want to see South Street's bommie,' Mitch said breathlessly to Terry. 'It's massive.'

'Have you been up?'

'I've been on th'Arches; you can see it easy. It's massive.'

Mrs Wellens from the corner shop was giving out little triangular bags of sweets, holding them in the fold of her apron and being followed everywhere by a gaggle of kids. Terry wouldn't have minded some but was beyond the age when he could stand in line for two ounces of dolly mixtures. The day sweets had come off ration he had gone mad, touring all the local shops and buying whatever they had left on their shelves, even stuff he didn't like, just to experience the heady freedom of walking into a toffee shop without coupons.

The fire had collapsed and lay like a huge glowing disc in the middle of the Common. Chair springs, door hinges, bolts, nails and assorted bits of metal pulsed white-hot in the ashes; the heat was tremendous. Bessie Smith called them over for their black peas and they stood in a special group – The Gang – slightly apart from the rest like battle-weary troops down from the front, slurping the salty mush into their mouths and catching it with spoons as it dribbled down their chins.

Terry's sister Sylvia ran up and asked them if they wanted some treacle toffee. 'Aye, go on,' Spenner said. 'Bring us some.'

Everybody seemed to be eating. Mrs Chadwick had bided her time, as she always did, waiting for the appropriate moment, and now brought forth three trays of parkin made to her own secret recipe. Everybody had a piece, and it was good, but Terry had never tasted parkin like his Auntie Martha made: dark, rich and succulent, it literally melted in the mouth.

'How much wood have we left?' asked Mr Heap, interrupting the lads' black peas, treacle toffee and parkin.

'Why dun't he fall in the brook?' said an anonymous voice.

Mr Heap pretended not to have heard: nothing would shake his good humour on this night or deter him from his set course: the lads were all right (as lads went) but they needed discipline, organisation, leadership.

Terry, Malc Smith and Danny Travis stole away to share a Woodbine. They found a little cubby-hole behind a stack of crates that had letters and numbers stencilled on them and the word 'CROFT', the name of a nearby mill. Terry puffed on the ciga-rette and felt a wave of dizziness and faint nausea pass over him, as it always did when the smoke first entered his lungs. He handed the fag to Malc, seeing his face light up in the reflected glow as he took a deep drag. Danny Travis said, 'I wouldn't mind groping Doreen Hartley.' (Doreen was Kevin Hartley's younger sister – the same age as Terry – and lived next door at number seventy-five.)

'I'd rather have Sandra Weeks,' Terry said. 'Have you seen her tits?'

'No. And you haven't bloody seen 'em either,' Malc said.

'How do you know?'

'You bloody haven't.'

'How do you know?'

'Bet you half-a-dollar.'

'You haven't got half-a-dollar.'

'And you haven't bloody seen Sandra Weeks's tits.'

This seemed to bring the exchange to a close. But it had put Terry in mind of Margaret Parry. He wished she lived nearer than Gowers Street and messed around with them instead of Tony Shapcott's lot. A vision of Shap pressing her up against the garages came out of nowhere and spoiled everything: him with his big yellow teeth, broad shoulders and arrogant stance. She wouldn't be the kind of girl to do anything with him, surely not. But then Terry wasn't sure of anything where girls were concerned, and least of all what Margaret Parry might or might not let Shap do to her. He had a half-formed suspicion that girls weren't as innocent or as unwilling as they made out, because while the secrets of their bodies were wrapped in pure virginal mystery, at the same time he detected a certain . . . sly curiosity, looseness even. He didn't know what it was exactly. Of course they did it against their will, that was only to be expected; but then again, why did they choose to do it with boys who weren't clean and healthy and respectful, and instead went for those who were rude, crude and with dirty minds? He was baffled.

Most of the adults had gone, taking their chairs with them. Terry's mam had told him not to stay out too late. The Gang sat close to the smouldering fire, black as the ace of spades, eyes red-rimmed, smelling strongly of smoke and gunpowder fumes. There was the usual round of dirty jokes, of which, Terry noticed, the two brainiest lads – Roy Pickup and Phil Kershaw – seemed to possess the largest and most varied collection. Spenner told them about a Hank Janson novel he was reading in which this ace newspaper reporter was forever walking into houses, hotels and 'apartments' and finding semi-naked girls in the process of taking, or having just taken, a bath. One girl had breasts 'like marshmallows', and there was another whose nipples 'pointed stiffly in different directions like accusing fingers'. Terry asked if he could read it but Spenner said he was too young and told him to stick to Just William for the time being.

Roy Pickup, from his superior High School position, said:

'There's a boy in our form who's got some Continental Art Studies. From abroad,' he added.

'Studies of what?' Alec Bland said.

'Camels, what do you think?' Kevin Hartley sniggered. He was a blond lad whose blondness was now concealed under a layer of soot.

'What do they show?' asked Malc Smith, the whites of his eyes gleaming out of a charcoal face.

'Women in different poses,' Roy Pickup said. 'You know ...' He was embarrassed and didn't want to put it into words. 'Women standing different ways. You know.'

'Naked?'

'Yeh.'

'All over?'

'Yeh.'

'Showing the lot?'

'Nearly. Except for their fannies.'

The word itself made Terry's stomach curl up into a tight hard ball. He said the word in his mind several times and tried to connect it with Margaret Parry. After all, she must have one.

'Go on then,' Dougie Milne said.

'Go on what?' Roy Pickup said.

'Tell us some more.'

Roy Pickup looked round awkwardly at the circle of interested faces. He said lamely, 'That's all there is.'

'Were they thin or fat?' Terry asked.

'What about their TITS?' Danny Travis said, contorting his face and lowering his voice to a husky whisper on the crucial word.

'Did they have nipples like stiff fingers pointing different ways?' Alec Bland wanted to know.

'Some of them had.' It wasn't clear whether Roy Pickup was actually remembering this or exercising his imagination. 'Some had big flat 'uns like saucers.' He made a circle with his fingers: 'Big as this.'

'That in't big for a tit,' Dougie Milne said scornfully.

'Nipples that big, pie-can.'

'Oh.'

'Bloody Nora ...'

The talk meandered on; the fire dwindled, flaring occasionally into brief life, and as the night advanced the wind changed direction and blew from the ash-tips across the river and moaned through the brick archways. The distant clank-clunk of wagons being shunted could be heard from the marshalling yards high up above Moss Brook. Somebody's mother called from Kellett Street and it was a signal for the Gang to drift away, kicking the pale dead embers into little flurries of powder, like miniature snowstorms. 'Not a bad bommie this year,' Spenner observed, and they all agreed, to a man, that it hadn't been a bad bommie this year.

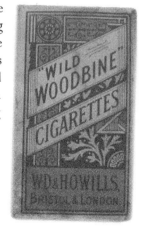

The Birthday Party

*

ONLY THE TOP PEOPLE WERE INVITED TO Yvonne Brangham's birthday party. Specially for the occasion Terry's mam had bought him a new white shirt and a green tie with black squares. The tie was made in a clever way that Terry was very proud of: instead of tying it you simply slipped it over your head and folded your shirt collar over the elastic band, which held the tie neatly in place. He was dead sure nobody else had a tie like it.

At the corner of Yorkshire Street and Halifax Road he met Betty Wheatcroft, decked out in all her finery, and they walked together past Heybrook School and up Park Road past the semi-detached houses with their own gardens. Some even had garages. Terry was nervous, but he felt very superior and rather honoured to be walking up Park Road with Betty Wheatcroft, conscious of the fact that only a chosen few received an invitation.

'What have you bought her?' Betty asked. Terry carried a paper bag stuck down with tape.

'Chocolates. What've you?'

Betty held up a pretty package tied with pink ribbon with a big bow on top. 'Vanity set.'

Terry nodded. He didn't know what a vanity set was but supposed it was something girls found a use for. They walked on. Terry was struggling to remember something he had read about what you were expected to say to girls when you took them out or met them at a party. He thought he remembered.

'I like your dress,' he said studiously, looking straight ahead.

'Thank you,' Betty said politely. She had her coat on, the dress showing at the bottom, about two inches of it. 'I like your tie.'

Terry said, 'Look at this,' and pulled the tie away from his collar and let it snap back; he did this twice more.

'I haven't seen one of them before.'

'No,' Terry said. 'It's brand-new.'

Yvonne Brangham lived in a large stone house with a bay window, set back a few feet behind green wrought-iron railings that were corroding. The enclosed 'garden' was a dozen square feet of damp earth with a couple of weary bushes with drab darkish leaves. The gate was missing, having been removed during the war for scrap metal. Yvonne's mother was Terry's idea of what Enid Blyton must look like, smiling, stoutish, smartly dressed in a fawn cardigan with two loops of pearls at her throat, competent but not fussy. She took Betty's coat, saying, 'Yvonne's in the sitting-room.'

Terry felt rather grand, standing in his best jacket, new shirt and tie in a house that actually had a hallway behind the front door (there was even a tall wooden stand with an oval mirror set in it); he was also slightly uneasy, not knowing what a sitting-room looked like or where you might find one.

'Don't wait, go on in,' Mrs Brangham said. What Terry liked about her was that she didn't pat the top of his head. Feeling grown-up and important, and clutching his quarter-pound chocolate assortment in its paper bag, he followed Betty's rustling dress and pink satin slippers along the hallway and into a bright sunny room with flowers, pictures on the walls and a piano in the corner.

He knew them all, thank goodness: Yvonne, Jean Ashmore, Brenda Harrison, Mary Macauly, and of course Betty. There were four boys, all of them in Terry's class. He presented the chocolates to Yvonne and she accepted them graciously.

'I like your dress,' he remembered to say, standing quietly and self-consciously just inside the door, and Rod Callaghan and Arthur Halliwell went into a fit of snorting giggles, punching each other's shoulders.

'Take no notice,' Yvonne said. 'They've been drinking cider.'

'Where'd you get that tie from, Webbie – Starkey's?' Arthur Halliwell said, gawping. (Starkey's was a rag-and-bone merchant.) Terry could feel his neck getting red but he refused to look at them. He thought: a couple of brainless louts, and nearly blurted out, 'You two won't pass for the High School at any rate,' but held his tongue. He was cleverer than they were, and knew it, and it was enough.

Mary Macauly was sitting at the piano, tapping out a few notes. She was a shy moon-faced girl who spoke very softly and correctly, and so it came as an even greater shock when she said out of the blue: 'I'd rather kiss Terry Webb than you two any day of the week.'

He could hardly believe his ears, and again a hot blush started creeping up from beneath his clean white collar. He jerked his head like a robot to look at her and she was quite calmly tapping out a little tune. He knew he had to get control of himself: this stupid blushing would ruin everything, especially in front of the other boys. He said rashly, 'I think Jean Ashmore's smashing,' and saw Jean look confused and uncomfortable and a shadow of disappointment pass over Yvonne Brangham's face, and realised he'd said the wrong thing. He knew now why he'd been invited.

They had their tea in another room (what Mrs Brangham referred to as 'the living-room'), Terry being very courteous, passing plates of sandwiches before he took one himself, holding his china cup by the handle, and only talking when his mouth was empty. At one point he said something funny and everybody laughed, and he experienced a warm satisfying glow deep within and could hardly keep his face from beaming with happiness. Yvonne kept glancing at him with what he took to be a look of secret admiration, and once or twice he caught the eye of Jean

Ashmore before the two of them looked hastily down at their plates. This was when you stopped being a kid, Terry realised, and started growing up: this was getting to know and like other people, and they to know and like you: it was terrific.

The girls helped Mrs Brangham clear the table, and she said: 'You boys run along into the sitting-room and amuse yourselves. Think up some games to play.'

When they were in the other room Arthur Halliwell said, 'I can think of a few games to play with Betty Wheatcroft,' and made a gesture with his fist. Terry was vaguely disgusted. They were supposed to be behaving responsibly, not like kids in the infants' class.

'Which one are you having?' Derek Cross asked Terry.

'Whichever one's left,' Terry said blandly, knowing full well he had the pick of at least two. It seemed to him now that he held some sort of power over the situation, and he had acquired the notion that the others were looking to him to give a lead. Even Arthur Halliwell and snide Rodney Callaghan had stopped throwing out taunts and insults, almost as if they had given way in deference to him. He suggested that they play Postman's Knock and when the girls came in they agreed.

It was gone six o'clock and quite dark outside. For a nasty moment Terry and the other lads thought that Mrs Brangham was going to spoil everything, but she'd only followed the girls in to draw the curtains and put some coal on the fire. The room was warm and cosy, the night shut outside, the firelight winking in the candlestick holders on the piano, and the moquette arm-chairs deep comfy pools of shadow. Terry had already noted that the carpet went right up to the skirting-board and that there wasn't a single frayed hole anywhere in it. Mrs Brangham went out, not even saying, 'Don't jump on the furniture' or 'Don't make too much noise,' and he imagined for a moment, wistfully, what it would be like to have her as a mother.

Of the five, Terry fancied Jean Ashmore the most, but he had to admit that Yvonne was great at kissing. They played Postman's Knock and then a simplified version of Truth, Dare, Force or Promise – simplified because the girls didn't want to get their party dresses crumpled and insisting that the boys didn't go too far. In paying one forfeit Rodney Callaghan had to kiss all the girls in turn and Terry couldn't help feeling a sneaking satisfaction at their lack of enthusiasm and the perfunctory way they pecked at his thin straight mouth.

After the games they switched the light off and settled down: a couple in each armchair, two couples sharing the settee, Derek Cross and Mary Macauly on cushions near the window. Terry had never known a girl's lips taste so sweet. He had kissed girls before – that is, pressed his mouth against their mouths – but this was the first time he not only enjoyed the sensation but could actually see the point of it. Yvonne's lips were soft and there was a smell emanating from somewhere that made his senses unsteady. He experimented with both hard and gentle kisses, with long and short ones, and discovered how it was possible to prolong a kiss for ages and breathe at the same time. Now and then he opened his eyes, just to see what she looked like while he was kissing her: the firelight wavering on her pale forehead, deep moving shadows in the hollows of her eyes, and glossy ringlets of dark hair burnished by the glow. He decided that kissing girls was all right; it just needed a bit of practice.

After a while they broke away and Terry didn't know

46

what to do with his eyes or what to say. He kept squeezing her shoulders for something to do.

At last he said in a whisper, 'I like your dress.'

'Are you glad you came?'

'Yeh.'

'You like Jean don't you?'

'She's all right.'

'Do you like her better than me?'

'No,' Terry said. He found that the lie came easily, and it was even possible to look her in the face as he said it.

Then she disconcerted him by closing her eyes and sighing, lifting her mouth blindly towards his. Terry kissed her, moving his lips up and down, from side to side. It was nice. They were in a private world of contentment, the room dancing with shadows, the huddled bodies passive and mute and lightly breathing, until somebody farted.

'Bloody Nora,' Derek Cross said from the floor.

Arthur Halliwell said, 'Pardon my friend the pig.'

'Shit down and make yourself cum-fart-able,' Rod Callaghan said.

Terry was trying not to laugh; he thought it would be undignified and give the wrong impression. Now the genteel atmosphere was shattered, the boys were saying the rudest things they could think of and some of the girls were stifling their giggles. Derek Cross recited:

'I wish I was a caterpillar

Then life would be a farce,

I'd climb up to the tallest trees

And slide down on my hands and knees.'

Mary Macauly said, 'Tell them to shut up, Yvonne.'

'I din't start it,' Derek Cross protested in the darkness, frightened at being struck off the guest list.

Yvonne snuggled under Terry's arm and murmured in his ear that she was glad he wasn't like the others. Terry replied that so

47

was he, yet felt his conscience rebel at such an untruth. And his pride was hurt too — that she should think him different from the others, incapable of a rude joke; in other words a Mummy's Boy. It was true that he was different from the others, he knew it in his bones, but he didn't want to be *that* different.

'Do you go to the Ceylon on Saturday afternoons?' Yvonne asked him.

'Sometimes.'

'Are you going next Saturday?'

'Might do.'

'Will you go if I go?'

'All right.' What else could he say? But he'd much rather go if he knew Jean Ashmore was going.

'I think you're the best boy in our class,' Yvonne Brangham said impulsively, aiming suddenly for his mouth and not quite hitting it dead-centre.

'I like you as well,' Terry said. 'I like your—' He nearly said 'dress' but reckoned he'd wrung that particular compliment dry.

'My mother likes you,' Yvonne said. 'She thinks you're very nice and quiet and polite.'

'Does she?' Terry said dully. He had a sudden yearning to break away from her embrace and run into the street and jump in a puddle or kick a tin can or swing from a lamp-post. Girls were all right to kiss (and he hadn't realised till now how enjoyable kissing could be) but he hoped it wasn't going to get in the way of messing round with the Gang; he enjoyed dirt-track racing on the Top Track and swaling the moors up Brown Wardle and lots of other things just as much as sitting in a comfy armchair in a firelit room with a girl in a rustling party dress, satin slippers and ringlets.

The Ginnel

*

THE GANG WAITED IMPATIENTLY FOR SNOW, THIS being December and December being winter and in winter the dirty white stuff supposed to fall from the skies. This year, however, it was depressingly damp and foggy, the mist tending to gather in hollows on the Bottom Track like pools of grey water, and hanging in vaporous ribbons close to the surface of the river. So while waiting for the time when they could bring their sledges up from the cellar and grease the runners, they had to find other diversions and amusements. Such as sneaking into the compound at the end of the Ginnel where rows of broken-down camouflage-coloured ex-army vehicles rotted away, their tyres deflated, their innards gone rusty. The idea was to dangle strips of cloth into the petrol tanks, soaking up the last precious drops, set them alight, and run amok like dervishes, whirling them above their heads to mimic helicopter blades on fire.

Another pursuit, known as the North-West Passage, required skill, cunning and nerve. First you had to climb over the fence into Sam Clegg's, the coal merchant's yard, then descend the vertical stone wall, hand under hand, to the hummocks of grass which bordered the river, feeling your way along in the pitch dark so as to avoid the patches of deep green slime which lapped the wall. Then came the section calling for stealth and nerves of steel: the pens and allotments running the full length of Kellett Street down to the river's edge. Chances were that some old geezer would be pottering about in his shed or greenhouse, and the trick was for ten of you to sneak by undetected in the tall, rustling marsh-grass, virtually under his nose. There was no escape-route – allotments in front, river to their backs – and when they'd negotiated it a surge of exultation swept through them all as they climbed over a couple of broken fences and came out at the end of the Figure 7, back in the world of gaslamps and safety.

During this time Dougie Milne broke his leg by falling off an air-raid shelter and was out of action for three months. He had been demonstrating how paratroopers land on the balls of their feet without hurting themselves.

Terry didn't mind the winter too much because the dark bitter nights brought with them an air of mystery and intrigue to Denby: you could play at spies, convicts or escaped prisoners-of-war, pressed rigidly in the shadows trying not to breathe when anyone passed by, burrowing your face in your windjammer to conceal its tell-tale paleness. And the darkness held a special kind of excitement: away from the brightly-lit main roads (where the rule of law and order prevailed) there was the possibility of escape into another kind of territory, the backstreets and alleyways, the viaducts and railway sidings, the ash-tips and allotments. This was a subworld in which adults, snug in their terraced blocks of brick, were an alien species. Tomorrow they would regain control but the night belonged to the Gang.

Sometimes, of course, the adults ventured out. Whenever there was a bob or two to spare they might go to the pictures, queueing with patient yet bright-eyed expectation to see Hollywood's version of How the War Was Won or the graceful Gainsborough lady with her large feathered hat introducing a home-grown production with stars such as Robert Newton, Patricia Roc, Margaret Lockwood, Dennis Price, Phylis Calvert, and Terry's mam's particular favourite, the suavely evil James Mason.

If there was nothing on at the flicks, then the Cloverdale on

Entwisle Road kept a decent pint of mild, or they could try the Trafalgar Hotel on the corner of Ramsay Street; but there wasn't, for most of them, a great deal to spare for booze, what with winter upon them and coal at 4/1d a bag. Mostly their evenings were spent listening to *Radio Newsreel* followed by *PC49*, or perhaps Valentine Dyall as *The Man in Black*, and on Saturday nights *Variety Bandbox* with top of the bill Frankie Howerd, and on Sundays *Palm Court*.

At weekends the Carlton was a big attraction (a shilling to go on the floor, sixpence on the balcony) with Emyrs Griffiths and the Carlton Band playing the usual medley of popular tunes in quickstep, foxtrot and waltz time. Under the revolving globe of tiny mirrors throwing its fragments of light along the ceiling, down the walls, across the polished wooden floor, the couples moved in dreamlike formation to a subdued shuffling of feet, the women humming *They Didn't Believe Me* or *As Time Goes By* into their partners' right shoulders, just above the place where the dusting of face powder smudged the wide pointed lapels and the trace of Californian Poppy lingered.

On the corner next to Wellens's shop, with its posters advertising Fynnon Salts and Dollie Blue, several of the Gang were already assembled, kicking a tennis ball about as they debated what to do. Spenner – who was fanatical about anything on wheels – wanted to break into the army vehicle depot and siphon petrol out of the tanks, but the others weren't too keen, having done this three or four times already.

'Knock-a-door-run!' Alec Bland said, as though coming up with a brainwave, and Roy Pickup, the High School boy, said uncharitably, 'Stick yer 'ead up yer arse, Blandie.'

'We could allus raid Shap's pigeon loft,' said Malc.

'What for?'

'Dunno,' Malc said. 'We just could.'

Sandra Weeks, Doreen Hartley and Fat Pat Sidebottom were coming along the street and Kevin Hartley shouted: 'Where you off to, our kid?'

'What's it to you?' his sister said, flouncing past the group.

'Oh, bloody Hell,' Spenner said in a prissy voice, sounding the *h*. 'Three tarts without a pair of knickers between 'em.'

Sandra Weeks said, 'Maybe we haven't, but at least we don't smell,' which was a taunt that hurt because there was some truth in it. Spenner ran after her and thumped her in the back.

'Bully!' Doreen Hartley screamed. 'Bloody big bully!'

Sandra was crying, her cheeks red and wet. She sobbed an insult and Spenner was about to strike her again.

'Lay off her,' Kevin Hartley said. 'You've hit her, now leave her alone.'

Terry was intrigued to see what would happen next. Kevin was the same age as Spenner, so he could stand up to him, but Terry had never seen the pair of them fight. Kevin said to the three girls:

'Go on, get home.'

'She's telling her dad,' Doreen threatened, supporting Sandra. 'Bloody big bully,' she added contemptuously.

Spenner turned towards her and there was a murderous look in his eye. Terry was nervous and excited. It was bound to start any second. The tension ticked in the air like an unexploded bomb.

'You better tell your kid to keep it shut,' Spenner said to Kevin Hartley.

'She will keep it shut,' Kevin said. 'But don't you lay a finger on her.'

Spenner's eyes were bloodshot. His hair formed a red halo round his head in the lamplight. He was blazing mad but he was unsure of Kevin Hartley; and he knew himself to be in a vulnerable position because hitting girls was something that went against the Gang's code of ethics: lads who hit girls were regarded as weak and unmanly, and nobody liked being labelled a bully.

'You'd better tell that sister of yours ...' Spenner's voice was shaking and there were flecks of foam at the corners of his mouth. Terry had never seen him like this. It was frightening to see somebody out of control, obsessed to the point of mindless rage, unable to overcome such a simple thing as the taunting of a young girl.

'All right,' Phil Kershaw said, 'we're not kids. This is daft, fighting over something trivial.' This was a word he'd probably picked up at De La Salle College.

'She'd better not call me that again, that's all.'

'You'd better not touch her either.'

'If she calls me that just once more —'

'Don't you touch her *at all*,' Kevin said.

'Are we standing here all night?' Terry piped up. 'Let's go to the army depot or over to Nile Street.'

Spenner wiped the spittle from his mouth and Terry noticed that his fingers were trembling. Kevin had relaxed his stance but he was still watchful. His short fair hair rested flatly on his head like a cap.

'Come on then, if we're going,' Roy Pickup said, and like a tableau coming mechanically to life the lads started to move down the dirt slope towards the Bottom Track, Kevin and Spenner walking on opposite sides of the group, looking straight ahead. Malc Smith said in Terry's ear: 'Bet Spenner would have pasted him easy.'

'Do you think so?' Terry said, and left it at that.

Down past the pens, along the pitch-black Ginnel with its matting of dead slimy leaves underfoot, and up into the sodium-yellow glare of Trafalgar Street, which butted onto the main road. There wasn't much conversation until they drew level with the telephone kiosk at the corner of Good Shepherd Church, when Roy Pickup said, 'I'll show you a great trick.' He went into the telephone box and the others scrimmaged round the open door. Roy lifted the heavy black receiver and tapped out a sequence of what sounded like morse code on the telephone rest.

'What you doing?'

'Listen,' Roy said, and held up the receiver so that they could hear the phone ringing at the other end. It rang for a while and then a woman's voice said: '4784.'

'Is that Brown's the Hundertakers?' asked Roy in a prim voice.

'This is 4784,' the voice said impatiently.

'I got the wrong number. Sorry. Thank you,' Roy said, and put the receiver down.

'You didn't put any money in,' Alec Bland said, stating the obvious.

'Me uncle told me how to do it; he works for't GPO. The only trouble is you can't hang about too long because the engineers know where you're phoning from.'

At that moment a police car went slowly by, a black Wolseley with a radio aerial, and the lads froze in attitudes of cautious panic, their senses alert like animals half prepared for flight. When the police car had gone Danny Travis said 'Steaming Nora' with heartfelt relief.

'You know what we could do,' Spenner said, always the delinquent schemer, 'split up and ring each other from different phone boxes. Pass coded messages like secret agents.'

'We need a password,' Phil Kershaw said, wanting to play the game properly if it was played at all. He tried to think of a suitable phrase before the others did but the only one he could come up with was 'Black Mask'.

They roamed along Ramsay Street, dodging into shop doorways to avoid the clinging drizzle and climbed the steep pavement of Copenhagen Street, passing the Ceylon with its dim blue gas globe over the entrance and the tattered posters flapping limply in the wind. In the murky night it was barely possible to make out the title of the big picture showing Thurs, Fri & Sat: *Badlands of Dakota*. Terry's Uncle Jack (his mother's younger brother) used to take him quite regularly when he lived with them on Cayley Street just after the war, but since he moved away Terry only went to the sixpenny rush on Saturday afternoons. His hero at the moment was Roy Rogers and Trigger.

'What time is it?' Malc said anxiously. 'It hasn't gone nine o'clock yet has it?'

Some of the lads made scathing remarks but this didn't matter to Malc: he was more afraid of his mam's heavy hand than all their scorn put together. Alec Bland decided to leave too, and they went off down Oswald Street, running on the slick pavement under the gaslamps' wavering beams.

The rest of them congregated round the chewing-gum machine outside a tobacconist's. Spenner squinted left and right along Yorkshire Street, and then instead of turning the knob slowly anticlockwise as the penny dropped, he jerked it rapidly to and fro and four packets fell out. They put some more money in and accumulated fifteen packets of XL for fourpence.

Finally they decided to split into groups and phone each other from different call boxes. Terry and Danny Travis returned to Trafalgar Street near Good Shepherd Church. All the way back Danny was fretting about how late it was, and the trouble he'd be in, and so Terry was left on his own to await the phone's ring, leaning against the misted glass watching the red tail-lights of the traffic disappearing towards town. He had no idea of the time, only that it must be getting late.

A few people passed by, couples mostly, wrapped up against the deepening chill of winter. He huddled inside his corduroy windjammer, numbed to the bone, wishing he'd had the sense to wear the woollen balaclava his mother had knitted for him. He could have gone home, there was nothing to prevent it –

except of course that the others would think him a soft cock –
and he had enough pride and ambition to want to be regarded as
a cut above the other boys his age.

Terry looked in the direction of the Arches, whistling a tune
and counting the streetlights, and so didn't see the man crossing
the road. The man wasn't old, thirtyish or thereabouts, though
Terry saw him simply as an adult of indeterminate age. He was
wearing a raincoat, shabby and frayed at the edges, with a scarf
tied in a big knot under his chin.

'Hello son,' the man said. Terry noticed immediately that his
shoes were old and worn, with grey knotted string in place of
laces. 'What you doing here?'

'Waiting.'

'What for?'

'Just waiting.'

'You must be waiting for something.'

'A phone call,' Terry said. He was wary but he knew that the
man wasn't a copper. At least he was reasonably certain, because
coppers shaved regularly and this man didn't.

'Who's going to ring you?'

'One of me pals.'

'At this time of night?'

'Yeh.' Terry widened his brown eyes innocently. 'He's poorly in
hospital and he's going to ring me to tell me how he is.'

'Oh aye?'

'Yeh. Honest.' But the man didn't seem to be taken in by
Terry's big brown eyes, because he said nastily:

'I've heard that tale before.'

'It's true. Don't believe me if you don't want to.'

The man looked up and down Entwisle Road. 'What have you
got in your pockets?'

'Nowt.'

'Let's have a look.' He ignored the scraps of paper and rubber
bands and crumpled packet of XL chewing gum and asked what

was in the tin. Terry opened it. 'Dimps. You're a smoker, are you? We've found a secret smoker, have we?'

He was looking at Terry and almost smiling. 'We have the odd crafty drag now and then, do we? You can tell me, I don't mind.'

'Sometimes.'

'Would you like a full one?'

'What?'

'A full fag. Here, have one. I don't mind kids smoking. I used to smoke when I was your age.'

'All right. Thanks.'

'Are you going to light it?'

'I go dizzy if I smoke a full one.'

'What's your name?'

'Terry Webb.'

'You're all right, Terry,' the man said. 'I like you.' There was an oddness about him that Terry couldn't place. Then the man said: 'You're a well-built lad aren't you? Do you exercise a lot?'

'I go to the baths.'

'A swimmer eh? How far can you swim?'

'I've done me six lengths.'

'Six lengths,' the man said, and whistled. 'Wish I could swim.'

'You can't swim?' Terry said. 'Honest?'

'Frightened of the water. Always wished I could swim.'

'It's easy. Nowt to it.'

'It is for you, Terry, because you're strong and well-developed. I bet you've got strong legs.' Terry looked down at his knees covered in bruises. 'You're a sturdy lad, aren't you?' said the man, gripping his shoulder.

He turned his head to look along the road and the streetlight overhead fell directly on his face so that the knifeblade shadow of his nose ran straight down over his chin. His eyes were hidden: the yellow light made his skin wan and anaemic: he looked back at Terry. 'Have you no pals, Terry?'

'Yeh, I've got loads of pals.'

'Where are they tonight then?'

'They're going to meet me.'

'Here?'

Terry nodded.

'They're a long time.'

The man grinned suddenly and gave Terry a friendly punch on the shoulder. 'You're a grand lad, Terry, will you do me a favour?'

'What?'

'I'll give you another fag.'

'What is it?'

The man seemed to hesitate. He said, 'I want to get to Kellett Street. Any idea where it is?'

'Down there,' Terry said, pointing behind him. 'You go down the Ginnel and through the allotments—'

'Come on then. Show me.'

'I can't. Me pals are coming soon.'

'It won't take a minute. Show me how to get there and I'll give you another fag.' The man was smiling in a very friendly way. 'Come on!' he said jovially. So Terry walked with the man along the street by the side of the church and down the dirt slope leading to the Ginnel.

Away from the streetlights it became so dark that Terry couldn't see his hand in front of his face, and he knew (as he had known all along if he had trusted his instincts) that he shouldn't be walking in pitch blackness with a man who was a stranger. But nothing seemed to be happening, thankfully, other than they were walking in single file (the Ginnel being narrow and closed in both sides with creosote fencing) with Terry in front, their footsteps deadened by the soggy carpet of decaying leaves, the man humming softly under his breath.

It was all right, Terry thought, it was going to be all right, because once through the allotments the gaslamp at the end of Hovingham Street could be seen, marking the outpost of ter-

raced houses with lights behind their curtains and people inside
doing ordinary things like sitting in front of the fire listening to
the wireless. The man stopped humming and they walked along
in silence, Terry placing one foot in front of the other and conscious of the breath entering and being expelled from his lungs.
Behind his back the man said:

'Do you ever play with girls, Terry?' And when Terry didn't
answer: 'I bet you like putting your hand up their dresses, don't
you?'

'I've never done that.'

'I bet you have.'

Terry said nothing.

'Girls like you doing things like that, Terry. They like boys putting their hands inside their knickers and having a feel.'

They were nearly at the end of the Ginnel. When they turned
the corner there would only be the allotments to get through.
Then he would be able to see the gaslamp and the lights of the
houses. As long as the man kept talking it would be all right;
nothing to worry about, Terry thought, taking a step and another
step and another step; nothing to worry about. It would be all
right...

'Has a girl ever felt your dick, Terry?'

He sensed that the man was doing something in the darkness
behind him, fiddling with something. The man's voice had gone
low and throaty. The man's low throaty voice was saying, 'Has a
girl ever played with your dick and made it stiff? I bet she has,
hasn't she, a sturdy lad like you?'

They turned the corner and at last they were in the allotments.
Terry knew every pothole, every patch of stunted dog-pee-
smelling grass. He could just faintly see the gaslamp at the end
of Hovingham Street.

'Stop,' the man said. 'Turn round.'

Terry stopped and turned round and saw that the man was
holding something pale. His hand was moving. 'Do you know any

girls who'd like to feel a big man's dick, Terry? I bet loads of girls have felt your dick, haven't they, and made it rise ...'

Before the man could call him back, imploringly at first, then with fury, he took off at top speed, the gaslamp like a welcoming beacon far ahead of him, pelting towards it and past it and between the houses, not stopping once the entire length of Cayley Street until he reached No. 77 and his mother had opened the front door, alarmed by his face, remarking that he looked as if he'd seen a ghost.

Saturday Morning

*

TERRY LAY IN THE LUXURY OF WARMTH,
listening to the gurgle of the brook at the bottom of the
yard: the smell of frying bacon wafted up the narrow
stairs and hung in the cold air. He was overcome, overwhelmed
by the strangest feelings. He found it astonishing that the actual
moment, even as he was thinking it, was existing here and now
and that he was part of it, a living breathing body. He looked
down at the front of his vest palpitating with life and was staggered by the miracle. He had almost to convince himself that it
was happening, it was real, and not just a figment of his own
imagination.

He was conscious of the whole world, filled with millions of
people, existing even as he thought about it. And the sky he could
see outside the window, a pale washed blue, was infinite space
going on forever, and all that space was looking down eternally
on this world, on England, on Denby, on Cayley Street, and on
him, the one and only Terry Webb. It was frightening.

A song he vaguely recognised drifted up the stairs from his
mam's favourite request show on the Light Programme, a catchy
tune with a swaying rhythm, and the intriguing words *Rum and
Coca-Cola ... Working for the Yankee Dollar*, sung in close harmony
by the Andrews Sisters. In his dreamy nostalgic state it trans-
ported Terry back to the time when his mam and Uncle Jack used
to sing it together, and in a trice he saw the figure in the army
greatcoat with a kit-bag slung over his shoulder marching down

Cayley Street while a seven-year old snotty urchin called Terry raced towards him yelling 'Uncle Jack! Uncle Jack!' at the top of his lungs.

'Can I carry it? Can I?'

'If you want to ruin yourself for life.'

'What've you got in there?'

'Bully beef, bazookas and Rommel's cap.' A broad grin from Jack at the puzzled look on Terry's face. 'Pressies – loads of pressies. For your mam and dad and Sylvia and er ...'

'Me?'

'Oh heck. I'd forgotten about you.'

'You haven't really. Have you?'

'No! I've got you three tins of real coffee, two pairs of nylons, a silk scarf, a Hasselblad camera—'

'Oh.' Terry was almost blubbing. 'Is that all?'

Jack picked him up by the waist and swung him round. 'Bars of milk chocolate with walnuts, sugared almonds, boxes of Turkish Delight, American gum in five flavours ...'

'Smashing Uncle Jack! Are you home for good?'

'Well, I'm home,' Jack said. 'Anyroad.'

Barbara couldn't hold back the tears when they were all sitting round the table in the front room. It was a very special occasion – as special as Christmas – because they'd lit a fire. 'We knew you were coming home, Jack. Auntie Polly read it in the tea-leaves.'

'That woman's barmy,' Joe mumbled

'She did, Joe! Just like she knew the war was going to end six months before it did.'

'You didn't need tea-leaves for that. It was on the front page of the *Daily Herald*.'

'She told me I was going to be a Spitfire pilot,' Terry piped up.

'Aye, when pigs can fly,' his dad muttered.

'I wrote and said I was coming down from Catterick two months ago,' Jack said. 'Just waiting for my demob papers to clear.'

'Is that in Egypt?' Terry asked. And after Jack laughed and shook his head, Terry explained, 'I thought it was 'cos you're so brown.'

It was true — Jack had a deep and even tan that made his eyes and teeth flash brilliantly, and with his black wavy hair he was the dead spit of the film star Tyrone Power in the pirate picture Terry had seen at the Ceylon a week or two ago.

'Here you are, Joe.' Jack held out the box with its frill of crinkly white paper. 'Have some Turkish Delight.'

'No thanks, it sticks to me plate.'

Barbara Webb dabbed at her eyes. 'Oh Jack, it's so good to have you back home again. You were so young, only a lad when you were called up.'

'Bit more than that,' Jack laughed. 'Nearly eighteen, sis.'

'Still young, I think ... that reminds me, Eileen Kershaw asked when you were coming home.'

'How is she?'

'She's working at Turner's, in the canteen. Why didn't you write to her?'

'I did write.'

'One letter and two postcards in nearly four years.'

'I'd nowt to say.'

'Thousands of miles from home in a foreign country and you'd nothing to say! You could have told her about North Africa.'

'What — that it's hot, stinks, and has millions of flies? Come as a shock to Eileen I daresay.'

... working for the Yankee Dollar ... !

As the record came to an end the memory snapped off, quick as a light-switch, and Terry was back in the snug burrow of his bed, following the cracks in the ceiling as an explorer traces the tributaries of a mighty river in darkest Africa.

Lying here at ease, his hand came to rest quite naturally between his legs and he tried, for the umpteenth time, to masturbate successfully.

'Your bacon butty's on the table,' his mother called from the bottom of the stairs, and Terry slumped back into the bed, defeated by a whisker.

When he had got dressed in front of the kitchen fire and eaten his breakfast, she said, 'I want you to go to the butcher's. I've written it down.'

Terry was still slightly adrift in the memory of Uncle Jack's homecoming, and something bothered him about it: that had been three years ago, in 1947. Why did Jack not leave the army until two years after the war ended?

'Because he wasn't called up till '42, a few days after he turned eighteen,' his mam said. 'The buggers nabbed him for two more years after the war. Never left Egypt except for a short leave.'

'Where is he now?'

'How should I know?' Barbara said. 'Stop asking daft questions,' and shoo'd him on his way.

Sylvia was playing outside the backyard gate in the dirt, serving tea to a circle of dolls. It was a fine day, clear and cold, with hardly a stirring of wind. Terry fed his pigeons and put the money and the list his mother had written in his pocket, thinking how funny it was that Saturday mornings had their own special flavour; even if you lost track of the days you'd still know when it was Saturday.

Mrs Heap was down on her knees on the strip of pavement, donkey-stoning her front step a vivid buttery yellow, and Bessie Smith, Malc's mam, was at the top of the step-ladder washing the fanlight over her door. Teddy Travis, Danny's elder brother, was tinkering with his Norton, lying flat on his back in the dirt surrounded by spanners, chromium-plated bolts, c-clips and oily rags. The one car in the street was owned by Sam Clegg, the coal merchant: an upright Austin Seven with a canvas roof on struts like a pram-hood and black wire-spoke wheels. It was always spotlessly clean and polished till it shone; he even washed the

tyre treads. Opposite Sam Clegg's were three garages which had once been used to house the Civil Defence fire-fighting equipment; now they were rented by a small round man with bright button eyes and a swarthy bald head who kept two ice cream vans there, painted with the name 'Granelli's' in gold circus lettering.

Alec and Malc were sitting on their bikes watching the traffic on Entwisle Road. Malc was counting the red cars and Alec the blue ones to see who could get most. Terry had pestered his mam and dad for a bike since he was seven or eight but his father said they were dangerous, which when interpreted in the language of the Webbs meant that bikes were too expensive and they couldn't afford to buy him one. Malc had managed to get his because Mrs Smith worked the housewives' shift at Oswald & Duncan's, while everyone in Denby knew how Dolly Bland, Alec's mam, earned a bit extra on the side.

Terry asked them what they were doing that afternoon: Alec's blank brown eyes were lost in counting, his lips miming numbers. 'Fourteen,' he said at last. 'Eleven,' Malc said.

'I might be going to the match with me dad,' Malc said.

Terry, who had no interest in football, said, 'Do you fancy the baths?'

'I'll have to ask me mam,' said Alec.

'Why do you always have to ask your mother before you can go anywhere?' Terry said. Secretly he thought Alec a bit of a mard-arse, though had never said so. 'Anybody'd think you were a kid.'

'I'm older than you, Webb.'

'Three weeks.'

'I'm still older.'

'Are you going or not?'

'Might do.'

'Call for us.'

'Call for me.'

'All right.' Terry was bored with the contest. 'About two o'clock.'

The butcher's was next to a chip shop, and next to that was the Trafalgar pub. Terry liked the butcher's shop: Arnold the butcher had a kindly face and a blob of a purple nose like a lump of plasticine. He wore a straw hat and a blue-and-white striped apron soiled with blood. He teased Terry and told him jokes and asked him riddles, and Terry would stand there, moving the toe of his shoe in the sawdust, making rivers, dams, bridges, exploding them with dynamite in his mind.

'What's the longest word in the world?' Arnold asked.

'Dunno.'

'Smiles,' Arnold said, forcing scrag end into the mincer with a wooden baton. 'There's a mile between the first and last letters.' He boomed a hearty laugh, his face going even redder, more amused than Terry.

'When is a door not a door?'

Terry knew this one but shook his head because he liked Arnold and didn't want to spoil his fun.

'When it's ajar. Get it? A jar.' His pink jowls trembled against his starched collar.

'Hey,' Terry said. 'That's clever.'

'How's your mam these days?'

'Swell.'

(This was a word he'd heard the Yanks using, who came over from Burtonwood, the US Air Force base, to whom the standard greeting was, 'Got any gum, chum?')

'Still go to the Carlton, does she?'

Terry shrugged.

'Terrif dancer, your mam.' He lofted a clotted clump of fatty mince onto the scales. 'Used to come to your house when you were a baby. Didn't know that, did you? During the war, in the blackout. Your mam and dad used to have parties —'

'Parties?'

'Don't look so flummoxed. Hey – your dad was a bit of a nifty dancer too.'

'Me *dad?*' Terry said. '*My* dad?'

'Big gang of us in them days. Carlton on a Saturday night, then back to Barbara and Joe's for supper. Course, you were tiny then, nobutt a babby.'

It did seem incredible, but even as he spoke a vision drifted on the edge of Terry's mind, imperfectly remembered, of being taken from a warm bed in his mother's arms and thrust into a crowd smelling strongly of something. There was noise, and heat, and lights that made him blink, and people standing close together holding glasses, breathing fumes over him. Ladies with strong perfumes clutched him to their bosoms, their brooches pointed and sharp digging into his chest, and many wet kisses on his smooth cheek. He was passed from hand to hand like a rag bundle, dazed by the light and the noise, buffeted to and fro before being returned to darkness and sleepy warmth. It was a memory and not a dream, though nowhere in it could he find a round-faced, red-faced man with a blob of plasticine for a nose and a jolly laugh that set window-frames rattling.

Arnold gave Terry his change with the same hand that had wrapped the mince, so that the coins were greasy, with bits of fat stuck to them. 'Why can't a cross-eyed teacher teach properly?' – and when Terry shook his head, wrapping the money in his handkerchief with a slight shudder of disgust – 'Because he can't control his pupils!'

Arnold laughed delightedly at his own wit as he wiped his blue hands on his apron.

For Saturday dinner they had liver and onions and chips, with strawberry blancmange to follow. Joe sat in his working shirt, his scrubbed arms resting on the kitchen table, devouring the food as might a starving man. Afterwards he would have a proper wash in the sink and get ready for the match. Usually the meal was a pleasant one, with the rest of the day stretching before

68

each of them to dispose of as they pleased, but today Terry made the mistake of asking his father what 'Fuck off' meant. It was a question he had not considered lightly, suspecting that it meant something very rude, not to be mentioned in polite society, ever since the Boy Scout had snarled it to his face one afternoon on his way home from school.

But Joe was in no mood for educational enlightenment, fetching Terry a beauty across the back of the head with a hand that felt like a shovel and knocking him clean off his chair.

Barbara said, 'The lad was only asking a question, Joe!'

'Don't let me hear you using that word again in this house,' Joe said. 'That filthy talk.'

Finding himself on the floor with a throbbing head in the middle of his dinner was an experience that Terry wasn't likely to forget; he was hurt and wanted to cry but he wouldn't give his father the satisfaction. Underneath the pain and the hatred he somehow sensed that Joe was the loser: that his adult strength was all he possessed, and without it he was a sinking man.

Barbara's face had closed up like a fist. She was making a clatter as she collected the plates and carried them to the sink, turning on the geyser and filling the kitchen with steam and the gush of boiling water. Joe said:

'How am I going to have a wash now?'

'You'll have to wait. Won't you?' Barbara said, spacing the words evenly and calmly.

'You know I'm going to the match.'

'Can't be too soon for me.'

'How can I, woman, when you're washing up? You could have left them till after.'

Barbara screamed, 'Do you want me to throw them on the floor? Do you? Because I bloody will!' She took hold of the enamel bowl and half raised it out of the sink: it was a gesture, nothing more, but the anger was real.

'Don't be stupid, woman.' Joe's voice had thickened. If this

69

went on much longer he would lose his temper and become dangerous.

From the back door, holding a doll in the crook of each arm, her muddy drawers at half-mast, Sylvia said in a cross little girl's voice: 'Stop shouting at my mummy.'

'Go out and play,' Barbara said. 'You and all, Terry.'

He was glad to get away out of that atmosphere. It didn't give him any pleasure to hear them arguing, even when he knew she was defending him. He went through the backyard and ran down the dirt back-entry, jumping over the sticky mud patches where the water had evaporated, and all at once, for no reason, felt tons better. It was Saturday afternoon. He was off to the baths with Alec. And (you never knew your luck) there was always the chance that Margaret Parry would be there in that pale-yellow cossie that was a size too small.

Christmas up Syke

*

I T SNOWED ON CHRISTMAS DAY. JUST AFTER DINNER
there was a taxi coming to take them all to Auntie Martha's
who lived up Syke near the ponds. Terry's sack contained the
usual packets of sweets, chocolate selection box, apple and
tangerine, a painting set, a ludo and snakes-and-ladders game
combined, and three books: *1001 Amazing Facts, The Boys Bumper
Book of Adventure,* and *Jets, Rockets and Guided Missiles,* which was his
favourite. He was expecting no more, and so the first sight of the
brand-new shining bicycle as he opened the stairs door and
stepped into the kitchen made the eyes bulge in his head. It was
a red Raleigh Sport with drop handlebars, a Sturmey-Archer 3-
speed and a hub dynamo. It even had whitewall tyres.

Terry hugged his mam, knowing the sacrifices it must have
cost, but he was too embarrassed to thank his dad directly or
permit a show of affection. He slapped Joe on the shoulder instead, and his dad feigned a punch in return, with a nod and sort
of a sheepish grin.

Terry put a Mars bar from his selection box in his windjammer
pocket and wheeled His Bike into the street: it made a smooth
well-oiled ticking sound: there was no one about to show off to,
but on this wonderful morning it didn't matter.

The snow lay thinly on the hard ground, heaped like powder
in the ruts and hollows of frozen mud. Denby was silent and
deserted as he rode along, the tyres crunching softly through
the snow, and everywhere the peaceful whiteness covering the

houses and pavements and making the stone setts into rows of little rounded hillocks. Terry had never been so happy in his life. He rode along Cayley Street, changing gear for the fun of it, past Wellens's shop, did a circuit of the Top Track and then down the slope and round the Bottom Track, making a detour to the dead end of the Figure 7 and back again. He liked watching the blur of the spokes and the mirror-bright rims reflecting the handlebars, himself, the sky, in narrow distortion. Everything he saw gave him pleasure: he was aware of his own aliveness, glad to be Terry Webb and no one else.

When he arrived back his mother said, 'Have a good wash and put your best clothes on. We'll have some hot mince pies round the fire.'

'But I had a bath last night.'

'You still need a wash, Terry, on Christmas Day.'

Terry sighed, docile and resigned. It seemed daft having a wash when you weren't dirty.

His father had lit a fire in the front room, this being Christmas morning, and all the family sat round the hearth drinking tea and eating hot mince pies. In deference to the occasion Joe was wearing a shirt with a collar, the trousers of his Sunday suit, and carpet slippers (though still no socks). There was wrapping paper and string everywhere – in the hearth, on the floor, under the cushions – and Terry's books and games and Sylvia's doll's house furniture and tea party set scattered over the rug. Joe was pacing himself nicely, smiling grimly through it all, averting his eyes from the mess and confusion, tapping his foot in time to Sandy Macpherson's medley of carols on the wireless.

Dolly Bland popped her head in to say 'Merry Christmas' and sip a glass of sherry, then a little later Dot Hartley, Kevin and Doreen came in from next door, bringing a jigsaw of Tower Bridge for Terry (he *hated* jigsaws) and a skipping-rope for Sylvia.

Barbara was doing a lot of nudging and winking with Dot, which Terry didn't twig till his mam asked him to get a chair for

Dot; and ten-year old Doreen intercepted him and plonked a big wet one in the middle of his face – right under the mistletoe.

'Come on, our Terry,' his mam said, 'that's sixpence you owe her ...' She was jigging about, as fluttery as a schoolgirl.

Terry had gone a deeper shade of red than his new bike. It wasn't that he minded being kissed so much, but to have been manoeuvred into position so effortlessly made him feel a right idiot. Ungraciously he handed over the sixpence, appearing flustered, and with everyone standing round grinning, he said, 'Mrs Hartley can have my chair,' and as she moved forward to accept he stood on the arm of the settee and kissed her on the lips, tilting his head to avoid the mole on her chin.

There was a moment's complete silence. Terry got down off the settee and held out his hand. 'Sixpence, please.'

'I'll go to the bottom of our stairs,' Barbara said, hand spead-eagled on her chest.

Handing over the money, Dot said, 'You won't have any need to worry about your Terry. Talk about sharp.' And in his private tally of victories and defeats Terry chalked up another Swastika on the side of his Spitfire: it was perfectly okay pretending to be a kid so long as the adults didn't rumble you.

The taxi came for them at two o'clock. It was a Morris Oxford with a faded pennant on the radiator, and Terry almost peed himself as the long black bonnet slid into view past the leaded window. He had been coerced into having yet another wash (he still wasn't dirty) and his face shone like an apple as he stood on the doorstep, his knees shaking with cold and excitement. Joe bustled about, turning off the gas, locking the back door, making sure the cat was out, while Barbara piled presents on the sideboard. Every two minutes she would say, 'Have we got everything?' – repeating it over and over like a chant, as much for her own benefit rather than actually addressing anyone.

The driver waited morbidly behind the wheel, an indifferent face beneath the shiny peak of his cap, and at last they were ready,

Bessie Smith and Mrs Heap and Mrs Travis peeking out from behind net curtains as the driver put the car into reverse and the Webb family moved majestically backwards down the snow-covered street. Terry sat next to the driver; the smell of leather intoxicated his senses. He breathed in luxuriously and tried to see over the dashboard: the long shiny bonnet sloping away and the pennant vibrating stiffly in the slipstream.

As they rode along with incredible smoothness he kept finding a smile on his face: he still couldn't get over the astonishing fact that he actually had a bike. Bloody Nora, wait till tomorrow. Malc and Blandie would be pig-sick: his Raleigh had a 3-speed *and* a dynamo and theirs didn't. He sat back and wallowed in a kind of smug inward rapture, the smile imprinted right the way through him like Blackpool rock.

Then they were at the door of Auntie Martha's and Uncle Cyril's: now Christmas would really begin.

Terry suffered the hugs and kisses stoically in the cause of peace, harmony and goodwill towards all relations. Already the big table had been opened out, the felt underlay to protect the polished surface placed in position and the best tablecloth, washed and starched till it dazzled the eye, smoothed by Martha's capable hands so that it hung down to regulation length. The great white rectangle commandeered the room like a coffin at a wake, which meant that everyone was obliged to sit in corners and against the walls, conversing at a distance while the sisters Martha, Polly and Emily passed constantly to and fro from kitchen to table, table to kitchen.

Joe was sitting as far away from the fire as could be managed; the heat of the room was formidable, and still he perspired even in shirt-sleeves. Martha, Polly and Emily were his sisters, who had married Cyril Shaw, Reg Smith and Jimmy Brackett respectively. Martha and Emily were childless, though Polly had a boy,

Norman, going on nineteen, who had grown beyond the family circle and went off drinking with his mates or perhaps to the Carlton. The only person of Terry's age was his cousin Valerie, a pale watery slip of a girl with hair like yellow fleece, the only child of Joe's brother Harry and his wife Ivy. Altogether the gathering numbered thirteen, counting the children.

'And what are you learning at school?' Cyril asked Terry. Unlike his wife Martha, he had no feeling for kids, regarding them as an alien species, almost like tiresome little Martians.

Terry gave the standard reply, and his mother added, 'He'll be leaving Heybrook next year and going to the High School.'

She was always making rash pronouncements and it annoyed Terry. 'I *might* be going,' he said. 'I might. I haven't even taken the exam yet.'

'Our Terry, you know you will,' his mam said. Her pride and faith in him were complete and unquestioning; yet had anyone asked her which subjects he excelled in she wouldn't have known what to answer.

'More expense, Joe,' said Reg.

'Aye,' Terry's dad said. He was actually smiling; but then Christmas came but once a year. He gave a short forced laugh. 'High School,' he said, as though naming some rare tropical disease. 'What would they do today, this lot, if they had to leave school at fourteen like we did? They don't know they're —'

'— born,' Emily said, adept at finishing off other people's sentences.

'Three-and-six a week I used to get when I started,' Joe said. He'd found a subject that interested him, but all of them – Terry included – could have recited the list of woes and calamities, hardships and deprivations just as capably. It had all been said before and would be again, and again, and again.

'Why do you always have to harp on about that?' Barbara said. 'Times change. We're not all living in the stone age like you.' (This was one of the standard dialogues between them, a pattern of words that went in endless circles so that each knew the response of the other before it was uttered.)

'Kids today, I don't know,' Cyril said, which was the truth. He talked with a Senior Service in his mouth, the front of his waist-coat and jacket lapels covered in ash which he forgot to brush off. Martha, his wife, laying knives and forks on the table, said:

'They're exactly the same as when you were a lad. Anybody'd think you'd been brought up in the workhouse with no shoes on your—'

'—feet,' Emily said.

'They're all the same, fellas,' Barbara said. 'Nobody had such a hard time as them to hear them talk.'

'We didn't have the same chances they have,' said Reg.

'That's what you've worked for,' Ivy Webb said. She was a wan creature, the same as her daughter; to Terry the pair of them seemed to fade insignificantly into the wallpaper. 'If you can't give your kids a proper start in life what's the use of it all?'

'There's no gratitude nowadays,' Cyril said, wheezing cigarette ash down his front. 'When we were given something we were grateful. Kids today want everything on a—'

'—plate,' Emily said, nodding.

Terry lost interest in the conversation when his Uncle Jimmy swallowed a sixpenny piece and pulled it out of Valerie's ear. He did the same trick every year and it never ceased to amaze and intrigue them. Jimmy had been in the RAF and on his sideboard at home were photographs in silver frames of groups of men in blue uniforms standing in front of a giant propeller and part of a wing that Jimmy said was a Wellington bomber. He had never actually made the claim that he was a pilot during the war but Terry had somehow gained that impression. And Jimmy had a real gun too, a Browning automatic, which he kept in a felt pouch in the top left-hand drawer of the bureau.

'Did you shoot anybody with it?' Terry had once asked. 'Only wogs,' Jimmy said, a reply which mystified him. For a long time afterwards Terry imagined wogs as small furry creatures with pointed ears and bushy tails, rather like foxes.

At one minute to three silence fell. Cyril switched on the radiogram and everyone sat motionless as the National Anthem swelled from the speaker; then the King spoke for ten minutes, the flat, tired yet kindly voice with the slight impediment droning out the Christmas message to his Subjects throughout Great Britain and the Commonwealth. Martha, Polly and Emily had ceased their preparations to listen, standing at the door to the kitchen in attitudes of sober respect.

When it was over everyone breathed and smiled again. The table was now fully loaded, containing everything except the turkey, whose arrival was the second major highlight of the day. (The first for Terry having been the ecstatic thrill of waking up and realising it was Christmas Day.) The men and children ate first, the women waiting on them, after which they would sit and eat together and indulge in women's talk before doing the washing-up.

Terry wasn't faddy about food and had a bit of everything: turkey, pork, stuffing, sausages, sprouts, carrots, peas, roast potatoes, mashed potatoes, cranberry sauce, apple sauce, pickles, beetroot, and to follow, Christmas pudding and white sauce (with a silver threepenny bit in the children's helpings), sherry trifle and cream, mince pies and chocolate biscuits. The crackers were pulled, the paper hats put on, and the room throbbed with the heat of the fire and the eating people.

'Would you like some more Christmas pudding, love?' Martha said, resting her hands on Terry's shoulders. 'Or there's plenty of trifle left ...'

'You've had enough, our Terry,' his mam said. 'He's had plenty, Martha, thanks. If he has any more he'll be —'

'—sick,' said Emily.

Terry left the table and went to sit quietly on the settee under the window, his belly distended like a hard rubber ball. He opened *Jets, Rockets and Guided Missiles* and showed Uncle Jimmy the pictures and cut-away diagrams; to his surprise Uncle Jimmy didn't seem to know how a jet engine worked or even the difference between a jet and a rocket.

'Bright lad you've got here,' Uncle Jimmy said to Joe.

'Aye,' Joe said. 'Thinks he is.'

'Will you have a drop of something?' Cyril said, getting up and opening the doors of the cabinet with the rows of bottles and glasses inside.

All the men had beer or a short, except Joe who had a glass of shandy. They talked about work, about how Brights' was doing (where Cyril was an overlooker and Martha a beamer), and about which mills were laying men off or going on short time. The room was oppressively warm and Terry began to feel queasy. It was dark outside; through the leaded window the snow gleamed faintly under the streetlights: a dim stretch of heathland merging into night. At hourly intervals the blue-and-cream buses rumbled past, going up to the terminus at Syke ponds and coming down again with an icy blast that blew grit under the front door and jarred the fluted glass panels in the vestibule.

Terry went into the kitchen to escape the heat and to get a drink of water. He drank it slowly, putting on a special smile for Auntie Polly who was washing up at the sink. She was an exceedingly short, squat woman with heavy brows and chin-whiskers, and to Terry it seemed that she was always wearing the same long dress with faded flowers on it and an enamel brooch pinned just above the shapeless swell of her bosom. He got the impression that she never knew what to say to him – even though she had a son of her own – and in a queer way this gave him a sense of adult superiority: he felt it was up to him to take the initiative.

He put the glass down on the draining-board and considered for a moment before saying, 'I like your dress.'

Polly looked at him through the rising steam; then she smiled, rather uncertainly. Terry saw that she had more hairs on her chin than last Christmas, and there were some growing on her upper lip, though he was polite enough not to use this observation as a topic of conversation. Instead he said, 'How are you keeping then?'

'Not bad,' Polly said. 'Considering.'

'Cold in't it,' Terry said, 'for this time of year?'

Somehow the conversation wasn't zipping along as he thought it should, and worse, he still felt sick. He opened the stairs door.

'I'm going upstairs.'

Polly accepted this information without comment or expression, so Terry left her at the sink, her thick red hands immersed in soapy water. Upstairs in Auntie Martha's front bedroom it was a blessing to breathe in cold air that didn't have the taint of hot rich food in it. And the darkness helped – just the one streetlight outside the window shining on the white fur rug and candlewick bedspread, slanting across the clutter of objects on the dressing-table. Auntie Martha lived in what Terry considered to be luxury; there was even talk of Uncle Cyril buying a television set in the New Year.

Syke was raised above the town on the slopes of the hills, lightly populated, which gathered in a circle until they adjoined the Pennines farther to the north and east. It was still working class but the houses weren't crammed together and some of them were semi-detached with gardens front and rear. Terry's teacher, Mrs Butterworth, lived in one of these.

From the window he could look down to the lights twinkling in the valley. His school was down there somewhere, and beyond it the maze of streets which encircled the Arches: at this distance and with the gloom pressing down no detail visible, no landmark clearly identifiable. He liked the feeling of being alone in the sumptuous bedroom, his breath making an oval of condensation on the window-pane, and everywhere in the town below on this Christmas Day the thought of people congregating in front rooms, oases of warmth and laughter in the cold and dark. It was at such moments that nostalgia infected him like a dull fever, as though he were totally alone and watching over everything: the silence, the icy stars, the misty town in the valley. Yet deep inside there was an immense store of pleasure because he knew that down there somewhere, in the kitchen of the house in Cayley Street, there was a red bike shiny and new and glistening with chrome – His Bike – waiting for him.

The sound of music wailed from the front room: Frankie Laine singing *Jealousy*. It wouldn't be one of his Auntie Martha's records because he knew that she liked Donald Peers and Charlie Kunz. He went down, feeling quite chirpy, and crept into the front room on his hands and knees, squeezing into the space behind the radiogram. The table had been cleared and folded away, settee and chairs arranged in a semi-circle, and everyone was holding glasses and eating nuts; all except Valerie and Sylvia who were sitting on the hearth-rug playing with their stupid dolls.

'Still following the Dale, Joe?' asked Jimmy.

His father laughed. 'Aye, me and a few other silly sods.'

'Any chance of promotion?'

'Not this season.'

'Never in a blue moon,' said Cyril, who was the local bookie's runner and therefore took pride in laying good odds on any sporting event.

'Harry goes up sometimes,' Ivy said. 'Stands up there in all weathers. I tell him it's bad for his chest but he just won't—'

'—listen,' Emily said.

'You won't listen, will you?' Ivy said.

'No,' Harry said.

'Where's your Norman gone to-neet?' Joe asked Reg.

'Couldn't tell you, Joe, not if you paid me. Off galivanting I suppose, but he never tells us owt.'

Terry was getting rather fed-up at not being missed. It was cramped behind the radiogram. He made a high-pitched beeping sound that no one took any notice of.

'Across at Waggon I expect,' Polly said – her sole contribution for the evening.

'Does he go boozing?' Ivy said disapprovingly. 'At his age?'

'He's nineteen,' Cyril said. 'Spends his brass how he wants.'

'He never is,' Ivy said, shaking her head. 'Nineteen! Well I never. Would you credit it. Doesn't time—'

'—fly,' Emily said.

The record had finished and Terry took the opportunity to emit another high-pitched beeping noise. Jimmy said in an unnaturally loud voice: 'Somebody's got the wind in this room.'

'Jimmy,' Emily said, scandalised. 'Don't be vulgar.'

Jimmy came to the radiogram to put another record on and winked at Terry over the raised lid. They mouthed their complicity at one another and made faces.

Cyril went round again, filling up the glasses. He was a dour man, and tight with his money, but he didn't begrudge spending a bob or two at Christmas and was never backward in offering beer and shorts from the well-stocked cabinet. As he moved from chair to chair the ash on the end of his cigarette wilted and fell onto his waistcoat before cascading to the carpet.

Jimmy said: 'We haven't drunk a toast yet.'

'Aye, the Christmas toast,' said Reg.

'Where's our Terry?' Barbara said.

'Come on, lad, get a glass,' Jimmy said, and Terry crawled out from behind the radiogram. Cyril was about to pour him a glass of lemonade until Martha said, 'Nay, give the lad summat a bit stronger. Get him a drop of sherry.'

Terry raised his glass with the others, clinking it against Uncle Jimmy's as Reg proposed the toast: 'A Merry Christmas and a

Prosperous New Year for all the family. Let's hope the coming year will be as kind to us as this year has been and that next Christmas we'll all be here in good health and spirits.' He raised his glass. 'To us all.' Everyone drank. Emily started weeping.

Martha said, 'A toast to Mother and Daddy Sam.' These were the elderly Webbs, Terry's grandparents, who lived on Belfield Lane and who hadn't been to the Christmas party for the past four years due to Mrs Webb being a semi-invalid. On Boxing Day several of the family popped down to see them and spend an hour or two.

They drank again, Emily's glass wobbling in her hand and Martha's eyes red and watery. There was a subdued atmosphere for a while, the women taking their handkerchiefs from their cardigan sleeves and the men staring into the flames. It seemed unreal to Terry, a roomful of people sitting silently holding glasses in their hands. He was moved without knowing why.

'When's Father Christmas coming?' asked Sylvia in her cutest voice, breaking the spell.

'He should be on his way any time now,' Emily said, looking at Jimmy and nodding to the kitchen. She pointed to the ceiling. 'Listen for the reindeers clip-clopping clip-clopping, their little silver bells jingling away...'

Bloody Nora, Terry thought. Not again.

'We haven't got his mince pie and drink of beer ready yet,' Valerie said, genuinely alarmed, and Terry crossed his eyes and made a grotesque face behind her back.

'Jingle bells, jingle bells, jingle all the way,' Emily began to sing. Valerie and Sylvia and the adults joined in, but Terry refused to open his mouth, even after a dark look from his mother. He sat on the rug with *Jets, Rockets and Guided Missiles* and pretended to read.

'Sing, Terry,' Valerie said, 'otherwise Father Christmas won't come and you won't get any presents.'

'Hard—' He nearly said 'crap' but clamped the word between

his jaws and gave her a sour, world-weary smile instead. Uncle Jimmy made some elaborate pretext to leave the room, receiving meaningful glances from everyone but Sylvia and Valerie, and Terry who pretended not to notice.

Barbara hissed, 'Why aren't you singing, our Terry?'

'Forgotten the words,' Terry said, turning a page.

They had got through *Rudolph the Red-Nosed Reindeer, Silent Night* and were well into another chorus of *Jingle Bells* before there was a knock at the front door and in came Uncle Jimmy wearing Emily's red dressing-gown trimmed with white fur, suede flying boots, and an economy packet of Boots cotton wool stuck to his chin, upper lip and eyebrows. On his cheeks were two circles of rouge and he carried a brown sack with Tate & Lyle stencilled on it.

Sylvia had risen and was standing transfixed at this apparition, clutching her mother's hand, and Valerie's pale blue eyes were hovering between excitement and a thrilling kind of fear. They each had to say 'Hello Father Christmas' before giving their names as Jimmy pulled presents from the sack. When it came to Terry's turn he looked Jimmy in the eye, between the rouged cheeks and the cotton wool eyebrows, and said flatly, 'That isn't Father Christmas, it's Uncle Jimmy.'

'Terry!' Valerie whispered. 'You won't get any presents!'

'Not bothered,' Terry said. 'It's still Uncle Jimmy,' and wouldn't be budged even when Barbara grabbed his wrist and tried to shake some sense into him. It didn't matter; he refused to be deceived – especially since Father Christmas had the same freckled hands as Uncle Jimmy and wore the identical ring on the little finger of his right hand.

Father Christmas ate his mince pie, drank his glass of beer, and went, leaving Terry's presents on the sideboard. He wouldn't ask for them and it was left to Auntie Martha to stop all further nonsense by bringing them to him where he sat calmly reading on the hearth-rug.

They sang more carols, Jimmy slipping in from the kitchen with a strand of cotton wool still clinging to the side of his neck. The men's faces were glowing with alcohol and the heat from the fire and the women were a little tipsy, yet well within the bounds of social propriety.

After the giddy excitement of Father Christmas's visit the mood became reflective, almost sombre; at such moments Martha couldn't help weeping at the memory of the baby girl she had lost – her first and only child – and had to be comforted by Emily, while her husband Cyril sat motionless in his chair by the drinks cabinet, the ash lengthening on his cigarette, successive layers of it trapped in the folds of his waistcoat.

A bus came down from the terminus, rattling the vestibule door, and Harry said, 'Is that the last one?' They finished running early on Christmas Day and Harry had booked a taxi for nine o'clock.

'Twenty-past-eight,' Reg said. 'It will be.'

Terry was fascinated by one of his presents, a puzzle which comprised three interlocking pieces of bent metal. He preferred games of skill to those of pure chance. Finally he managed to do it and challenged Uncle Jimmy to a contest to see who could solve it the quickest. Uncle Jimmy beat him twice in a row.

'Are you going to be a pilot when you grow up?' Uncle Jimmy asked.

'Yeh. A jet pilot.'

'You have to be brainy, good at sums.'

'Do you?' Terry said, dismayed. Arithmetic was next to his weakest subject, after history. He tried to imagine what use sums would be to a jet pilot: if you could read the dials and work the joystick what good were division and multiplication?

Sylvia was leaning sideways on the hearth-rug, her eyelids drooping slowly shut and blinking open again. It came as a faint shock to Terry to realise that he couldn't have been much older than Syl – six, seven at the most – when he, Alec and Malc had played doctors and nurses with Sandra Weeks, Doreen Hartley and Fat Pat Sidebottom.

It had started quite innocently: the six of them crawling through the broken fence at the end of Arthington Street and sneaking into the lavatories at the back of Good Shepherd Sunday School, a ramshackle construction of whitewashed brick split into cubicles with a corrugated asbestos roof. Somebody suggested they play this game, taking it in turns to examine each other. In his private consulting room (the middle cubicle) Terry politely asked Sandra Weeks to remove her knickers so that he could carry out a thorough examination. Sandra did so and stood there patiently while he squatted in front of her, not knowing what he was supposed to be looking for or whereabouts it was located. He prodded and poked, sighing loudly and shaking his head, occasionally muttering to himself.

'It looks very sore to me,' Terry told her, upon completing the examination. He made Sandra turn round and pressed himself against her small cold buttocks; he hadn't gained a great deal from the experience, certainly nothing pleasurable, and couldn't even explain to himself why he had done it. For her part, Sandra remained compliant and completely passive all the while.

Terry recalled how puzzed he had been afterwards: to hear the big lads gabbing on about it you'd think that taking a girl's knickers down was better than rafting across the river or swaling the moors up Blackstone Edge.

'Joe,' Barbara said. 'Look at our Sylvia.' The little girl was fast asleep on the rug, snoring softly, curled up in that position of perfect peace and relaxation that only cats and small children can achieve. Terry felt weary too but wouldn't give in.

'I'll make a drink before you go,' Martha said. 'I bet Terry would like some orange squash and a mice pie.'

'Oh no Martha,' Barbara said, 'sit down. You've been on your feet all day.' But this didn't prevent Martha from going into the kitchen and putting the kettle on.

'Well, it soon comes,' said Reg, 'and it soon goes.'

'Aye, over for another year,' Joe said.

Cyril had fallen asleep with a smouldering cigarette in his mouth.

'That sounds like our taxi,' Ivy said. 'Harry, put Valerie's presents in that carrier-bag.' She called out: 'Don't brew for us, Martha, the taxi's here.' They found their hats, coats and scarves and stood by the vestibule door saying goodnight. Terry wished that he was going home in a taxi instead of having to walk.

'See you all again soon,' Ivy said, which she knew wasn't true. They lived on the new Kirkholt Estate on the other side of town and it might be next Christmas before the rest of the family saw them again. 'Take care now. Look after yourselves. Happy New Year. Give our love to Mother and Daddy —'

'— Sam,' Emily said, waving.

Terry went to the door to watch the taxi drive away, its tail-lights burning fiercely in the sharp clear air. Valerie's face appeared for a moment in the oval rear window, unsmiling; she didn't even bother to wave. He had never liked her, soppy little sod.

Martha brought in cups of tea and a plate of mince pies. Cyril started in his chair and an inch of cigarette ash fell intact and lodged in his waistcoat. Barbara said, 'Thanks for having us, Martha, we've really enjoyed it. Lovely meal. I've never seen our Terry eat so much. It's a wonder he wasn't sick.' As she said this Terry did begin to feel slightly sick but he finished his mince pie all the same.

'Back to the grind on Monday, Joe,' Reg said.

'Aye,' Joe said. He didn't sound particularly upset; it was a fact of life that you had to work; you could moan about it, fair enough, but it still had to be done.

'Are you sure you won't stop?' Martha said anxiously. 'We could put Sylvia and Terry in the back bedroom and you could sleep with me, Barbara, and —'

'No, we'll get down,' Joe said. 'Brisk walk will do us good.'

Buggeration, Terry thought. His eyelids were stinging with tiredness. He got to his feet and struggled into his coat. Sylvia was fast asleep. Joe picked her up and cradled her in his arms.

'Kiss everybody goodnight,' Terry's mam said, meaning his aunties. He kissed Auntie Martha and Auntie Emily and steeled himself to kiss Auntie Polly, closing his eyes so as to avoid seeing her bristly chin. Her lips were like cardboard, hard and stiff and tasteless. He wondered if Uncle Reg ever had to kiss her properly.

Everyone came to the door to wave them off, a wedge of light imprinted on the cold black pavement. Joe carried Sylvia, and Terry walked in-between, holding his mother's hand. Already his knees were freezing. 'All the best,' Jimmy called after them, and the last sound Terry heard was the door closing.

Rugby Road was long and dark, the gaslamps diminishing in the distance, the farthest away no bigger than a match's glow. Terry put one foot in front of the other like a sleepwalker, not thinking, just listening to the sound of footsteps and his father's harsh breathing. Nobody said anything all the way home.

Across Yorkshire Street, down Oswald Street, under the Arches, and then they were turning into Cayley Street. The house was cold; but in the kitchen His Bike gleamed and shone redly. It stayed with him, this image, until he had pulled off his clothes and got between the sheets and then it snapped off as quick as a light-switch the instant his head touched the pillow.

Part 2

On the Embankment

*

TERRY DIPPED HIS HEAD IN THE BOWL OF WATER, shook himself like a dog and combed his hair into a huge glossy quiff. His bike leaned against the backyard gate waiting to take him to adventure. He looked past the mirror's rust-coloured spots into the depths of his own eyes, trying to see what others might see, what impression he would make, whether he possessed that mysterious something that girls found attractive.

Barbara came down the stairs with her arms full of bedding. She dumped it on the kitchen table and the castors squeaked. 'Are you still at that mirror?' Irritation and tiredness dragged at her features. 'Hurry up, I want some hot water.'

Terry pulled the comb along both sides, squeezing out water so that it dripped warmly inside the open collar of his shirt. He hadn't decided yet where to go; that was the terrific part of having a bike. He might ride over to Gowers Street and see if Margaret Parry was knocking about. Or he could hang around Heybrook schoolyard where Yvonne Brangham, Jean Ashmore and Betty Wheatcroft played.

'Don't be late,' his mam said. 'Nine o'clock. Think on. And if you go on the main road make sure your lights are switched on.'

'Yeh,' Terry said, not listening. He had just this minute remembered, with a slight tug of conscience, that the practice exams for the eleven-plus started next week and his teacher had advised them all to do some extra work at home.

He took a last look at himself in the mirror and ran through the backyard. A pigeon – his blue bar hen – was coming in to land, a fluttering ball of feathers poised above the lavatory roof. He cooed to it softly, holding out his hand, though he knew it wouldn't come to him, and the hen strutted on the grey slates, its neck jerking forward with each stride, its white-rimmed eyes cautiously spying out the lie of the land.

Doreen Hartley was skipping in the back-entry with Fat Pat Sidebottom. Terry swung onto his Raleigh and wolf-whistled as he went by; as he turned the corner the two girls began to sing:

'Georgie Porgie pudden 'n' pie

Kissed the girls and made them cry

When the boys came out to play

Georgie Porgie ran away.'

Mr Heap was coming home from work as Terry cycled along Cayley Street. There hadn't been any snow since Christmas, though they'd be lucky to escape February without a blizzard or two. The ground was rock-hard under the tyres. He could smell fog in the air and already the waning light seemed to give everything the quality of a pencil sketch: colourless houses in varying tones of greys.

There was nobody about; he decided to try Gowers Street.

On the cinder track behind the garages he spotted Shap and two of his pals standing outside Shap's pigeon cote looking at something on the ground. Terry propped his bike against the hut, which was covered in tarpaulin and painted in black and white stripes.

'What's up?' Terry said, joining the group.

Shap laughed. 'Just screwed a piddie.'

On the ground was a headless pigeon staggering about in its own blood. The head lay a few feet away.

One of the lads said, 'You missed the best part. You should have seen it. Splashed blood that far' – indicating a spatter of dark spots on the white stripe of the hut.

The other lad said, 'It was squirting out like a fountain.' He performed a swishing noise with spit to represent the sound it had made.

'You wouldn't think they had that much blood in them,' said the first lad. 'Look, it's still coming out.' The pigeon had fallen on its side and the blood had oozed to a trickle. Even now its legs were twitching.

'I'm going to screw another,' Shap said. He opened the door of the hut. For some reason he seemed highly pleased with himself.

'Why do you have to?' Terry said.

'They're my piddies,' Shap said from inside the hut.

'I'm not saying they're not your piddies. What do you have to screw them for? Are you going to eat them?'

'I had pigeon pie once,' one of the others said. 'Yuck!'

Shap came down the steps of the hut holding another pigeon, a hen with dark bars on its wings and flight feathers. He held it correctly, the body resting snugly in the palm of his hand with the legs trapped gently between his fingers.

'Are you going to screw that one?' Terry said. 'It's a nice bird.'

'I've got eighteen,' Shap said. He laughed. 'Seventeen.' His mother ran the Post Office on Entwisle Road and his dad was a manager at Fletcher Bolton and so he could afford to buy and kill as many as he liked.

'Do you want to sell it?'

'How much for?'

'How much do you want?'

Shap thought for a moment. 'No, it's not worth owt. It came in as a strag.' He pretended to throw the bird up into the air so that it thought it was being released, but kept hold of its legs. The wings fanned the air and then settled back into place.

Terry said, 'I'll give you five bob.'

'Have you got it on you?'

Terry took out his money and counted it: he had fivepence ha'penny. He offered it to Shap. 'I'll give you the rest on Saturday when I get me spence.' In actual fact he only got half-a-crown in spence, but he could ask his mam to lend him the extra.

Shap sniffed and shook his head. He gave a sudden laugh, his large flat teeth flashing in the dusk. He didn't need the five bob. If he'd felt like it he could have given the pigeon away for nothing. But he wanted to screw it: there was nothing to stop him: it was his. 'If you don't want to watch you'd better get lost,' he said, 'because blood's going to spatter.'

Terry didn't want to watch but he wasn't going to let them scare him off and then snigger behind his back. He stood his ground.

'Is he soft or something?' one of the lads asked Shap.

'Mard-arse Webbie,' Shap said, and still grinning took the pigeon's head in his fist and used it as a handle to spin the body as you would a football rattle. The body came off and landed several feet away in the dirt.

As he rode along the cinder track between the garages Terry heard Shap and the other two screaming at one another that this time the blood had spurted even farther, a good ten feet at least, as far as the rotten tree stump.

He rode round aimlessly for a while, turning this way and that, following the streets haphazardly; at one point he saw Betty Wheatcroft and waved to her, but she was carrying a shopping-bag on her way to the Co-op. The gaslamps were lit as he came into Oswald Street. There was a grocer's on the corner and it occurred to him that he still had the money in his pocket: he went in and bought two sticks of liquorice, a packet of sherbert dip and a Mars bar, and when he came out his bike had gone. There was nobody in the street.

He looked wildly up and down, knowing they couldn't have ridden far. What a bloody daft thing to do; he should have put the padlock and chain on as his dad was always telling him.

A choking self-pity descended from nowhere and large perfect tears formed in his eyes. The light from the lamps was streaky and fragmented, and he could hardly breathe for the pain in his chest.

Behind the grocer's shop the railway embankment rose steeply, separated from the street by a fence of upright railway sleepers with pointed tops. And somebody's laugh came from beyond it – a laugh full of confidence and boastful strength, not a fear in the world – and when he went to look Terry saw Colin Purvis riding his Raleigh Sport over the sandpits and tussocks of grass. Colin Purvis's dad owned a butcher's shop and he was a tall lad, a year or maybe eighteen months older than Terry, but even so very big and powerful for his age, thanks probably to all the free steak and liver he consumed.

There were three others watching him, a girl of about thirteen, and two boys. Terry knew the girl by sight (she lived near Margaret Parry on Gowers Street) but didn't know her name. The two lads he had never seen before. He shouted over the fence: 'What do you think you're doing?'

'What's it to you?' one of the lads said, whose hair looked as though it had been cropped under a pudding basin. Both boys were about the same age as Colin Purvis, twelve or thirteen, and rough-looking.

'That's my bike.'

'Come and get it.'

Terry climbed over the fence.

The lad with the pudding basin haircut came straight to him but Colin Purvis said, 'I know him, it's Terry Webb,' and the lad halted a few feet away. He had thick eyebrows with no space between them and a pugnacious expression.

'Don't wreck the gears,' Terry shouted to Colin Purvis. 'It's brand-new. If you break anything I'll get skinned.'

Colin Purvis rode the bike into a sandpit and nearly fell off. He wrenched it out, stamping on the pedals, and said, 'Who says it's yours anyway?'

'You know it's mine. It was outside the shop.'

'Finder's keepers,' said the lad standing in front of Terry, staring him in the face.

'I've got a big brother,' Terry said unconvincingly.

'So what?'

'I'll go and fetch him.'

'Fetch him then.'

Terry tried to get past the lad with the short haircut and was punched on the arm. It wasn't a hard blow but the threat of what it might mean made his insides shrivel up. He ran on and tried to intercept Colin Purvis, begging him to be careful and not damage anything. It was becoming too dark to see clearly, the pitted grass at the bottom of the embankment illuminated only faintly by a single lamp. Colin Purvis evaded him, skidding the back wheel through 180 degrees and laughing when Terry went stumbling in the wrong direction.

'Come on, Colin, please,' Terry said, detecting in his own voice a thin whine of fear and abject pleading. He didn't know what else he could do except run vainly about in the darkness, lunging after the shadowy bulk of the boy and the bicycle; and even if he managed to grab the handlebars there was nothing he could do to make Colin Purvis get off. Terry could only hope that sooner or later he'd get fed-up with his silly clowning and let him go in peace.

The girl said in a bored voice, 'Give the kid his bike back and let's go.'

'He can't prove it's his,' the lad with the thick eyebrows and pudding basin haircut said.

'You bloody know it's mine!' Terry said, balanced precariously between anger and tears. He hated them all: the two lads and the girl and Colin Purvis most of all. He was a big dumb fat bloody sod.

'Here you are then, mardie,' Colin Purvis said at last, throwing the bicycle on the grass. Terry ran up to get it and Colin

Purvis grabbed him and pinned both his arms behind his back. Terry yelped and struggled to get free and Colin Purvis held him tighter.

'He's our prisoner,' said one of the other lads, who had some sort of impediment in his speech. In the darkness it was difficult to make out who was who, except for the girl, who had long fair hair. In the dim lamplight it looked like straw.

'What we going to do with him?'

'Scrag him.'

'He's only weedy,' said the lad with the impediment. He sounded as though his nose was blocked and his mouth full of phlegm.

'Let him go,' the girl said boredly. 'He's just a kid.'

'A cheeky kid,' the lad with the pudding basin haircut said, and in a little fit of spite kicked at the frame of the bike. Terry tried to move but his wrists were held firmly in Colin Purvis's meaty grip.

'Hey Carol,' Colin Purvis said suddenly. 'Show him your tits.'

'Get stuffed,' the girl said.

'Yeh, go on Carol,' the lad with the pudding basin haircut said, just as keen himself to see her body.

'What do you think I am, a stripper? Get lost.'

'You've stripped before now,' Colin Purvis said, grinning. He had a broad fleshy face, pockmarked, almost tending to fat, yet saved by the hard bulk underneath. His arms were round and packed solid and hardly narrowed at the wrists before opening to the wide spread of his hands. Terry's own wrists felt hot inside them, chafed and sore.

'Shut up,' Carol said.

Terry gave up the struggle and tried to reason with them. By getting them to talk it seemed to push the danger away, as though words were some kind of soothing balm.

'I haven't done owt to you, Col, have I? You've had a go on me bike, fair enough; if you let go of me wrists I won't run away, honest. They're getting really sore now.'

'Oh dear his wrists are getting sore,' the lad with the impediment said solicitously. 'What a shame. Oh dear.'

'If I let go will you run away?' Colin Purvis said. He winked at the others but they couldn't see his face properly: it was just a broad pale smudge in the lamplight.

'No,' Terry said. Colin Purvis let go. The danger seemed to have passed. They weren't going to harm him after all. Now if he could keep them chatting till he got his bike over the fence . . .

'What you doing?' Colin Purvis said as Terry bent down and took hold of the handlebars.

'I was just —'

'No you're not. You're not going yet. We haven't done with you.'

'What you on about?'

'We want to see your dick.'

'No,' Terry said.

'Carol wants to see it.'

'I don't,' Carol said. She shook her long fair hair back. 'Are we going to mess around here all night? Let him go home to his mam.'

Colin Purvis was standing casually with his hands by his sides, confident that he was within grabbing distance should Terry decide to run for it. He liked tormenting people. He was aware of his size and strength and employed them to make kids walk in fear of him – just as this snivelling squirt was frightened now. What he liked most, though, was the feeling that they were in his power: they stayed when he said stay and could only go when he said go. And part of the kick was to have an audience for his tricks and stratagems and cunning deceits, which was why it was necessary to have Carol, Eddie and Shaz there to witness the proceedings.

'It's getting late, Col,' Terry said, trying to keep his voice calm. 'Me mam'll be wondering where I am.'

'She'll have to wonder then, won't she?'

'You've had a go on me bike, what else do you want?'

'Wait and see,' Colin Purvis said softly, a little malicious grin creeping over his face. Without taking his eyes off Terry he went over to Carol and whispered in her ear. She said fiercely, 'No,' and there was more whispering. 'Why not?' he said, raising his voice.

'I don't want to.'

'But why not?'

'I don't want to.'

'What you going to do?' Eddie (the one with the speech impediment) asked Colin Purvis.

'I want to watch him shag Carol.'

'I won't do it,' the girl said. She folded her arms across her chest as if in self-defence.

Colin Purvis said deliberately: 'Why not? You let me.'

'I'm not having that little squirt poking up me.'

'I bet you'd hardly feel it anyway,' Shaz said. His shorn head gleamed like a close-fitting cap. Terry wanted to kick his dull stupid ignorant face in. He wanted to kill them all, even the girl.

'Come on Carol,' Colin Purvis said coaxingly. His hand was inside her coat and he was unfastening the buttons on her blouse. 'Show him what a big pair you've got.'

'I don't want to, Colin,' the girl said, though she made no attempt to resist the progress of his fingers. It was as if he had power over her – she had no choice but to obey him.

Colin Purvis said, 'Bring him,' and the five of them walked into the shadow of the fence, Colin Purvis draping his heavy arm across the girl's shoulders and Shaz forcing Terry along with spiteful jabs in the small of the back. Carol leaned against the fence, indolent and resigned. She gave the impression that her body didn't belong to her; it belonged to Colin Purvis, or Eddie, or Shaz, or anyone.

The lad with the pudding basin haircut held Terry lightly by the arms, not so much to restrain him but rather as a gesture that he was captive, under their control. But Terry knew full well he couldn't escape, not with his bike to hump over the fence. He had no choice but to go along with it and pretend he wasn't bothered. Colin Purvis said:

'Have you ever seen a tart's titties?' – and standing in front of the girl with his legs astride hers opened her blouse all the way down and flipped up her brassiere with his thumb so that her breasts were exposed to the cold night air, pale spheres in the dimness, the focal point of attention.

Terry didn't know why but he was frightened. There was something unnatural and obscene about Colin Purvis's disinterested treatment of the girl, as though she were a lump of meat.

'Have a feel.'

'I don't want to.'

'Have a feel,' Colin Purvis repeated in a voice that suggested it might be unwise to refuse.

Terry put out his hand and touched the girl's flesh. It was like touching putty. Her skin was cold and flaccid. He experienced nothing.

'Not like that,' Colin Purvis said. 'Like this.' Carol stood passively against the fence as he fondled her with both hands, moulding his hands to her body. Then he leaned forward so that his pelvis was thrust into hers, and started grinding. 'This gets her going,' he said in an aside, and Terry noticed that the girl had closed her eyes and was breathing through her mouth.

'Let's make him do her,' Shaz said close by Terry's ear.

'No,' Carol muttered. 'No.'

'Come on Col,' Eddie said in his queer nasal voice.

'Fuck off you lot,' Carol said, opening her eyes. Her hands were on Colin Purvis's buttocks. She said, 'Tell them to get lost, Col.'

'The kid wants to watch,' Colin Purvis said, and in another aside to Terry: 'She's like a rattlesnake when she gets going.'

'I don't want to watch,' Terry said. 'I want to go home.' He was very scared and didn't feel well; his insides were upset because all this seemed like a nightmare: the half-naked girl in the shadow of the fence and Colin Purvis leaning against her and the two rough lads like evil phantoms in the darkness. Denby, Cayley Street, No.77, weren't all that far away but they might have been a million miles. Somewhere nearby – from a back door left open while somebody went to the lavatory – a snatch of music drifted for a moment like sanity (it was Kay Starr singing *Wheel of Fortune*) and he had to make a supreme physical effort not to break down and scrike. He knew that if he cried it would be the end.

Colin Purvis was fumbling below. Carol made a sound in her throat and her head fell back against the fence. Her body began to move. Colin Purvis said calmly: 'Give us his hand,' and when Terry resisted Shaz held him round the neck while Eddie forced his hand down until it had made contact with something hot and open and wet.

'No, no —' Terry said, and collapsed at the knees. What happened next he wasn't fully aware of: he was on the ground and for some reason Shaz was kicking him. But what hurt him almost as much as the pain was that he didn't know why Shaz was kicking him, it was mindless. He hadn't done anything to them. 'I haven't done anything to you,' Terry cried.

Eddie stood on his hand. 'Get Carol to toss him off,' he said to Colin Purvis.

'You must be bleeding joking,' Carol said, fastening her blouse.

Colin Purvis buttoned his trousers. 'Denby lot.' He looked down at Terry on the ground. 'Soft as pig shit.'

Shaz said, 'Let's cob house bricks at his bike.'

'Chuck it under a lorry on Entwisle Road,' Eddie said, 'best thing,' and honked a few notes of his peculiar foghorn laugh.

'You've got stuff all over me skirt,' Carol complained, bending down to see in the weak lamplight.

'Wipe it on't grass,' Colin Purvis said, turning his attention elsewhere. He got hold of Terry by the hair and kept pulling until Terry was standing up.

'What we going to do with him?' Shaz asked avidly.

Eddie leered into Terry's face, enjoying the response it evoked.

'You better not do anything to me,' Terry said.

'What will you do if we do?' asked Shaz. 'Tell your dad?'

'Me uncle's a policeman,' Terry said hopelessly.

'Oh aye?' said Shaz. 'Will he come if we blow a whistle?'

'Let me go,' Terry said, starting to cry. 'You lousy buggers.'

This was the wrong thing to say because it provoked Colin Purvis into hitting him in the stomach. He was crying hard as they picked him up and bundled him over the fence. The back entry between the fence and the row of houses appeared as a black tunnel, the dirt worn into ruts by the vehicles that used it to gain access to the garages huddled together under the corroding walls of the viaduct.

'This one'll do,' Colin Purvis said, opening the door of a midden where the dustbins were kept. It was a windowless brick box with a thick stone flag roof. They pushed Terry inside and bolted the door; his shoes crunched on cinders and there was a smell of fish, wet newspapers and rotting vegetables. He sat on the edge of the dustbin, his chest shuddering, wondering in his terror what they would do next. They might drop lighted papers through the gap at the top of the door and choke him to death. But even worse than this was the fear that they would take his bike somewhere and wreck it. The impotence of his revenge overwhelmed him. He wanted fists of iron to smash the door down and batter Colin Purvis to a pulp of glue. It wasn't fair, three onto one; the injustice of it made the blood sing in his ears and his throat close up.

When he had ceased to cry he realised that they had gone away. In case they were playing a trick he put his hand cautiously through the gap at the top of the door, then tried to reach down to unfasten the bolt. He couldn't get anywhere near it: his fingers scratched feebly at the woodwork. Panic overcame everything and he kicked the door and yelled like a madman and didn't stop until he heard the scrape of a back door thresher and footsteps crossing the yard. The bolt slid back and a man with a bald head and a long thin nose was looking at him suspiciously. The metal tabs on his braces caught the faint light and winked dully. He held the door open with a hairy arm and said, 'What's the bloody game? Playing at silly sods are we?'

'I got locked in,' Terry babbled. 'Some lads—'

The man jerked his thumb. 'Come on, out of it. You don't live round here do you? Where you from?'

'Denby.'

'Then get back to Denby. And don't let me catch you round here again.'

Terry said, 'It wasn't my fault. I couldn't help it if they—'

'Go on, you little squirt, sod off,' the man said and clouted him hard on the back of the head. Terry ran down the back entry seeing stars and nearly ran into a wall.

He shouted: 'I'll tell me dad over you!'

'*I'll* tell your dad,' the man said. 'Bloody vandal.'

His bike was lying where Colin Purvis had thrown it down. He lifted it over the fence, switched on the dynamo, and rode the quickest way home without stopping once.

The Engine Room

*

BARBARA WEBB HAD GOT A JOB ON THE HOUSE-wives' shift at Oswald & Duncan's and in the evenings Terry and Malc would walk down Belfield Lane past the Croft Mill and turn up the track alongside the slipper works which led to the wire enclosure stacked with crates and bits of old rusting looms. Usually they didn't go directly into the spinning shed (which meant sneaking by the chargehand) but went through the scarred green doors into the engine room and stood on the metal gantry watching the huge shining steel arm of the beam engine sliding through the hot moist air with a power and ferocity that was compulsively hypnotic. The noise and vibration trembled in the soles of their feet and they had to mouth their conversation above the pounding roar of oiled machinery. Terry thought it magical: he had never seen anything like it: in his imagination it was the boiler room of an ocean liner ploughing through the Atlantic or the main propulsion drive of a rocketship in deep space, en route for Mars.

The air was heavy like syrup, the dense smell of machine oil catching the back of the throat. Pungent steam drifted from somewhere, a faint pall of it obscuring the gauges and levers and polished brasswork; and everything was so spick and span that the engine room might have been prepared specially for display at an exhibition. The engineer in charge didn't mind them coming in to look, although this was implied rather than stated because he never spoke to them or even nodded. He walked everywhere with a wad of cotton waste in his capable hand, automatically caressing the dials and copper pipes, the green gantry rail, the large brass-rimmed glass-fronted gauges. But it seemed that the machine didn't need looking after: it pounded remorselessly onwards under its own volition, never pausing or faltering, obeying some secret, hidden law of its own creation.

When they came outside it was like stepping under an icy shower. The perspiration froze on their bodies and Terry shivered all over, feeling the sweat cooling on his neck. Malc said, 'Do you think we'll get spotted if we go in't mill?'

'What can they say if we tell them our mams work here?'

'The chargehand had a fit last time.'

Terry said, 'He's not the boss.'

They pretended to be escaped prisoners-of-war dodging the Nazis, slipping into the shadow of the crates and working their way towards the open double-doors from which the roaring clatter of the looms escaped into the night. If the engine room was magical and romantic, the looms were vicious and terrifying. They chattered non-stop like maniacs, endless rows of spinning metal and blurred white thread, working themselves into a frenzy. The heat and speed were hideous.

Bessie Smith was piecing up a broken end, her fat red arms inches above the whirling conical bobbins. She frowned when she saw them but couldn't spare a split-second's concentration in case the thread burnt a gash in her hand or flicked away a fingernail. Some of the women had the tops of their fingers missing. Terry's mam was unloading a skip, stacking the full bobbins in the gangway: there were bits of cotton in her hair and stuck to her stockings. She shouted in Terry's ear to keep a look-out for the chargehand.

'Can we do owt?' Terry shouted back.

She shook her head. 'Unless you want to go and ask Ellis to make me a brew.' She had to repeat this before he understood. The racket was tremendous.

Ellis was the man who operated the hoist – a man in physique but a boy in his ways. Sometimes, when he was in the mood and not sulking, he would make tea for the women, either in separate mugs or in a large aluminium teapot with a broken spout. Terry knew where to find him, in his cubby-hole lined with hot pipes next to the lift-shaft.

As he walked along the narrow gangway leather belts slapped and creaked overhead, spinning on large spoked wheels near the ceiling before disappearing through holes in the whitewashed walls. The heat came at him in successive waves, fanned by the looms: the warm fetid breath of machines.

Ellis was reading an old issue of *Picturegoer*. He had on just over-alls, vest and underpants, his thin bare ankles protruding from a pair of rope-soled slippers with canvas tops. Terry asked if he wouldn't mind brewing two mugs of tea, one for his mam and one for Mrs Smith. Ellis gave him a grin in which there were more gaps than teeth and wiped the rims of two pot mugs on the sleeve of his overalls. He scooped tea from the caddy using his fingers and then pushed a tap with his elbow and scalding hot water spluttered from a pipe sticking out of the wall.

The chargehand said from the doorway, 'What's all this then?' It was quieter here, so he didn't have to shout.

'I'm just getting a brew for me mam,' Terry said. He smiled his most ingenuous smile. The chargehand wasn't impressed, his face tightening with impatience, but then decided it wasn't worth the bother and went away, shaking his head wearily.

'What does he get mad for?' Terry asked.

'Piles,' Ellis said. He giggled.

Terry thought about this on the way back with the mugs of tea, wondering 'piles of what?'

When he and Malc were outside and walking up Belfield Lane Terry began to feel wary and nervous. Twice in the past week he had woken sweating from nightmares in which he was tied down, unable to move an inch, while Colin Purvis (who was bald in his dream with tattoos on his arms) gave certain precise instructions to Eddie and Shaz – instructions that were unintelligible but which Terry knew were pure evil.

They passed the Cloverdale Hotel and walked along Entwisle Road, and the farther they walked, the more nervous he became. He was half-prepared to run at any moment, staying close to the houses and shop-fronts as if they might offer protection. A few feathery flakes of snow wafted down under the yellow lights and lay like soft confetti on the pavement.

'It's snowing,' said Malc. 'Great.'

Terry was thinking: once we get past Oswald Street and under the Arches I'll be all right; we can cut across the Common and climb over the railings at the end of Cayley Street ...

'Hiya,' somebody said and Terry jumped. Whoever it was moved forward into the light and Malc said, 'Hiya Shap.'

He had been standing deep inside a shop doorway on the corner of Gowers Street, which was why they hadn't seen him.

'What's up with you, Webbie?' Shap asked Terry.

'Nowt. Why?'

'Somebody after you?' His wide confident grin revealed the row of off-colour teeth, big as tombstones. It was hard to imagine Shap without his yellow smile. You got the impression that he carried it with him wherever he went, ready to be slapped on at a moment's notice. Terry thought that he too would probably have a smile like Shap's if his mother ran the Post Office.

'Do you want a fag?' Shap said, surprising them both. He gave them a full Player's each, which felt like a cigar in Terry's mouth.

'Where's the rest of them?' Terry asked, meaning Shap's pals.

'Gone in,' Shap said.

They moved into the doorway with him, watching the snow thicken and come flurrying down onto the road in a deathly hush; a bus came by and spoiled the bland smoothness, sending slush curling into the gutter.

'What time is it?' Malc asked.

Shap looked at his watch and said that it was five minutes past nine. This gave Terry an idea. He had been puzzling over what to buy his mother for her birthday in March, and thought now of a watch. He'd seen some advertised in the back pages of the *Sunday Pictorial*: 'Ladies 17-jewel Swiss-movement Cocktail Watches. ONLY 15/- DEPOSIT! £1.7.6d a month. Cash Price £5.19.6d.' If he could get a paper round at 12/6d a week he could easily afford the payments. He tried to work out how much £1.7.6d was by the week.

'Bet you don't know who I've bin with tonight,' Shap said.

'Who?' Malc said.

'Guess.'

'We haven't a clue,' Terry said.

'Margaret Parry.' Shap was grinning. 'Behind the garages.'

Terry didn't want to hear any more but he had to stay. It was the price of the cigarette he was smoking.

'What did you do?' Malc said.

'I didn't actually stuff it,' Shap said, an admission that surprised Terry by its honesty. 'But I pulled it out and she held it.'

'Go on,' Malc said with unfeigned interest.

'Well,' Shap said, 'we were messing about round the back of the garages, nothing dirty, just creeping up on the girls and frightening them. Margaret was hiding so I went looking for her. She was hiding behind the concrete garage with the flat roof and when I found her she said "Keep quiet. Don't tell the others where we are". Anyway, then we started snogging – proper French kisses – and I had a feel up her legs. She didn't say owt, didn't even pull me hand away. She was wearing these kind of silky knickers and I put me finger inside and rubbed her up. She was giving me belting kisses: you know, slavvery. Anyway, after a bit I thought I'd try it and see what she did. She got hold of it, really tight. I thought "Bloodyhellfire" and put me finger up her fanny.' He held up the finger in question as if in evidence of the truth of his claim.

It might have been true, it probably was true, every word of it, but Terry didn't wish to hear any more. In one way he could visualise Margaret Parry doing precisely what Shap was describing, and yet in a curious contradictory way he found it impossible to believe that such a sweet attractive creature (as he imagined her to be) could participate in anything so blatant and disgusting. It degraded her in his eyes to the level of gross bodily appetite and cheap crude sensation. The rather disturbing notion entered his head that perhaps girls were attracted by such behaviour: he thought of Carol and how crudely Colin Purvis had treated her and how she had never once complained, allowing him to do and say anything he pleased. Were all girls like that? Did they want a big rough moron like Colin Purvis or Shap to put his hand inside their knickers and tickle their fannies? Was that all there was to it?

Terry looked at Shap's mouth splayed in a vast stupid grin; he felt weary and despairing – of ever being able to understand. Did Shap know the secret, and did the secret consist of nothing more mysterious than the cruder the better?

Malc said reverentially, 'Steaming Nora,' in wonderment and envy at Shap's tale, and flicked the fag-end into the steadily falling snow, now obscuring the lights as it swept down in a thick silent curtain.

'Wait till next time,' Shap said smugly. 'I'll go all the way.'

'She won't let you,' Terry said.

'She's dying for it.'

'How do you know?'

Shap said, 'You're only a kid. You've never touched a girl or played stink-finger with her.'

'How do *you* know?' Terry said, throwing the cigarette-end into the snow.

'Who then?' Shap challenged him.

'I'm not telling you.'

'Because you've never bloody done it.'

'Neither have you. I bet you've never even kissed Margaret Parry.'

'I've just been telling you haven't I?' Shap said, the smile finally extinguished.

Terry made a scoffing sound.

'Look,' Shap said dangerously, 'I don't want a kid like you telling me I'm a liar. If you don't believe me, smell it,' holding up the index finger of his right hand.

'What does that prove?'

'It bloody proves——' Shap said, and then must have realised there was no need to prove anything, least of all to a squirt like Terry Webb who everybody knew was a cocky little know-all. This infuriated Shap, mainly because it threatened the mellow good mood that had enveloped him so snugly; fortunately he had a method for dealing with kids who thought themselves smarter than everybody else, and also the strength to implement it: Terry was sent slithering on his back in the snow and was momentarily lost to sight, a dark huddled shape obscured by the whirling flakes.

Shap waited for retaliation, his broad pale fists poised ready, but Terry had risen and gone, swallowed up in the blizzard of white.

After Dinner

*

ON SATURDAY MORNING THE SNOW LAY DEEP and crisp and even. Along the Top Track it was packed hard and glossy from the wheels of the coal wagon and the horse-drawn milk float and the van delivering bread to Wellens's shop. The Gang were out in force with their sledges, sliding one after the other down the Brew so that the slope was buffed and burnished into a channel of glass upon which it was impossible to stand upright.

Terry's sledge had been made by his Uncle Jack, when he stayed with them after his demob: a rigid box construction with a pair of cast-iron runners that Terry had polished with Brasso and rubbed up with lard. It wasn't the fastest sledge (Roy Pickup had an all-metal one that went like greased lightning) but it was strong enough to carry two, three, even four lads all at once. This could be hazardous if the sledge went out of control halfway down and skewed ninety degrees, throwing the top three onto the icy slope, then overturning with the steerer hanging on and sliding the rest of the way upside-down and arse-about-face. The year before, Danny Travis had been thrown off and semi-concussed, lying in an awkward heap with a purple lump the size of a half-a-crown gathering nicely on his forehead.

Spenner, as usual, came up with the craziest schemes. 'Five of us on one sledge. How about it?'

They tried it, Roy and Kevin lying flat, Terry and Malc astride them, Spenner standing at the back holding the rope like a stagecoach driver whipping a team of four across the prairie. It nearly worked, very nearly, except that Spenner's weight upset the equilibrium of the sledge which reared up like a bronco, throwing Spenner off the back, dislodging Terry and Malc, leaving Roy and Kevin hanging on to finish at the bottom of the Brew on their backsides with the sledge on top of them.

Spenner came limping through the frosty grass, red-faced with laughing, and Malc was jumping up and down to shake out the snow that had been scooped inside the legs of his short trousers.

'You're all looney,' Teddy Travis said, sitting on his Norton at the top of the slope. 'You could have broken your bloody necks.' He was fair, like his brother Danny, with a fresh open face that the sun, when it came, would bring out in a deluge of freckles.

'Are we having another go?' Spenner said.

'Bugger off,' Kevin Hartley said. 'I'm not committing suicide for you or anybody.'

'We could tie three sledges together and all the lot of us pile on.'

'You're cracked,' Teddy Travis said. Only three years separated him and Spenner, yet they were the vital years that marked the division between sledging with the Gang on the Brew and inhabiting the grown-up world of jobs, money, girlfriends and gleaming black Nortons. Already Teddy had forgotten how he used to roam the ash-tips and swale the railway embankment, paddle across the river on a raft of planks and oil drums, raid the pens down the Figure 7 for crab-apples. What he saw was a bunch of crazy kids with not a ha-puth of sense between them, unable to distinguish danger from tomfoolery; Spenner especially, who Teddy thought a complete raving nutter.

Terry went to stand in the respectful group round the Norton, breathing in its throat-filling smell of oil and leather and metal-polish. The lads already knew the answers but still asked the questions:

'What will it do?'

'How much was it?'

'Will you give us a ride?'

'Where've you bin on it?'

'Will it beat an AJS?'

'Will you give us a go round the block?'

Sometimes, when he felt like it, Teddy would take one of the younger lads on the pillion and do a circuit of the Top Track, hammering the throttle along the length of Kellett Street and bouncing over the potholes, the confined roar of the twin exhausts banging back and forth from the house fronts. Terry had been round twice, but today Teddy couldn't be bothered. Besides, he said, it was too dangerous on the ice and snow.

At twelve o'clock Terry and Malc went in for their dinners, no bones broken but the tops of their legs smarting with frost, and with sore red rings where the edges of their wellies had been rubbing. The Gang had already decided to go sledging that afternoon on the hill behind Heybrook School: a terrifyingly steep slope which finished up – if you weren't quick enough – in the shallow but ice-flecked water of the brook.

Terry kicked the snow off his wellies against the back step and went into the kitchen. His mam said: 'Don't tramp slush in here. Throw 'em under the sink.' Turning from the stove she said: 'Wait till Denis gets to be his age' – this to Mona Sysons who was sitting in the rocking-chair nursing a six-month-old baby boy. Mona was the eldest girl of Barbara's friend Madge who lived on Ramsay Street; she was a thin waif of a creature with dyed red hair, a sallow complexion, and a tiny cracked voice that sounded to Terry as though it had a struggle to get out of her throat. Mona had been married for thirteen months. The little boy on her knee looked the picture of health.

'Say hello to Mona,' his mam said.

'Hello,' Terry said.

'Say hello to little Denis.'

'Hello Denis.'

'How's our Terry then?' asked Mona.

'All right.'

'In't he getting a big lad now?' she said to Barbara.

'Eleven on Tuesday. Wash your hands and sit down.'

Terry sat down at the kitchen table and ate his dinner. He was wiping up the gravy with a piece of bread when Sylvia came in and got told off for being late. Barbara put her dinner on the table and resumed the story she was telling Mona about this woman who'd had to have an operation, and when she came to a certain word lowered her voice to the level that made Terry prick up his ears. The word was 'abortion'; probably Spenner or Roy Pickup would know what it meant.

The kitchen was becoming perceptibly darker. Behind the window the sky – a sluggish dirty grey – was an unbroken layer of cloud pregnant with snow. The light over the ash-tips was unreal, like that of a stage set, the undulating horizon glowing whitely under the sameness and drabness of light.

'Looks like we're in for it,' Barbara observed, switching on the single bulb which threw a wash of yellow over everything: sink, stove, coconut matting, the few sticks of furniture. She took a postcard from behind the clock on the mantelpiece. 'Guess who this is from, Terry...' Her whole being seemed suddenly, vivaciously alive. 'Your Uncle Jack!' The smudgy colour picture was of what looked like a town hall or a railway station.

'He's working in Leicester,' Barabara said, switching from Terry to Mona. 'You know, Jack tried all over round here, he really did, but couldn't find a thing...'

Mona unbuttoned her blouse and began breast-feeding the baby. Terry tried to drag his eyes away from the magnetic sight. The baby found the nipple and snuggled onto it with a grunt and a sigh.

'... cotton trade's dead as a doornail. You know, I think it's so unfair on all these fellas who lost out during the war. They came back to what – bugger all.'

'Does he know where babies come from?' Mona asked, nodding in Terry's direction, the cracked voice like a rusty penny whistle.

'Hah. They think they know everything nowadays,' his mam said, though the way she said it implied that they didn't.

'Have they told you about the facts of life at school?' Mona said.

Terry hesitated, feeling the stirring of a blush below the line of his collar. He said, 'No,' in a gruff voice. It was too soon to make his escape immediately because this would be tantamount to a confession of knowledge, and for them to know he knew would shame him.

'I've certainly never told him,' Barbara said.

'You ought to, he's getting to be a big lad now.' She beckoned with her free hand. 'Come on, Terry, look at little Denis having his dinner.'

Terry approached as though he were dragging his sledge, one foot reluctantly in front of the other, curiosity and embarrassment in equal measure. He had never seen a full white breast in a baby's mouth at such close quarters before. The sight transfixed him so that he stood, the socks around his ankles, his knees burning from the fire, staring with absolute fixedness at the girl, conventionally dressed except for the upper part of her body bared to the air. He knew, as he looked, that it was an image he would never forget: she wasn't beautiful, he felt no desire, yet the simple act she was performing seemed to him almost miraculous. He had never before realised the true function and purpose of a woman's breasts.

'Greedy little bugger,' Mona said in a reedy affectionate whisper. The baby's eyes were closed, his round red cheeks like tiny balloons pressing against the breast, and, somewhere between, hidden from view, the eager sucking mouth.

Terry went upstairs to the cold back bedroom. He could have done with a smoke but daren't risk it, not with his father due home at any moment. He stood at the window looking out at the river sliding blackly between the white banks, overcome by a kind of frenzy – the feeling that his head was unable to contain the thoughts rushing madly within it and the breath in his body compressed to suffocation point. He had never felt so odd in his life.

Without willing it to come, the vision floated up of Shap and Margaret Parry standing in darkness behind the garages. It didn't matter any more whether it was true or not: the image was lodged permanently in his brain. He fell on the bed, clutching the pillow to him in a passionate embrace, pressing his lips to what became in his imagination Margaret Parry's lips, the dark recess of her mouth open and vulnerable in a fantastic French kiss.

From the next door backyard he heard Mrs Hartley say, 'Don't forget the washing-up, Doreen. And no more than two in the house. Think on now.'

There was the sound of a latch and then the backyard gate banged shut.

During the afternoon he suffered a brainstorm; at any rate he lost possession of his faculties. Had anyone known what he planned they would have thought him deranged, yet everything he did was as a dreamlike trance, not at all real, as though happening to someone else down the far end of a long echoing tunnel.

Even so, he noted and committed to memory every detail of Doreen Hartley's dress as she opened the door to him with wet hands, a ring of suds clinging to her forearms. The kitchen was as familiar as his own: the wall of tongue-and-groove boards painted green with the stairs door and cellar door adjacent to each other, the cupboard set in the opposite wall, the black-leaded grate in the corner near the window, the gas-stove with its rack of plates, the big pot sink on cast-iron legs where Doreen stood with her hands immersed in greasy water. Kevin wasn't in, she said, he'd gone with his Uncle Ted to watch the rugby. Terry stood behind her, unable to speak or move; in the mirror he could see her pale round face surrounded by crinkly brown hair, eyes downcast to the dishes in the sink which she mechanically washed and stacked on the red rubber mat. She hummed something tuneless.

The kitchen was dark, the drab sky seeming to draw what light there was and absorb it like grey blotting paper. Without giving it much thought Doreen said, 'How did you get on in the practice exams, Terry?'

'I passed.'

'Eh?'

'I passed,' Terry said, clearing his throat.

'I didn't. Mr Reagan said Arithmetic and English let me down. He said if I can improve them two I might have a chance.' She blew out some air in a sigh of bored restlessness. 'Just think, another five years in that dump. Drive you potty.'

Terry was sitting on the corner of the kitchen table, the palms of his hands resting on his knees. He thought he must be choking to death. Doreen rinsed the last plate and wiped her hands on the towel hanging on a nail behind the back door. He noticed how the flesh on her upper arms wobbled with the movement: he wanted to feel what it was like, pinch it between his fingers, knead it. She was wearing a blue dress with buttons down the front and the buttons followed the gentle curve of the swelling underneath. All he had to do was stand up. Reach out his hand. Touch her. What could she say? There was nothing to stop him.

Doreen finished wiping her hands. She wasn't a pretty girl, neither was she plain. Her face was pleasantly rounded, her eyes were round too, and her body obeyed this genetic law of roundness: ample and at the same time unsure what was expected of it, what it might be capable of. As for Terry, he could only marvel that Doreen Hartley had lived next door for eleven years and he had never before understood how desirable she was; he convinced himself that she was very desirable.

Doreen stepped back as he slid stealthily off the table and put both feet on the floor. It must have been that movement or the look in his eye that made her say, 'What do you want?'

'You.'

'Me?' Doreen said. 'What you on about?' – but she was getting the gist of the idea quite rapidly as he advanced towards her and she noted, for the first time, the expression on his face. In an instant she was terrified and thrilled, and like those cartoon faces in a children's comic which when turned upside down reveal another totally different person, she suddenly saw him in a new light. It was still Terry Webb but now a Terry Webb with a glazed look in his brown eyes and a deliberate purposefulness in his movements. She said in a fierce whisper, 'Terry – don't,' as he wedged her body against the back door and tried to force his lips on hers.

'What's up?' Terry said under his breath. 'Come on, Doreen, come on.'

'Terry, me mam —'

He stopped her mouth with a kiss placed inexpertly off-centre, his hands all over the blue dress like ferrets. She fought him off and he released her mouth, panting, whispering urgently, 'Let us have a feel, Doreen, come on, a quick feel —'

'No, I don't want.'

'Come on.'

'No.'

A silent deadly struggle ensued in which he pulled her away from the back door and got her down on the floor. His hands plucked at the buttons on the dress, trying to unfasten them, until he realised they were purely for decoration and in his frustration tore at the neck of the dress.

'Terry,' Doreen said, 'if you don't let – me – go —' frightened now by the intensity and purpose in his face. He was an animal and there was no way she could control the animal or turn it back into the familiar Terry Webb who lived next door.

There was a hand squeezing her breast and another inside the neck of her dress. She had this feeling of being held down and overpowered by a dead burdomsome weight. 'Terry,' she managed to say, and pulled him by the hair-roots till he yelped like an animal and rolled off her, his knees inflamed where they had been rubbing on the lino.

Terry sat up massaging his scalp. 'Bloody hell, Doreen.'

Doreen was on her feet moving towards the back door and watching him, pulling the hem of the blue dress down below her knees. Strands of crinkly hair adhered damply to her forehead. She said with a little scared laugh, 'What were you trying to do?'

Terry wouldn't look at her. 'Bit of fun,' he said emptily; the blood had cooled, his eyes were back to normal, and he felt daft sitting on the floor in the middle of Doreen Hartley's kitchen with red knees. As he rose to his feet she put her hand on the latch, prepared for flight, and said, 'Go out the front way, Terry.'

'Don't be silly, I'm not going to touch you.' But he knew that if he got within grabbing distance he wouldn't be able to resist the tantalising buttons on the front of the blue dress and the warm mounds residing ever so slyly beneath the thin material. Doreen stood palpitating by the back door.

She said, all humour gone, 'Are you going to go, Terry, or do I have to tell your mam?'

'All right,' he said. 'Wait your sweat.'

He moved towards the back door and Doreen scuttled away and stood with the kitchen table between them. Points of colour burned in her cheeks. His throat was dry with disappointment.

How was it that somebody like Colin Purvis or Shap knew the secret, and he didn't? What could he, should he, have murmured in Doreen's ear to make her lie down quietly with him on the kitchen floor? He wouldn't have hurt her, that was the last thing he wanted to do.

As he went across the yard he heard the door slam and the hollow rattle of the bolt. Under the leaden sky it was the most desolate sound Terry had ever heard, the sound of being shut out, and he really had to check himself in case the tears started to flow.

Odds and Sods

*

ON TUESDAY AFTERNOONS MR REAGAN TOOK the boys of 4A and 4B up to the playing fields behind Howarth Cross School. On the timetable this was known officially as 'Games', though the only game played was football. There were enough boys in the two classes to make up two teams of eleven, with a dozen or so left over as the 'odds and sods' who kicked a football about in lackadaisical fashion in a parody of a match. The odds and sods didn't have enough skill to be considered for a team place, and Terry was one of these. He resented this, though laughed it off whenever Arthur Halliwell or Vic Crabtree asked sneeringly what it was like to be one of the deadlegs. 'So what?' Terry said. 'You lot only get muddy.' And went on smiling grimly all the time he was kicking the scarred leather ball about in the corner of the field where the grass grew ankle-high.

What irked him all the more was that his two best pals, Alec and Malc, were both selected to play for the proper teams. He refused to believe they were that good, or, conversely, that he was that bad. He put it down to Mr Reagan not liking him because he was good at art and had played the main part last term in the school play.

The afternoon dragged on. The days were becoming longer now, so that it was possible to see the ball even at four o'clock. The final whistle blew and the boys straggled tiredly into the dressing-room – a draughty shelter with a concrete roof and wooden benches along the dank brick walls. There were no baths or showers, and most of the boys simply pulled their clothes over the top of their football strip, one or two of them not even bothering to change their boots.

'How many did Stanley Matthews score?' Vic Crabtree shouted to Terry, which provoked laughter from the lads sitting close-packed on the benches. The smell was overpoweringly of sweat and damp cotton, with a taint of trampled grass-seed. Clods of mud littered the floor.

Terry said, 'Shut your gob, rat-face.'

'Or what will you do Webbie?'

'Boys, boys,' Mr Reagan said mildly. 'Don't be spiteful. We can't all be good at football.' Terry felt his face go hot. He bent down and pretended to be having trouble with the laces on his boots.

Mr Reagan went on, 'Perhaps if Terry Webb tried a bit harder he'd get on the team.'

'We don't want any invalids, sir,' Arthur Halliwell said.

'Don't be disrespectful,' Mr Reagan said. 'You shouldn't talk about invalids in that way. They can't help how they are.'

'Brought your crutches with you, Terry?' a voice called from the end of the dressing-room.

'He doesn't need crutches,' Rod Callaghan said, 'he's got a wheelchair.'

There was more laughter and then a sudden lull during which Terry's muffled voice was heard to say distinctly, by everyone including Mr Reagan: 'I wouldn't be on your shitty team if you paid me.'

He was still bent over, blinded by tears, unable to see the laces he was supposed to be untying.

'Who said that?' Mr Reagan said, knowing very well who it was.

'It was the Invalid, sir,' Derek Cross said, snorting.

'Be quiet,' Mr Reagan said. 'Was that you, Terry Webb, who used that disgusting word? Stand up.'

The laces were fastened in a hard wet knot. Terry picked at them hopelessly. His neck, cheeks and ears were on fire.

'He's gone all red, sir.'

'Shut up, Halliwell,' Mr Reagan said. 'Did you hear me? I said stand up.'

Had he considered the matter more rationally Terry might have obeyed. But he had no respect for Mr Reagan, and besides he wasn't really Terry's teacher, he only took them for Games. He also suspected that Mr Reagan had a disdain for clever kids who came top in the classroom and were hopeless on the football field. It was an opportunity Mr Reagan couldn't let slip by, and he didn't, lifting Terry by the short hairs at the back of the neck and making him stand up.

'Get outside,' Mr Reagan said, an unreasoning spite making his voice sharper than he had intended. Terry stepped over legs and discarded boots to reach the open air and waited on the edge of the pitch where the corner flag flapped in the stiffish cold breeze. He thought that he had never hated anyone as much in all his life, not even his dad.

Alec and Malc hung about waiting for him at the junction of Albert Royds Street and Halifax Road, pirouetting to make their boots swing round their necks and strangle themselves with the knotted laces. The three of them walked in the direction of Heybrook, and after a while Malc said:

'He's a pigging sod, that Reagan.'

Terry was very calm. With an insight beyond his years he said, 'He's jealous, that's all. Teacher of a B class in a dump like Heybrook, what a life.'

They walked on in silence for a while, until Alec Bland said, 'Have you heard this one?

Mrs Brown went to town

To buy some macaroni,

She had a fart behind a cart

And paralysed a pony.'

They were passing a newsagents-cum-sweetshop and Terry asked the other two if they had any money on them. Alec had threepence, Malc didn't have any.

Terry said to Alec, 'When we go in, take your time deciding what you want. Then ask for summat on one of the shelves.'

'What if I don't like anything on the shelves?'

Terry and Malc looked helplessly at each other.

'Dun't matter,' Terry said slowly and patiently. 'Ask for anything. We'll get you summat you *do* like.'

Alec got it. He looked happy, then nervous

They went in and luckily there was another customer who couldn't decide what colour of writing paper she liked. While she dithered Terry and Malc idled near the sweets counter, the banked array of chocolate bars, wine gums, gobstoppers, lollipops, liquorice sticks, peppermint and coltsfoot rock set before them like a feast before a king. As the owner of the shop ducked below the counter to rummage for yet another shade of writing paper, Terry dipped into the treasure and slid a bar of peanut brittle into his trouser pocket, maintaining an expression of bored innocence when the owner reappeared with a brown cardboard box.

'Pink,' the woman said. 'I don't know about pink.'

'What can I get you lads?' the owner said over her head.

Alec's voice was a squeak. 'Chewing gum.'

'Spearmint or PK?' the owner said. As he came round to the side counter Terry saw that the chewing gum was near the front of the display, behind the glass panel in its shiny metal frame. He said quickly:

'Don't get chewing gum, Alec. Get summat else.'

'What?' Alec said, his eyes bulging.

'Get some ... liquorice torpedoes,' indicating the jar behind the man's head.

'Fourpence a quarter,' the man said, reaching down the jar, and by the time he turned back Terry had a twopenny bar of Fry's Five Boys chocolate and a packet of sherbert dip concealed about his person. Malc had been at the treasure too.

'You'd better get two ounces,' Terry said when he saw the owner weighing out a quarter-pound. 'You've only got thrupence.'

'T-t-two ounces please,' Alec said.

'I've settled on the blue,' the woman said from the other counter.

'Won't be a tick,' the man said, sliding the sweets into a triangular bag. He put the jar back on the shelf and Terry took a Mars bar and – rashly – a crinkly packet of Butterkist. He coughed to camouflage the noise.

The three lads walked some distance along Halifax Road before sharing the spoils; it was a pretty good haul. As they turned the corner into Entwisle Road the streetlights came on and they strolled past the Cloverdale Hotel, its name spelled out in big golden letters standing in relief against the dirty cream-coloured façade of the building. In his days as an amateur boxer Terry's dad had trained there in one of the upstairs rooms.

'*PC49* tonight,' Terry said happily. Ever since *Dick Barton Special Agent* had finished, this was his favourite programme, with *The Man in Black* a close second.

'I'll miss it,' Alec said. 'It's the Brigade tonight.'

'What are you doing?'

'Mr Skeels has got us making model aeroplanes.'

Terry said, interested, 'What kind?'

'Spitfires.'

'Are you making one each?'

'Yeh. Ten of us.'

'I might join again.'

'You're too late,' Alec said. 'We've already cut the frame out and we're on to the wings.'

'Who wants to join the bloody Brigade?' Malc said. 'All they do is shout at you to line up, stand to attention, stand easy, stand on yer arse ... and you've got to go to Church *twice* on Sundays.'

'You don't.' Alec said.

'You do.'

'Don't.'

'You do,' Terry said, 'otherwise you can't have a drum. I missed one parade and Skeelsie said I couldn't be in the band.'

This shut Alec up and Terry was appeased. But as they approached the hoardings near the Arches his heart contracted into a small painful lump in his chest: he was scared and wanted to urinate. Colin Purvis, Eddie, Shaz and Carol were coming towards them on the opposite side of the road. They hadn't seen him, Terry believed. They were walking past. Then at the last moment they crossed over and blocked the pavement.

'What you lot eating?' Colin Purvis asked. Under the streetlights Terry could clearly see the blackheads on his bulbous nose.

'Toffee,' Malc said. If there was any fear in him Terry couldn't detect it.

'Give us some.'

Alec Bland offered his bag of liquorice torpedoes.

'Bin playing footie?' Shaz said, ignoring the other two and looking directly at Terry.

'Yeh.' Terry kept his face impassive. A sixth sense told him it would be fatal to show fear. Anyway, they were on the main road. They wouldn't try anything on the main road. He hoped.

Then Carol said, 'You're the mard kid, aren't you?'

Terry shrugged. He felt himself colouring.

'Yes, it's you,' Carol said aggressively. She thrust her breasts out assertively. He had thought, mistakenly it seemed, that she would respect him for not wishing to treat her like a tart; he really thought he'd done the right thing that night on the embankment by trying to behave decently towards her. He was utterly at sea so far as girls were concerned, not knowing what they wanted, or how to treat them, or what went on in their heads. It was bewildering.

'Shall we lock him in the midden again?' Colin Purvis said silkily, putting his broad heavy hand on Terry's shoulder.

'Still got your bike?' Eddie said, and the sound of his hollow nasal voice brought the nightmare back in all its fear-crawling intensity. He wanted to run, now, fast, away, yet it would mean running through the cordon and it was certain he wouldn't get ten paces.

'How old are you lot?' Shaz asked, staring from beneath the single thick eyebrow that went across his forehead like the mark of a crayon.

'Eleven,' Alec said.

'Eleven,' Malc said.

Two answers, one true, one false, trembled on Terry's lips. He opened his mouth and heard himself say, 'Ten,' actually believing in the moment he said it that it would save him, this tiny insignificant lie, from further punishment: the truth was that he had been eleven for two full weeks now.

'Are you lads from Denby as well?' Eddie asked.

'Yeh,' said Malc. 'Where you from?'

'What's it to you, shortarse?' Shaz snarled.

They were moving closer and closer, crowding them into a crushed group against the hoardings. 'Are all the lot of them soft as pigshit round here?' Eddie asked Colin Purvis. Shaz trod slowly and deliberately on Alec's foot, adjusting his stance to increase the pressure and grinding down. It was horrible to be so close to safety – so near the Common, a few yards away – and not able to reach it, like one of those technicolor dreams where you're being chased by a monster and can't move because your feet are stuck in treacle.

Eddie said to Terry, 'Give us your wrist,' and twisted it behind Terry's back until his elbow was bent double. He obviously derived some pleasure from doing this because his mouth opened in an empty black hole of a grin.

'I bet he starts crying,' Carol said. She was looking at Terry with the utmost loathing.

'I bloodywell won't,' Terry said, but he was forced to yell out when Eddie jerked his wrist even higher, turning the joint.

'Go on, make him bawl!' Carol said.

Colin Purvis made Malc empty his pockets. He put the sweets in his own pocket, crammed the half-eaten bar of chocolate into his mouth.

'You wouldn't like it if I told your dad,' Malc said.

'You do *what?*' Colin Purvis gaped at him incredulously. His mouth stopped moving; there was chocolate stuck to his thick lips. He hit Malc in the stomach with his fist and Malc slid down the poster advertising Dinneford's Milk of Magnesia to sit on the pavement. Terry wished with all his might that Spenner would magically, miraculously appear, as he had at Shap's bonfire, but it didn't seem to be the kind of day for magic or miracles.

Shaz said, 'What shall we do with 'em?' But before Colin Purvis could reply Alec said, 'There's your mam.' His voice was shaking with relief.

Everybody turned to look, except Malc, who was staring groggily at the pavement, and there, marching under the Arches with a shopping-bag over her arm was Bessie Smith, on her way to the UCP tripe shop. She was a vision, the most beautiful sight Terry had ever seen.

'Whose mam?' Shaz said quickly.

Colin Purvis moved off, the others followed, pretending to take their time but hurrying all the same. 'Mard-arse,' Carol said under her breath.

Terry helped Malc to his feet and Malc said, 'I'm going to tell his dad over him, the pigging swine.' His eyes were brimming with tears, not so much from the pain as the monstrous injustice of it all. 'I bloody am and all,' Malc said vehemently. 'I'm going to tell his dad.' But Terry wasn't listening. He was thinking of Carol and how he would never understand girls if he lived for a million years.

Dead Sunday

*

SUNDAY WAS TIME OUT OF TIME, A VACUOUS HOLE of a day without shape or pattern. When he'd been a member of the Church Lads' Brigade there had been early-morning parades followed by an hour in church, and, though tiresome, this had at least got the day started and under way; now, too lazy to make the effort, Terry felt the day drag wearily from minute to minute, a limbo of dead time hanging in perpetual suspension. He got up late, round about ten-thirty, made his own breakfast, which usually consisted of toast and jam, and mooched about the house listening to Billy Cotton's Bandshow or a programme from a log cabin in which various cowboys showed up with guitars and banjos to sing about life on the prairie. In between, Terry lay indolently on the settee reading the *Hotspur* and *Champion*, the latter being his least favourite comic; his father kept the *People* and especially the *News of the World* well out of harm's way and Terry's reach.

In deference to the Sabbath, Joe wore a shirt over his vest and socks as well as slippers, though he didn't bother to shave. By midday he and Terry were like two lone survivors during the final lingering moments of an ill-fated submarine trapped on the ocean bed, both suffering from claustrophobia and fighting over the last gasp of oxygen.

'Why don't you clean your bike? The rims are filthy.'

'I'll clean it tomorrow.'

'Do it now.'

'I might be going out on it later on.'

'Put some newspapers down. That bike cost fifteen pound. It's going rusty.'

'It'll soon come off.'

'You'll soon bloody come off if you don't get it cleaned.'

'It's Sunday,' Terry said. 'Can't I have a bit of a rest?'

'Rest?' Joe said. 'Rest? You do nowt as it is.'

From bitter past experience Terry knew there was no point in defending himself. Only one thing to do: he got his shoes from under the sink, his windjammer from behind the back door, and went out. He called for Danny Travis, who wasn't in (visiting his grandma for the day), then went further up Cayley Street to Spenner's house where he found Dave helping his father to point the wall of the outside lavatory. This kind of co-operative activity always made Terry envious and, for a reason he couldn't define, vaguely sad. He watched father and son for a while, going to fetch water when Spenner's dad asked for it, mixing the water with sand and cement and blending it in with a stick. When one side of the wall was finished Mr Spencer gave Dave two bob and Terry a shilling. Wellens's corner shop was closed on a Sunday so they went to the off-licence on Ramsay Street and each bought a bar of Cadbury's chocolate and a quarter-pound of sweets.

Without a definite plan in mind or consciously making any decision they walked in the direction of the town centre. As they were passing the Municipal Baths, Terry asked in a casual fashion how Spenner got on with his dad.

'Do you ever have a laugh with him? You know, a joke?'

'Yeh, sometimes. Why, what's up?'

'Nowt. Do you ever have rows?'

'He gets on at me if I forget to turn the lights off or if I let the fire go out.'

'I suppose they're all like that.' Terry said, feeling a mite more cheerful.

The town centre was an expanse of tarmac, bare as a military parade ground, just the blue-and-cream buses lined up one behind the other outside the glass shelters. The town hall clock in its fake Gothic tower was striking one o'clock as they paused for a minute outside the Regal to look at the tinted photographs advertising the coming week's attraction: *Mr Drake's Duck* starring Douglas Fairbanks Jnr and Yolande Donlan. Neither of them fancied it. They dawdled past the granite-based banks and building societies, to where the Packer Spout fountain spluttered into a pool containing three or four murky goldfish; there was nothing much to see and even less to do. Sunday was a real dead hole of a day.

'Hey,' Spenner said suddenly. 'Mellor Street Depot.'

'Where's that?'

'On bleedin' Mellor Street, where do you think?'

'What's there?'

'Wagons,' Spenner said, his face lighting up. Even his hair seemed to blaze a fiercer shade of red when he got excited. 'We can sneak in and drive 'em. They don't have keys. You just switch the ignition on and start 'em by pressing a button.'

It took them ten minutes to walk to the Mellor Street Depot, an area of waste ground backing on to a steep sandstone cliff in which birds had tunnelled to make nests. A high wire fence with strands of barbed-wire along the top separated it from the main road. At one end of the compound stood a decrepit three-storey building with dirty windows, and, Terry noted, a fire-escape covered in red rust. There didn't seem to be anyone about – at least there was no watchman's hut. The wagons stood in rows three deep, their radiator grilles emblazoned with the names Leyland and Albion and Foden. Some were fully loaded, though most were empty.

Terry felt a familiar movement deep within his bowels, compounded of thrilling anticipation, excitement, fear. Half-hoping that Spenner wouldn't know the answer, he said: 'How do we get in?'

But Spenner did. 'Round the back and shin down the cliff, or . . . ' and looked meaningfully towards the bottom rung of the fire-escape, about six feet above their heads.

'We'll be seen,' Terry said in a dreadful whisper.

Spenner said in a normal voice, 'Who by? There's nobody about. I'll give you a leg-up. Nowt to it.'

This they did, withdrawing the ladder to its usual position once Spenner had climbed it, going quick and silent as cats up the rusty iron treads. The warehouse (for that's what it was) unsettled Terry with its gloomy echoing interior, though it was far from empty. Wooden pallets were stacked from floor to ceiling, loaded with huge flat packages as big as billiard tables which, when Spenner ripped one open, contained nothing more interesting than hundreds of sheets of greaseproof paper. They wandered along the centre aisle, amusing themselves by switching the labels on the pallets so that the consignment marked for Swindon would go to Peterborough, the one for Galashiels to St Helens.

'Do you think anyone comes here on Sundays?' Terry asked.

'Why should they,' Spenner said, unconcerned. 'What's up, are you chicken?'

'Who says I am?'

The rear of the building was the loading area, with several adjacent bays like little dry wharves deserted by the sea. Spenner jumped down and slid open a small panel in the big sliding door and stepped outside into the watery sunshine. Terry ducked through after him and they ran swiftly across the open compound to the back row of vehicles whose tailboards butted up to the base of the cliff; two more rows of lorries in front hid them from the main road.

'How do you start 'em up?' Terry asked Spenner, who had clambered up into the cab of a Seddon, his grimy freckled hands with the black-rimmed nails holding the enormous steering-wheel which sprouted out of the floor on a metal post. The handbrake was as huge and as cumbersome as a points lever in a signals box. Spenner went through the procedure, showing him where the ignition switch was and telling him to wait for the light to come on before thumbing the big red button behind the driver's right elbow. 'Then you press the clutch down, put it in first, take the handbrake off and you're away.' He was in his element.

There was a Leyland three vehicles along whose door wasn't locked. Terry climbed up into the cab, feeling like a dwarf with the enormous steering-wheel in front of him and the expanse of glass as wide as a shop window: the ground seemed far below. One of the first problems he encountered was that his feet dangled uselessly several inches above the floor. To reach the clutch pedal he had to slide off the seat and stand on it with both feet. The handbrake required all his strength to release it, clicking over the ratchet, until both his arms were fully extended.

A roar that almost made him crap his pants reverberated across the compound as Spenner's lorry started up. The noise was enough to wake the dead, and if this wasn't enough the clouds of blue smoke billowing out must have been visible the length of Mellor Street. Looking through the passenger side window, Terry saw Spenner give a wild triumphant grin accompanied by a thumbs-up sign. Terry nervously watched the road through the gaps in the row of vehicles in front, expecting to see a black Wolseley with a POLICE sign on the roof appear any second. There were no immediate escape routes except a vertical one – straight up the sandstone cliff.

All afternoon they played in the lorries, starting them up, revving the engines, driving imaginary journeys to Liverpool and Cardiff, stopping at transport cafes for baked beans on toast, then clocking-off after the day's shift. When a black Wolseley with a POLICE sign didn't arrive – and didn't look like arriving – Terry began to enjoy himself: swaggering up into the cab, slamming the door and nonchalantly stabbing the red button which brought the big vibrating engine to life. He wasn't as ambitious as Spenner, who actually drove his wagon a few yards, stopping it behind the tailboard of the lorry in front and then reversing back into position against the cliff.

Later on the clouds thickened overhead and the sky grew black. A premature theatrical dusk descended on the compound and large globules of water clunked on the roof and smeared themselves down the windscreen. Terry ran across to Spenner's lorry and climbed up into the passenger seat; soon the rain was pelting down, obscuring the road and the lorries in front, and with the unreal darkness a cannonade of thunder rolled across the sky, working itself up to a dramatic climax that crashed directly above them.

'Shit and corruption,' Terry said. 'It's pissin' down.'

Spenner switched on the wipers and they staggered and whirred across the glass.

'Are you going to be a lorry driver when you grow up?' Terry asked. It seemed a good time to talk, sitting here dry and warm, watching the shifting broken images as the rain washed them down the windscreen.

'Think I'll join the Forces. Me dad was a sergeant in't Fusiliers.'

'There's nobody to fight any more.'

'They still need soldiers though.'

'What for?'

'To train.'

'Train what for?'

'So they can be in th'army. Pillock.'

The thought of joining the army in peace-time had never occurred to Terry. He said, 'What do you do when you've trained then?'

'You go on manoeuvres with tanks and guns. They send you all over't world. You've heard *Forces Favourites* haven't you? They have soldiers everywhere. Germany. France. Hong Kong ...' He couldn't think of any more places.

'America?'

'Yeh, America. Timbuktu.'

'I thought that were in Africa?'

'It *is* in bleedin' Africa. I'm just saying, Timbuktu as well as America. Me dad went all over the place. He even went to Burma. Brought loads of stuff back: flags, a Jap bayonet, a grenade – no pin in it – American chocolate, chewing gum.'

'Me Uncle Jack brought some spoons back with swastikas on them.'

'Spoons?' Spenner said, gawping.

'He said he captured them from a machine-gun post.'

'I bet.'

'He did,' Terry insisted. 'He was in the desert during the war with Monty and the Desert Rats. Nearly got taken prisoner.' This last was a bit of embroidery to make the story more convincing.

'Did he get the Victoria Cross?' Spenner asked, twisting his mouth into a funny shape. He started flicking the headlights on and off.

'I'm not sure. He might have. He's got one medal, a big 'un, with a ribbon.'

'He didn't get the Victoria Cross.'

'How do you know?'

'He'd be famous. He'd be a hero.'

'He might have been a hero.'

'He couldn't have been 'cos it wasn't in the papers.'

'Might have been.'

Spenner shook his head dismissivley, which really annoyed Terry. 'What's his last name anyhow?'

Terry had to think. Then he realised that of course Jack was his mam's brother so they'd share the same name his mam had before she was married.

'Marsh.'

'It would have been in the *Observer* then. "Jack Marsh, VC".'

Terry could see no way of refuting this assertion, and this

annoyed him even more. He wished, right now, this very moment, that he could produce a newspaper cutting from his pocket with a photo of his Uncle Jack wearing a medal, and above it the bold black headline: JACK MARSH, VC.

Spenner said, 'Wish I had some fags.'

'I left me dimps at home,' Terry said.

The windscreen wipers ticked in front of them.

'We're going to get pissed wet through in this,' Terry said, staring out.

'Wait till it stops,' said Spenner, yawning.

They waited, but the rain showed no sign of slackening.

'Have you got your results yet?' Spenner said after a while.

'Few more weeks.'

'Do you think you've passed?'

'Haven't a clue,' Terry said, which wasn't strictly true. On some days he felt certain that he must have passed while on others he had doubts. He very much wanted to pass for the High School, though he wouldn't have admitted it to anyone, not even a close pal like Spenner. He knew he was brainy, and as Mr Buckley, the headmaster, had told 4A: 'Only the cream of the cream go to the High School.' Just as he didn't like being beaten in an argument, perhaps for the same reason he couldn't accept second-best in the exam results.

'Your mother told my mother you'd passed.'

'She's always telling folk that,' Terry said with real exasperation. 'I don't know what's up with her.'

'Who wants to go to the bleedin' High School anyway?'

Terry chose not to respond to this remark, suspecting that if Dave Spencer had been offered the chance he'd have gone like a shot; but having failed the eleven-plus two years before, this was just sour grapes.

Spenner sat forward in the driver's seat.

'I can see a light.'

They both tensed.

Through the wavering patterns on the glass a splintered star of light was approaching, swaying to and fro as though coming from a torch or lantern being carried by somebody. Somebody, say, like a watchman. They opened the doors and jumped simultaneously. The teeming rain struck Terry in the face. He turned and ran straight at the cliff. The sand clogged under his heels and his legs moved ridiculously fast without getting anywhere. There were no handholds in the smooth damp wall of sand. To his left Spenner was clawing at the weedy plants that grew along a fissure, moving steadily upwards one hand at a time. Terry followed his example and scrambled through a thick patch of stinging nettles. Sand and small pebbles slid under his feet. He got near the top and started slipping backwards. Spenner held out his hand and hauled him over the edge, the two of them collapsing on the thin layer of grass which rested like a hairpiece on the flat clifftop. They crawled back to the rim and looked over. Through the driving rain they saw the light below and the foreshortened figure of a man in a raincoat reaching almost to the ground.

'Bleedin' close 'un,' Spenner said, and shouted down: 'Can't catch me for a penny cup of tea.'

'Bloody shut up,' Terry said breathlessly. 'He might send for the rozzers.'

Spenner threw a clod of sand, which splattered with a dull thud on the flat wet boards of one of the lorries.

Terry stood up, soaked to the skin, and felt a burning sensation in his knees. He looked down and saw that they were covered in small white blisters.

'Jesus,' he said. 'Je-*zuzz*.'

'What's up?'

'Look at me legs.'

Bloody Nora, they were *on fire*.

'Stinging nettles.'

'Oh swinin' hell,' Terry said. 'Oh. Oh. Oh shit and corruption.'

They walked through the unceasing rain back to town and Spenner had just enough to pay their fares to Copenhagen Street. They cut through the Ginnel, along the Bottom Track, and went down the alleyway and into Spenner's kitchen. His parents were out. Terry was suffering: he sat with his bloated legs stuck out in front of him, unable to bend them. Spenner boiled the kettle and bathed them in warm water and afterwards dabbed them with a pad of cotton wool soaked in Dettol. This stung like fury, but in a while the pain seemed to go numb and he was able to stand up and walk about.

Then Spenner opened a tin of baked beans and emptied it into a saucepan while Terry toasted some barm cakes in front of the fire. They sat at the table covered with oilcloth and ate the baked beans on toast, followed by half a Swiss Roll between them and a beaker of tea each. Spenner switched the wireless on but there was only somebody sawing away on a screeching violin (the announcer called it the Palm Court or something), so he switched it off.

'I bet that watchman's mad,' Spenner said, puffing away on a Woodbine.

'Yeh,' Terry agreed, relaxed and happy now that the adventure was over and they were safe in Spenner's kitchen, warm and full-bellied, the rain streaming down outside. The pain in his knees had nearly gone, leaving a faint prickly sensation.

'I nearly hit him when I cobbed that sand down,' Spenner said, chest shaking, red in the face. He was laughing so much he started choking.

'That bloody raincoat he had on,' Terry said, gasping for breath, 'touched the floor.'

'Can't catch me for a penny cup of tea —'

'Hey – them big packages in that warehouse. They'll be going all over't shop —'

'Liverpool.'

'Glasgow,' Terry said, holding his stomach.

'John O'Groats!'

'Land's End!'

They fell on the floor. They were helpless for several minutes. When they had calmed down, still whimpering, they went into the front room and Spenner sat down at the rosewood piano and began to play a medley of popular tunes: *Don't Fence Me In, You Are My Sunshine, Maisie Doats and Doasie Doats* and *Little Brown Jug.* Terry was filled with admiration and envy; he had no hidden talents that he could think of.

'Do you know any others?'

Spenner thought for a second and then began to play what sounded to be an extremely complicated piece with lots of crashing chords, his fingers running magically up and down the keyboard and crossing his hands over for a particularly clever bit towards the end. Terry asked what it was called and Spenner told him it was his latest exercise by somebody whose name sounded like 'Show-pang'. Terry wished they had a piano at home: he imagined himself rattling off a medley of popular tunes while (unknown to him) Margaret Parry eavesdropped outside the front door. She had never guessed till now how talented he was, because, of course, he had modestly kept it to himself.

They went back into the kitchen and Spenner disappeared upstairs for five minutes to scrounge for cigarettes and came back with two reasonably-sized dimps he'd found in his father's suits in the wardrobe. The two lads lit up and talked about the films they had seen recently: *Captain Boycott* with Stewart Granger, *Landfall* with Michael Denison, *Ma and Pa Kettle on the Farm, Commanche Territory* with McDonald Carey, *Battle of Powder River, The Blue Lagoon* starring Jean Simmons (they both agreed she was fit as a butcher's dog), and *No Place for Jennifer*, a crummy film that had bored Terry stiff and had his mother in tears. Both he and Spenner agreed that *Commanche Territory* was far and away the best. Terry still went with his mam every Friday night to the Regal or the Rialto, and on the way home they usually stopped at the chip shop on Smith Street for their suppers. But Fred the sailor hadn't been in since that first time last November.

Spenner asked Terry if he'd ever read any Biggles books. 'They're fantastic stories,' he said, rummaging in a cupboard and producing a book called *Biggles & Co*. 'This one's about some crooks trying to smuggle gold bars from France and Biggles and his two pals, Algy and Ginger, have to foil them.'

Spenner said that he could borrow it, and in return Terry promised to lend him *Jets, Rockets and Guided Missiles*.

The rain had stopped and was dripping from the guttering as he went through the backyard and walked down the cobbled alleyway. Framed at the far end was the kind of sunset that some-times follows a thunderstorm: spectacular shooting rays of red and purple and orange forming an irridescent arc in the sky. The rooftops and upper halves of the houses were bathed in a beneficent golden light, illuminating each brick and slate with absolute clarity and in the most exact detail.

On Cayley Street rainwater was running in streams into the grids, carving channels through the dirt along the edge of the pavement. Terry went into the house and got told off for not telling them he wouldn't be in for tea. This was another baffling paradox of the adult mind, because how was he supposed to inform them of the fact when he hadn't known it himself in the first place?

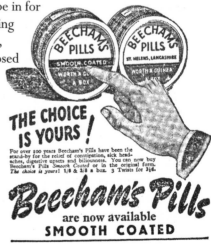

Behind the Garages

*

URING THE EARLY SUMMER OF 1951 THE RAIN fell on Denby from overcast skies, awakening the ground and bringing forth a profusion of fresh green grass that soon hid the scars of winter. Across the river, swathes of nettles sprang up on the grey ash-tips, while below in the swampy hollows the brown needles of marsh-grass thickened in dense intermittent clusters.

Before long the unpaved section of Cayley Street became a quagmire so that it was necessary to step circumspectly between the wide sticky pools and over the thick ridges of mud churned up by Sam Clegg's coal wagon and Teddy Travis's Norton. Bessie Smith forbade anyone (except the insurance man) to use the front door because of the trail of mud traipsed through the house, while Mrs Heap had to set to and donkey-stone her front step at least three times a week to keep it unblemished and pristine. But Ma Rigall was worst off: with her poor eyesight, thin pointed shoes and tiny hesitant steps, the mudbath of a street must have stretched before her like no-man's land in the First World War, with the dry solid pavements of Hovingham Street in the remote, unseeable distance.

Dolly Bland, so the neighbours informed one another, had been out gallivanting as usual – which meant that on Wednesday and Friday nights she was seen trotting down Kellett Street dolled up to the nines, the seams in her 9-denier silk stockings plumb accurate to within a few thousandths and her new suede wedge-heeled shoes with the fancy ankle-straps raising her normal five-feet-two by at least three inches. It was either the Carlton, they told each other, or the Flying Horse, and possibly the Robin Hood, two town centre pubs. But even more scandalous was that she'd been seen, it was whispered, in Yates's Wine Lodge, brazenly standing at the high polished bar with the men while she supped a port and lemon and the occasional Guinness. There wasn't much further to fall, unless it was the Grapes on Baillie Street, which had a reputation it was impolite to even mention in mixed company.

Mrs Pickup, Roy's mother, contracted pleurisy and the cream-coloured ambulance arrived to take her to Marland Hospital. A small gathering of neighbours watched in silence as the ashen face above the grey blanket was ferried into the cool green interior and whisked away; while on the credit side of the Denby account, Spenner's dad, also called David, won two hundred pounds on Vernon's (the first rumour of the windfall had said £2000).

Real excitement of the stomach-churning variety, however, came towards the end of May when a bullock escaped from a wagon on Entwisle Road and roamed the streets and alleyways, placidly raising its moist black snout over backyard gates and sending Mrs Banaitis, a Lithuanian lady, into hysterics. The Gang stalked the animal, taunting it with shouts and handfuls of gravel, daring each other to get as close as possible, then vanishing like quicksilver the moment it lumbered in their general direction. Spenner, as ever the daredevil, ran right up to the beast and yanked its tail. As it about-turned three times as fast as anyone (including Spenner) could have imagined, he took a running jump, cleared a fence four feet high, and landed perfectly in a pile of horse dung shovelled off the streets by Mr Sims for his allotment.

Eventually men wearing leather gaiters and hobnailed boots

and carrying long poles came along and cornered it between the pens at the entrance to the Ginnel – the Ginnel being too narrow for the bullock to enter – and locked it securely inside the cattle-wagon. But it had been a smashing afternoon and the memory of it lived for a long time and became part of Denby folklore.

With the lighter evenings the normal summer pastimes were resumed: dirt-track racing round the Top Track and down the Figure 7, swaling the railway embankments, sailing home-made rafts on the river, and later on, as darkness advanced, playing at werewolves and Frankenstein's monster in the eerie yellow lamplight. One time, racing near the pens, Terry ran through what he thought was a gap in the fence, and a horizontal strut of timber caught him smack across the forehead and knocked him flat on his back. An inch lower and it would have broken his nose and possibly altered his looks for life; Spenner fell down and rolled over, laughing like a drain.

Barbara came to the bottom of the stairs and shouted, 'One of your pals is here for you, Terry.'

From where he lay on the crumpled sheets Terry could see a section of the parapet that topped the Arches: a row of black millstone blocks sharply etched against the evening sky. The brook gurgled on the far side of Ma Rigall's backyard, trickling through the rusty springs of old bedsteads and over corroding bicycle frames and threadbare tyres green with slime. It wasn't yet warm enough to ferment the smell, which in summertime would rise in heavy sluggish vapours like the sweetish-sickly stench of gangrenous breath.

'Terry!' Barbara shouted, her voice near nagging frequency.

'Yeh, all right, I'm coming.'

'Hurry up then. Don't keep the lad standing here all night.'

Terry put aside the book he had been reading: *The Adventures of*

Brigadier Gerard. It had been recommended to him by Mrs Butterworth, and it was a smashing story. He pulled his stockings up and went downstairs. Spenner was bouncing a hard rubber ball against the lavatory wall and catching it with alternate hands. His fingernails, Terry couldn't help noticing, were rimmed with dirt, and on one of the sleeves of his grey pullover there was a streak of something green that looked suspiciously like snot. Spenner said:

'Have you got that copy of th'*Eagle?*'

'Which one?'

'The one I lent you.'

'When?'

'The one I twatting lent you last week.'

Terry glanced towards the kitchen window in case his father might have overheard the bad language. 'I'll have to have a look for it.' He suspected that Spenner made things up and sometimes told deliberate lies.

Spenner said, 'Let's call for Danny and Malc. We can get our bikes and go over to Nile Street.'

'I think I'll stay in tonight,' Terry said. 'I've got some homework to do.'

'You don't do homework.'

'I've been given some.'

'Since when?'

'Mrs Butterworth said we had to do some reading at home. I have to read a book before Friday.' This was a lie too, but only a small one.

'See you then,' Spenner said, catching the ball and opening the backyard gate.

'See you.'

Terry had a quick glance in the pigeon cote to see what the young squeakers were up to (offspring of the blue bar hen and dark speckled cock) and went into the house. Barbara was putting plates and cups away in the corner cupboard, and it came as a little shock of surprise to realise how frail and washed-out she looked: the mousy hair and thin neck and hollow cheeks.

Terry put his arms round her waist; he came up to her shoulder. 'What time is it?' he asked – a private joke between them because it was just an excuse for her to look at the Ladies' Cocktail Watch with 17-jewel Swiss-movement. She lifted her wrist and the cheap imitation stones and gilt surround caught the light from the window and glinted weakly.

'Just gone half-six. It keeps good time.'

'Do you like it?'

'Of course I do. It's a smashing present, our Terry.' She hugged him to her in a moment of real affection and ruffled his hair, which when not flattened with water and combed straight grew in a tangled mop. 'Are you staying in tonight with your old mam?'

'I'm going out on me bike.'

He went upstairs and put on a clean white shirt, then stood in front of the dressing-table mirror in the front bedroom and tried out a few expressions. When he came downstairs again Joe was yawning and scratching his armpits, his eyes bleary from having that minute woken up in the rocking-chair.

'Where you off to?'

'I'm going out on me bike.'

'I asked where.'

Terry shrugged. 'Just riding round,' and went on casually as if he'd just thought of it, 'I might ride over to Gowers Street.'

'Don't forget your lights on the main road.'

'No.'

'And don't be late in. Nine o'clock.'

'Dad—'

'Nine o'clock. You've got to get up at seven for your paper round.'

'I always do.'

'Aye,' Joe said, 'after your mother's screamed her head off for ten bloody minutes.'

Terry got out of the house, wheeling his Raleigh Sport across the buckled flagstones and bumping it down the backyard step. It was like being released from prison: he took a long deep breath and lifted his head: he could scent freedom.

Gowers Street was silent and deserted. He rode along the cinder track past the garages, a few stray cats and a solitary dog the only signs of life. Still sitting on his bike Terry leaned against the creosoted wall of a garage and lit the dimp of a Woodbine, feeling a slight wave of dizziness pass over him as the first drag entered his lungs. Above him the solid edifice of the Arches seemed to loom larger and blacker as the light drained from the sky.

A Jowett Javelin lurched and rattled along the track and stopped. A man got out and wedged the garage doors open with house bricks; he didn't notice Terry in the shadows. When he had locked the garage and gone away Terry cycled slowly back towards Gowers Street. The gaslamps had just come on. The street was part dirt, part paved, the setts extending from the main road as far as the green wrought-iron gates of the Clover Mill. Behind them the millyard was vast and empty, stretching away to the square bulk of the mill itself, absolutely rock-solid on its foundations, five storeys of white-leaded windows rising in perfect symmetrical rows.

It had always seemed a forbidding place to Terry. He had been inside just once, with Alec Bland (whose mother worked in the canteen) and walked the full length of the basement, which was used mainly as a store. He could only recall an endless succession of huge dim caverns with low concrete ceilings, stacked with dusty bales, splintered crates and broken machinery, and occasionally, through the gap in a wall of crates or behind the greasy innards of a silent loom, glimpsing a solitary workman involved in some mysterious, secretive activity. They were like lost souls to him, these lone people, hidden from the world in gloomy, dusty chambers in the depths of the mill. He had a horrible vision of one of them dying and being forgotten, rotting away to dust in the darkness behind the crates and bales and machinery.

Terry circled the lamp at the far end of the street and rode slowly back in second gear. Margaret Parry and two other girls were standing talking outside Margaret's house; he rode onto the pavement and put his foot on the window sill, leaning back in the saddle like a cowpoke after a long trail drive.

'You sit next to Betty Wheatcroft, don't you?' Margaret said.

'Yeh,' Terry said. 'Why?'

'She likes you,' Margaret said. 'She wants to go with you.'

He was genuinely surprised by this but didn't show it. He watched her with a kind of lazy indifference.

'How do you know that?'

'She told me. She said she liked you but you fancied Yvonne Brangham.'

'I don't.'

'She said you did.'

'Well I don't.'

They looked at each other in the gathering dusk. Her hair was short and curly and her eyes dark with thick lashes. Her teeth were incredibly white and she had what Terry considered to be extremely kissable lips, slightly pouting, a ripe cherry-red.

'Do you like Betty?' Margaret asked.

'She's all right.'

'Are you going to go with her?'

Terry didn't reply immediately, knowing he had to be careful what he said. With a cunning he didn't know he possessed he asked her what she thought he should do.

'Up to you,' Margaret said. She raised herself on tiptoe and balanced delicately on the pavement's edge, looking at her feet with rapt concentration.

One of the other girls suggested helpfully: 'You could go with her for a bit and see if you like it.'

'Yeh,' Terry said dully. Not the right answer.

Margaret teetered on tiptoe and it was all Terry could manage not to make a sudden grab for her, as he had Doreen Hartley. A prickle of sweat broke out on various parts of his body: he badly wanted to touch her hand or her shoulder: he knew already how soft she would be. But how to set in motion the mysterious process that would transport the two of them to the shadows behind the garages, that was the baffling problem. Above all he didn't want to be so bloody *nice*; niceness had to be avoided.

'You're too nice for Betty Wheatcroft,' said one of the other girls, and Terry's confidence drained out through his feet. A frozen sickly smile was clamped to his face like a mask. He took out a full Woodbine and lit it.

'I suppose Shap's nice too,' he said bitterly, his stomach deep and empty as a pit. One of the other girls said in a low voice:

'He's dirty.'

'Oh?' He thought his face was under control.

'Tries to make you do things,' said the girl.

'We daren't tell you what he did to Muriel,' the other girl said.

'Who's Muriel?'

'Me,' the first girl said.

'Why not?'

'Nasty,' Margaret said, crinkling her pretty nose. 'Dirty.' She was looking at Terry in a calculating way. Her eyes were wonderful. Terry basked in them as in a shaft of pure sunshine. 'You wouldn't do anything like that, would you?' she said.

Terry was more confused than ever. What did they want him to say? Was it better to be nice or dirty? He was completely flummoxed. He had to consider his reply most carefully, and finally said lamely, 'Depends.'

'On what?' the girl who wasn't called Muriel asked.

'On who it was.' He had begun to perspire again. This was worse than an interrogation, than torture. He felt to be on a tightrope of question-and-answer, question-and-answer, afraid at any moment he might get it wrong and fall off.

A woman in a faded pinny and curlers came to his rescue. She poked her head out of the door farther along the street and said, 'Muriel. Come on, it's gone eight o'clock.' Muriel sighed and grumbled and went in.

The other girl said, 'I'd better be going in as well.' Neither Terry nor Margaret made any attempt to dissuade her; nevertheless she lingered for several minutes more, the three of them seeming to draw closer together as the weight of night pressed down. When she had gone they continued to talk in low voices as if afraid someone was listening. Terry was thrilled to the core at the intimacy of their conversation: Margaret told him all about her parents, and her little sister Lyn, and their cat Blackie, and all the while her pale oval face and dark lips hovered in the centre of his consciousness and he felt himself to be drifting, sliding, sinking down and down until he was lost in the depths of her lustrous eyes.

'Are you going to let me have a go?' Margaret said.

'What? How do you mean?'

'Can I have a go on your bike?'

'Yeh,' Terry said, getting off, 'if you want.'

'No,' Margaret said, 'I meant on the back. You pedal while I sit on the saddle.' She tucked her pleated green skirt between her legs and climbed up behind him. Terry pushed away from the window sill and the bike juddered over the kerb and onto the setts; Margaret put her hands on either side of his waist to steady herself and they rode along the street. 'Down here,' she said, and he obediently turned onto the track, the tyres crunching through the cinders and bits of broken glass. The places where her hands held him were burning him through his clothing.

'Can you see all right?' Margaret asked.

'Yeh. Just about.'

At one point they went over a big stone and she fell forward against him, her arms around his waist, her fingers laced together across his stomach. Near the Arches, where the track narrowed and petered out into the long grass, they had to dismount. It was dark here, the lamps of Gowers Street some distance away.

'What time do you have to go in?' Terry asked.

'What time do you?'

'Oh ... anytime,' Terry said with an indifferent shrug, though he knew it must be getting on for nine o'clock. They walked between the garages, Terry wheeling the bike, and it was as if there was electricity in the air. They both could feel it. Terry's mouth was parched and he could hear his own breathing: he wondered whether he ought to say or do something: he wanted the walk between the garages to last forever. Margaret said:

'Let's stop and have a smoke.'

That was something else he liked about her. She had a quiet even voice that didn't offend the ear. It spoiled some girls, he reckoned, no matter how pretty, that their voices were flat and ugly.

He leaned his bike against a garage and lit a cigarette. He passed it to Margaret; she was resting the back of her head on the creosoted wood, her face upturned, and in the glow of the cigarette he saw that her eyes were looking towards the sky where a few stars glimmered behind the drifting patches of cloud. Should he do it now? Was this the moment?

'I didn't know you smoked,' Terry said.

'I don't much. Muriel smokes like a chimney.'

'Does she?'

'She pinches her mam's Park Drive.' Margaret inhaled once more and passed the cigarette back to Terry. As he took it in the darkness their fingers touched and it was as though a current had been transmitted between them. He drew the smoke in deeply and the dizziness expanded inside his head, making his skull tight. He couldn't let anything spoil it now, throwing the unsmoked cigarette into the grass, saying in a strange croaky voice, 'Margaret,' as he kissed her satisfactorily on the lips and felt her hands on his shoulders. While it was happening he couldn't believe it was happening – until the kiss was finished and she said in a single breath in the darkness, 'Will you go with me?'

Then it was true. He was actually here behind the garages on Gowers Street with Margaret Parry and he had just kissed her and she had asked him to go with her. Terry kissed her again and this time her mouth was open and he thought his senses would explode. It had been worth throwing nearly a full Woodbine away, and he didn't even care any more what Shap had done, or might have done, or said he'd done. If Margaret Parry was his, and wanted to go with him, then he could knock Shap and his gleaming quiff into the middle of next week.

'Will you?' she said more urgently.

'Yes.'

'I've liked you a long time.'

'I've liked you.'

'You promise to go with me. Honest and truly.'

'Honest and truly.'

'Swear on the Holy Bible?'

'Yes.'

'You've got to say, "I swear on the Holy Bible".'

'I swear on the Holy Bible.'

Margaret took his hands and placed them on her small developing breasts. She said, 'Do you want to open me blouse?'

Terry nodded dumbly.

'Well, do you?' Margaret said impatiently, unable to see him.

'Yes.'

'Go on then. I'll let you.'

Terry did as he was told and cupped her breasts in his hands; it was an instinctive gesture, almost mechanical, because he was still floating in a delirious dream. She pressed her mouth against his in a long hard kiss and he felt the first stirring of genuine desire. Her hand was touching his thigh. She hooked her fingers under his trouser-leg; it was as though a light had been switched on in his brain and he suddenly realised what was happening. The warm curved objects in his hands became Margaret Parry's breasts and the tickling sensation on his thigh Margaret Parry's fingers.

'Let's lie down,' Terry said.

'I'll get me skirt dirty.'

'In the grass.'

'It's too wet; I have to go in soon anyway.'

'Not yet.'

'In a few minutes I have.' She said, 'You're still going with me aren't you?'

'Yeh,' said Terry, smiling to himself in the darkness. This is what it felt like to be holding a girl's breasts. It was a nice feeling. He said truthfully, 'I think you're great. You're the best-looking girl round here.' He pressed and kneaded and massaged her breasts, enthralled by their softness and shape and texture.

'Have you done this to other girls?' Margaret whispered.

'Some,' Terry said. 'One or two.'

'What are their names?'

'I don't think you know them.'

'Who though?'

'Just some girls.'

'Were they as nice as me?'

'No.'

'Honest?'

'I swear on the Holy Bible.'

Margaret's hand was inside his trouser-leg. 'I can feel your thingy.'

'I know,' Terry said, dry-mouthed.

'Does it feel nice?'

'Mmmggghhhnn.'

'Why does it go all stiff?'

'Um. Dunno.'

'Doesn't it stick out of your pants when it's like that?'

'No. Yeh. No,' Terry said, finding it difficult to concentrate on the conversation. This was how he dreamed it would be but it was still too good to be true.

'Aren't boys funny?' Margaret said. She paused. 'It's wet at the end. Is it wee?'

Terry swallowed and shook his head. 'No,' he said.

'What is it?'

'It's stuff... that comes out.'

'All the time?'

'No.'

'Just when somebody holds it?'

'It does, yeh; sometimes.'

'It's slippery, isn't it?' Margaret said, interested and yet detached. She removed her hand and fastened her blouse. 'I have to go now. Will you be coming round tomorrow?'

'I have to deliver the papers first. Give us a kiss before you go in.' When she had kissed him he said, 'I think you're fantastic, Margaret, honest I do.'

They walked holding hands towards Gowers Street and said goodnight on the corner under the gaslamp. Before she left him Margaret said anxiously: 'You still want to go with me, don't you?'

'If you want to go with me.'

Terry rode home along Entwisle Road, a great bursting bubble of happiness inside. He had no words to describe how he felt, except to say that he was joyously, helplessly, hopelessly in love.

VE Day

*

IN THE WEEK THAT A COACH PARTY FROM DENBY went on a trip to the Festival of Britain (Terry mithered and mithered to go but his dad said it was a waste of money, which in the language of the Webb family meant he hadn't the cash to spare but wouldn't admit it) Teddy Travis, Danny's big brother, ran into a wall on his Norton at sixty miles an hour and was killed outright. What was left of him they buried in the local cemetery, which by a black quirk of fate was situated on Bury Road: there was a saying that sooner or later, whatever happened, you'd end up on Bury Road. Teddy Travis had managed it – sooner rather than later – at the age of seventeen and three days.

The school holidays began in the middle of June. While everyone in 4A was looking forward to four weeks of freedom, the last days of term were tinged with sadness because some would be returning to Heybrook (having failed the eleven-plus) and others, the clever buggers, would not. And it was very emotional, on the very last day, parting from Mrs Butterworh, who treated every member of the class to a cream cake and a bottle of pop; in return they presented her with a Real Leather writing case and a potted plant, the collection organised by Terry and Betty Wheatcroft, who also went to buy the presents.

Ever since he had been told that she fancied him, Terry had been casting sly sidelong glances in Betty's direction, hoping that a covert look of understanding would flash between them. Sometimes he imagined that it had, though being together in the same class for five years had hardened their relationship into a mould of friendly yet innocuous intimacy that was hard to break. He had always liked her, but now he saw her not merely as a friend but as a potential conquest. Since the episode with Margaret Parry he had cast himself in the role of the sexy-eyed predator whose fixed burning gaze was enough to have the girls queuing up behind the garages one by one to gratefully receive his expertly lethal attentions.

Strangely, however, Betty Wheatcroft failed to respond to his burning eyes and petulant lower lip. She once asked him, solicitously, if he was sickening for a cold, to which Terry replied, his face an indignant shade of beetroot, that even if he was it was nowt to do with her.

'I only asked,' Betty said, 'because your voice sounded funny. Have you got a sore throat?'

'No, I bloody haven't,' Terry answered sullenly, at a loss for a suitably crushing reply, and ran off to join Alec and Malc playing Desert Rats in a corner of the schoolyard, vowing never again to waste his time with stupid soppy boring girls.

Leaving Heybrook – and he assumed it was for good – put Terry in one of his introspective moods. The first two or three days of the holidays he spent lying in bed till nearly dinner time, listening to the brook trickling and gurgling at the bottom of the backyard, watching the golden trapezium of sunshine imperceptibly changing position and shape on the flowered wallpaper. From outside came the cries and screams of kids playing, and these sounds plunged him into a deep and painful sadness that was baffling, going over in his mind the tiny store of memories he had accumulated.

Terry thought it strange that even at his young age he should feel a yearning pang of nostalgia for things that had happened only last summer or the previous winter; it was almost as if, once experienced, these events and happenings turned into little romantic playlets inside his head, and he held them intact, their colours and sounds and smells still bright and fresh and real – more real now than then, in fact, because with the progress of time they had gained the quality of permanence, of being an essential part of the paraphernalia he would always carry with him.

He could recall with perfect clarity, for example, the day they had hung the Union Jack out of the front bedroom window, little pouches of sand stitched to the corners to keep it hanging straight, to celebrate the war ending. There were flags all along the street and lines of bunting and everyone seemed to be smiling, even Mr Heap, who had given Terry a boiled sweet. People seemed to spend all their time standing on doorsteps or out in the street in groups or going in and out of each other's houses.

Some time after this – weeks or months, Terry wasn't sure – it was VE Day, when once again the flag with the little pouches of sand was propped on its pole through the bedroom window. His dad, as usual, hadn't wanted to go into town that evening, so Terry and his mam got dressed up in their best clothes and walked to the town centre, stopping outside Fashion Corner on Drake Street, which was lit up with hundreds of fairy lights. He must have been five at the time, chubby-cheeked, big-eyed, with fair wavy hair cut short at the sides and long on top, a lock of it hanging over his left eye. (He knew the details by heart from the artificially-tinted photograph in the silver frame above the fireplace.)

The fairy lights had gone straight into his head and stayed there, standing on the pavement outside the Champness Hall, his neck craning upwards and his eyes dazzled with twinkling pinpoints of light – though the words they illuminated on the long white streamer had been lost and forgotten, probably because at the time he was too young to read them.

Then the scene changed to the town hall square, jam-packed with hundreds of people standing in row upon row outside the Empire Cinema and Flying Horse Hotel, watching those in the main square dancing to a band whose tinny strains came and went on the breeze. At first he had been unable to see, until a man hoisted him up onto his shoulders and he had a giant's-eye-view of soldiers, sailors, airmen and men in ordinary suits swirling in a huge circle with women wearing dresses cut severely square, with vee-necks and padded shoulders. The women's stiff waved hair never altered a fraction, despite the breeze and movement and giddy excitement.

The two visible faces of the town hall clock looked impassively over the motley, over the bunting and the strings of lights suspended from the iron lamp standards: an impression so firmly embedded in Terry's mind that whenever he saw the town hall clock it reactivated the memory of that night in the square when the crowd danced and sang; Barbara had wanted to join in but she couldn't leave Terry on his own or with strangers, no matter how friendly, and had to make do with singing along and moving her feet to the rhythm. After what seemed like hours they walked through the thinning crowd and Terry was handed a greasy bag of fried potatoes by an anonymous reveller which he and Barbara ate on their way to catch the No.6 back to Cayley Street.

He pondered all this, lying in bed watching the trapezium of sunlight moving down the wall. Recently he had started keeping a diary and one of the entries, even though he himself had written it, bewildered him: 'My mother and father are people'. They were individuals, separate from himself. The world hadn't been created the day he was born. Incredible as it might seem, Joe and Barbara had met and married and had a life together in the limbo of non-existence before he was thought of. Of course they must have existed before he was born. The trouble was, he couldn't conceive of a world which didn't contain *him*, Terry Webb. No matter how hard he thought about it, his imagination failed to conjure up a credible picture of what it must have been like. It seemed to have the same level of reality as a scene in a Biggles book.

*

'Are you going to feed your pigeons or not?' Barbara said when he eventually made it down to the kitchen and washed the daydream from his eyes.

'I've no food left.'

'There's some black peas you can give 'em. In that jar on the top shelf.'

Terry sometimes wondered what he would do without his mam. He said, 'Was it in the paper about Teddy Travis?'

'What paper?'

'The *Observer*. Alec Bland said it was in about the funeral.'

'Then it must have been.' Barbara went into the front room and came back with the hearth-rug which she threw over the clothes-line in the backyard and started to beat. Dust swirled and eddied in the shaft of light slanting through the back door.

'Are we going away this year?' Terry asked from the step.

'Going away where?'

'Auntie Hylda's in Wales.'

'I don't know; you'll have to ask your father.'

'We never have a proper holiday,' Terry said in a peevish sulking voice. 'Alec Bland and his mam and dad are going to Scarborough.'

'Alec Bland's mother can afford it,' Barbara said enigmatically.

'Why can't we then?'

'You wouldn't understand,' his mam said, whacking the rug with gusto so that dust rose up in a cloud over the lavatory roof. 'You're too young.'

'You're always saying that.'

'Because you are.'

Terry sighed. 'Can I have two bob, mam?'

'What do you want two bob for?'

'Some of the lads are going up to the Lake this aft and they're buying crisps and lemonade to take with them for a picnic.'

'What about your spence?' She paused, wiping her forehead with her pinny.

Terry shook his head. 'I'm skint.'

'Run an errand to Wellens's, I need some bread and potatoes. Then I'll see how much I've got left.' Barbara carried on beating the rug. 'It'll have to last you all week though, I can't spare any more.'

Terry did his errand, not at all conscience-stricken about the lie he had just told. None of the Gang, as far as he knew, were going up to the Lake that afternoon, but Margaret Parry was. He'd promised to meet her outside the Post Office on the corner of Gowers Street at two o'clock and instead of catching the 8A bus they planned to walk to the Lake through Belfield council estate and over by Clegg Hall, an ancient ruined manor house that had the reputation of being haunted.

After dinner he spent a long time combing his hair and polishing his shoes, all the while a sluggish flutter of excitement mounting in his chest. Barbara said, 'What are you titivating yourself for?'

'You moan when I don't clean me shoes,' Terry said defensively.

'Who's going with you, Betty Wheatcroft?'

Terry snorted and pulled a face, as though he found the idea ludicrous and offensive. 'I told you, just some of the Gang.'

'She's a nice girl, Betty; thoughtful and quiet.'

Terry had a last look at his quiff in the mirror, kissed Barbara on the cheek, made sure he had the two-shilling piece safe in his pocket, and ran out of the gate into the back-entry where Doreen Hartley was playing three-balls against the door of the dust midden. She stopped her game when she saw him and shrank back, standing close to the wall.

Terry ran past her, his eyes agleam, and said in a hoarse demon's whisper: 'Don't worry, kiddo, I'm not going to stuff you.'

A Walk to the Lake

*

HE HAD TO WAIT A FEW MINUTES BEFORE Margaret arrived, and to pass the time he studied his dim relection in the Post Office window amongst the pencil sets and notepads and tubes of glue. He tried to see what his smile looked like, but in the glass there was just a black gap that made it look as if he didn't have any teeth at all. At least his ears didn't stick out like Malc's did, and he didn't have a gobful of protruding wet teeth like Roy Pickup. He wished, though, that he was an inch or two taller. Margaret was the same height and it would have been great (he visualised it in his mind) to look down on her as they walked along and put his arm protectively round her shoulders.

When Margaret did appear he was taken aback by the vision of dark eyes and hair, fresh skin, and by the summer dress she was wearing, gathered in short puffy sleeves that left her arms bare. He could hardly speak, swallowed hard. 'We can get the bus if you want. Me mam gave me two bob.'

'I'd rather walk it,' Margaret said, smiling. She must have known how fantastic she looked, and she did, the smile said so. Doreen Hartley couldn't have smiled like that, and he doubted whether even Betty Wheatcroft could have. She stood for a moment like a bright generous child, with perfect confidence in herself and the afternoon and perhaps also – this he fervently hoped – in him.

'Come on,' she said. 'Let's go if we're going.'

Terry walked beside her, courteously taking the outside of the pavement, and was happy to see that she was wearing delicate white slippers, which meant that he was taller than her by a fraction – enough, at any rate, to inspire in him a measure of the confidence that Margaret exuded like perfume. He found himself smiling too; it was a wonderful day.

By the time they had walked along Hamer Lane and were crossing the iron bridge over the railway line Terry was engrossed in relating to her the plot of *Biggles & Co,* which Margaret seemed to find interesting. Thinking he might have been going on a bit, he asked her which books she liked.

'I don't read much,' Margaret said. 'I get *School Friend* every week; I like the Silent Three.'

'What are you reading at school?'

'We're not at school.'

'I meant before the holidays,' Terry said, feeling daft; she was so self-possessed and in control that he felt like a small child, shy and unsure.

'The last one we read was *The Adventures of Brigadier Gerard.*'

'Was it really?' Terry was delighted that they should have both read the same book. 'I've read that too,' he said eagerly, staggered by the coincidence.

Margaret shrugged her soft round shoulders under the thin covering of gingham. 'The boys liked it but the girls weren't all that keen. It's about these soldiers in Napoleon's army.'

They came to the end of a row of semi-detached houses, grey pebble-dash with red-tiled roofs. Ahead of them the lane narrowed to a single track as it disappeared into the gentle folds of the hills: farmhouses of black millstone were placed at irregular intervals over the green landscape and there were cows grazing in the fields. Grassy banks rose on either side so that the track became a deep line carved in the earth, following the contours of the countryside. Insects droned and whirred in the hot sunshine. Terry took Margaret's hand. After a few moments, he didn't know why, but he felt compelled to ask:

'You're not going with Shap, are you?'

'Who told you that?'

'I just wondered.' He looked into her green eyes, which he could have sworn were blue, and the breath quivered in his throat. She had very long thick black eyelashes.

'I thought I was going with you.'

'You are,' Terry said. 'You are.' Buggeration, he was making a botch of it, all for no reason.

'You said behind the garages that we were ...'

'Yeh,' Terry said, annoyed by his own stupid clumsiness. 'Forget it.'

They walked deeper into the countryside, the rutted track overgrown with weeds and the banks dense and heavy with vegetation. Occasionally a small animal – a rabbit or a hedgehog – would appear for a fleeting moment in the undergrowth and then vanish in a rustle of leaves. The silence afterwards was almost suspicious, as though pairs of tiny unblinking eyes were watching them from secret places.

As they approached the ruin of Clegg Hall Terry said, 'There are supposed to be ghosts in that place. Do you want to have a look inside?'

The main door of the house was hanging by a single rusty hinge. Inside, the crooked stone floors were covered in rubbish, plaster and broken laths that had fallen from the ceiling. It wasn't all that spooky because the sunlight was everywhere, broad shafts of it filling the rooms and illuminating the dust motes suspended in the warm air. Obsenities were scrawled on the bare plaster and there were explicit drawings of male and female genitals accompanied by explanatory text. In one corner a pile of excrement attracted the flies, and when disturbed they rose up in an angry buzzing cloud. Terry and Margaret came out again into the sunshine.

'I wouldn't fancy being a ghost in that place,' Terry said.

They walked along the track.

'Do you believe in ghosts?' Margaret asked, swinging her hand in his.

'I don't know. There was this story in the *Rover* about a bloke who kept having these dreams of things that had happened a long time ago, and when all comes out he'd actually been alive then and died and been born again.'

'I saw a picture like that once,' Margaret said. 'Only it was about this girl who they hypnotised and she started telling them what it was like in the olden days. She was in a trance and she didn't know what she'd said after.'

'Do you go to the pictures a lot?'

'Now and then. I go with me mam and dad sometimes – I saw you in the Regal one time.'

'Yeh, you did. And your dad goes with you?'

Margaret nodded. 'Why, doesn't yours?'

'He never goes anywhere. Well, he goes to watch football on Saturdays and to pay his union sometimes on a Thursday night, but he never goes anywhere else. Me mam's always on at him not to be such a stick-in-the-mud.'

'Do they row a lot?'

Terry was tempted to say yes (if only to make Margaret feel sorry for poor Terry and his wretched home life) but in all honesty he didn't suppose they rowed all that much. Anyway, he'd nobody to compare them with; for all he knew other kids' parents might be ten times worse. 'Sometimes.'

'Me mam threw the clock at me dad one time,' Margaret confided.

'Did it hit him?'

'No. It broke the clock though and knocked the tap off the geyser.'

The track opened out and the dirt gave way to cobbles where another lane joined it at right-angles. At the junction an old woman sat behind a trestle-table loaded with bottles of lemonade, cream soda, Vimto and Tizer. There were cardboard boxes full of loose sweets, and jars of liquorice twists and sticks of barley sugar. Underneath the table were two square metal tins with labels saying 'Smith's Crisps' in blue letters on a white background.

'I'm parched,' Terry said. 'Let's get a bottle of pop.' He bought a small bottle of lemonade (twopence deposit on the bottle) and two packets of crisps, which left him with elevenpence out of his two shillings. They walked up the lane until they were out of sight of the old lady and found a fairly flat comfortable spot on the grassy bank. It was now mid-afternoon and the sun was at its strongest.

Terry allowed Margaret to have the first swig, then took a deep gulping swallow himself, the lemonade warm and slightly flat-tasting. He lay back in the grass and ate the crisps, gazing up at the faultless blue sky. It was very still, with no breeze, and peaceful. A ladybird landed on his shirt and took off again.

'It was stupid, me asking about Shap,' Terry said. 'Sorry.'

Margaret leaned on one elbow, the soft round muscle in her shoulder straining against the gingham, pulling the seam taut. She was looking straight ahead into the field across the lane. From the corner of his eye he could see the line of her profile silhouetted against the blueness. He said:

'I'm glad you're going with me.'

'So am I,' Margaret said, not moving.

'You'll never go with anyone else, will you?' He turned his head to look at her fully and saw the rhythmic movement of her breast rising and falling, rising and falling.

'No,' Margaret said, not looking at him.

She seemed to be breathing quite heavily and Terry was disturbed because he didn't know why. Was it something he'd said? Was she angry or annoyed about something?

'Is summat wrong?' he asked, almost without thinking placing his hand on her arm. The feel of it was like no other sensation, as though he had touched something warm and soft that tingled under his fingertips. He became aware of the breath expanding inside his chest, of the familiar dull throb rising up as if

it might choke him. He looked at her lips, which were nicely shaped – a defined line to them and deep red in colour – not like some girls' lips which were slack splodges in the area roughly between nose and chin.

Margaret turned her face, unsmiling, towards him, and Terry felt his senses slide away. She didn't smile all the time she brought her head nearer to his, her eyes wide and green, and kissed him. The smell of her made him feel faint.

He had seen himself in the orbs of her eyes, his face getting bigger and bigger, until he had shut his own eyes to darkness and felt the pressure of her lips. It was, and he knew it well enough, the first proper kiss he had ever had in his life. He held her close with both arms pulled tight so that he could feel his chest pressing hard on hers.

It lasted a long time – long enough for him to register the clicking sounds of insects close by in the grass, the aimless drone of flying creatures over the hedgerows – then felt her arms tauten as she raised herself above him.

'Jesus Nora,' Terry said in a hoarse whisper. 'You can't half kiss.'

Margaret smiled, her eyes looking into his, and he would have done anything for her. To think that this wonderful beautiful girl was actually going with him: that she was his sweetheart: it was incredible.

And when an insect flew into her hair and was caught struggling amongst the strands he laughed out loud, involuntarily, from sheer joy.

'What's up?' Margaret said, and he untangled the creature and set it free.

Even then it seemed to Terry that he would remember that \afternoon, the walk to the Lake with Margaret Parry, that first real kiss, for the rest of his life. He knew that he would remember it because everything he saw, every sound and smell, was sharp and alive and vibrant to his senses. The springy undergrowth beneath his head was like a cushion and he closed his eyes as a great luxurious calm overwhelmed him. The sun beat hotly on his face, its intense light glimmering behind his eyelids.

'Do you like kissing?' Margaret asked.

'Yeh,' Terry said, smiling with his eyes shut. He opened one eye. 'Do you?'

'Sometimes.' She rested her forearm on his chest and propped her chin on it.

'Why did you ask if I like kissing?'

Margaret thought what to answer and wrinkled her nose. 'You imagine lads would think kissing stupid and – you know, sloppy. When you go to the Ceylon on Saturday afternoons all the lads start groaning and booing if there's a girl being kissed in it.'

'Them are kids,' Terry said. 'Kids are like that. Young 'uns of seven or eight.'

'How old are you?'

'Nearly twelve.'

'When's your birthday?'

'February.'

'You're not nearly twelve, you've just gone eleven.'

'Eleven-and-half.'

'Nearly eleven-and-half.'

'Yeh, all right, nearly.' He didn't feel any inclination to argue; life was too good. He said, 'You can have what's left of the lemonade if you like.'

Margaret shifted position slightly to make herself more comfortable. 'You're two months older than me,' she said. 'My birthday's on the fourth of April.'

'You just missed being an April Fool.' Terry opened his eyes and looked at the sky. He said, 'Will you still go with me when I'm at the High School?'

'How d'you know you've passed?'

'Well ... I don't,' Terry said, caught out. 'I think I have. You don't want to stay at Howarth Cross, do you? Wouldn't you rather go to the Girls' High School?'

'Depends if I've passed or not.'

'Can your mother afford to buy you a uniform?'

Margaret shrugged. 'If I had to have one.'

Terry put his hand on the gathered blue-and-white gingham just below her shoulder. 'Will you? Still go with me?'

'If you want to.'

'I'm asking you if you want to.'

The two perfect green eyes were looking into his, the curling black lashes surrounding them like a burst of dark spiky rays around the sun. His heart turned over: her beauty was just too perfect.

'I'd like us always to be together,' Margaret said.

Terry felt the urge to rashly confess: 'You're the first girl I've ever gone with. I mean – you know – properly.' It seemed right, somehow, to unburden himself in this way. He was so unsure of her, deeply frightened that her affection was only fleeting. He knew that by this act of confession he was, in a sense, throwing himself upon her mercy, believing, perhaps foolishly, that it would rob her of the right to reject him. If he could make her see how vulnerable he was she wouldn't have the heart to betray him. That's what he reasoned.

Margaret too felt the need for confession. She said, 'Shap did ask me to go with him once.'

Terry didn't say anything. This was his blackest fear come to haunt him, and in the broad light of day. He wanted to know everything and yet be told nothing.

'He asked me but I said I didn't want to.'

'Didn't you?' Terry said, torturing himself. He was struggling inside with a stupid uncomprehending rage because Shap lived nearer to Margaret than he did. Why couldn't she live next door to him on Cayley Street instead of Doreen Hartley? Then he would know she was close by, protected, safe from temptation.

'You held his thingy though, didn't you,' Terry said. 'His dick,' finding a perverse satisfaction in saying it so crudely to her face.

'I didn't,' Margaret said, rather too quietly.

'He told me,' Terry said with sadistic pleasure. (Oh why was he saying this? Why?)

Margaret stood up and brushed bits of grass from her dress. There were spots of red in her cheeks. She said, 'If you'd rather believe him than me.'

'Well didn't you?' Terry said hopelessly. 'In't it true?'

(What was the matter with him? Did he want to deliberately spoil everything on this perfect day?)

'You won't believe me whatever I say.'

'I might.'

'You won't.'

'In't it true then?' Terry said, when really what he he was saying was *Please make me believe it isn't true. Please.*

She stepped down off the bank into the lane. He had made a right bloody cods of everything. Pain twisted somewhere inside him, so acute and physically real that he felt sick; unshed tears pricked behind his eyelids. The insects in the grass around him suddenly irritated him with their mindless whirring and ticking; their disinterested activity was like an insult.

He jumped up and stamped on the grass in childish fury.

'What's up?'

'Nothing,' he said savagely. 'Nowt.'

They walked apart to the Lake and spent what was left of the afternoon miserably. The sun sparkling on the water, the little white yachts with their neat triangular sails, the pleasure boat with its striped canvas awning – everything that was delightful to the eye now seemed to Terry pointless and hateful. The afternoon, that had begun so magically, had ended up as a bitter, repugnant taste in his mouth, as unpleasant as copper pennies.

Margaret remained withdrawn and uncommunicative, only responding once when he offered to buy her some candy floss, or, if she preferred, a bag of fried potatoes. She said no thank you, very politely with a perfectly calm face, and in that instant he wanted to grab hold of her, in anger and remorse, and shake her until she fell into his arms. Her green eyes refused now to look into his, instead gazing across the water to the little yachts or looking intently (so it seemed to Terry) into the faces of the boys who passed in groups of three or four. He knew that she was only waiting for the flimsiest excuse to leave him, waiting impatiently for a friend to show up, and then without a word or a backward glance she'd be off, and that would be the end of that. The last he would see of her would be the flouncing of the gingham dress, the dainty white slippers walking away, the head of dark curls gradually becoming lost in the summertime crowd.

This didn't happen: they went home together on the bus with Terry's last fourpence, sitting on the back seat upstairs with a precise distance between them that never altered despite the jolting on Smithy Bridge Road as the bus went over the level-crossing. They got off at Heybrook corner and walked along Entwisle Road. It seemed to last for hours, this walk, in dead silence, until they came to the Post Office where Terry had looked at himself in the window, and where he finally mustered the nerve to say, 'Margaret —'

But she turned into Gowers Street without breaking her stride, in cool possessive control of her movements and emotions. With her, it seemed to Terry, went a complete world of soft sweet kisses and tender young breasts: a lost world in which he had lived for a single day, amongst the dry grass and mad clicking insects.

King Kong

*

ERRY SAT ON THE LAVATORY ROOF NEXT TO the pigeon-cote. He had taken to studying cloud formations, watching them come sweeping over Denby, lofty pinnacles of cumulus moving slowly and gracefully from the south-west like galleons under full sail. He forgot himself in the majesty of the clouds, became a mere speck of nothingness, as if he was up there sailing along with them. It never failed to stagger him, how puny and insignificant he was in relation to the whole vast universe.

He thought about it but never seriously considered for a moment wheeling his Raleigh Sport out of the gate and cycling over to Gowers Street. He could never summon the nerve to admit to Margaret Parry's face that he had behaved foolishly and said stupid things which he now regretted.

From his perch on the lavatory roof he agreed to go with Spenner and Alec Bland to the matinee at the Regal, scrounged ninepence off his mam, and the three of them set off for town. Spenner led the way up the slope to the rear of the cinema on Baillie Street and managed to prise open a large metal door with FIRE EXIT stencilled on it; they sneaked down a flight of stone steps into the Gents, and after a suitable pause came out one at a time into the auditorium, the rendezvous being the ninth row from the front, a dozen seats in from the right-hand aisle.

The film was *King Kong*, and Terry had never seen anything like it.

When the first close-up of Kong's grinning face filled the screen, with teeth that could snap lampposts, he nearly wet his pants. This – the frightening nature of the film – combined with the fact that they had sneaked in illegally meant that Terry sat uneasily, half-on and half-off the seat, prepared at any moment to drop to the floor out of view, or run like the clappers, or surrender himself to the usherette. As it was, he crept to the toilet four times during the picture, on one occasion to do his number two.

When the lights came up the three lads crouched in their seats, talking out of the corners of their mouths and passing a Park Drive back and forth inside their cupped hands. Terry knew that he ought to be getting back (his tea would be in the oven waiting for him) but he wasn't brave enough to embark on the lone walk through the glare of the marble foyer under the suspicious glinting eye of the manager. He preferred to wait for Alec and Spenner, safety in numbers, and, if need be, endure his mam's angry remonstrations.

It was odd coming out of the cinema into the daylight world, the sun still in the sky and people arriving by the busload, streams of them disgorging outside the Electricity Showrooms with that air of eager anticipation of a night on the town. It had the same disorientating effect of having slept during the afternoon and waking to find the day almost gone and night-time approaching.

Naturally they played at monster gorilllas all the way home, Spenner bagsing the part of the mighty Kong, chasing Terry and Alec with shoulders hunched and arms swinging, grunting and slobbering. The film had been so real to Terry that at any moment he half-expected the head and shoulders of Kong himself to appear over the rooftops, a hairy paw plucking double-decker buses from the main road and ripping the tops off like boxes of liquorice allsorts, crunching any stray hapless pedestrian between slavering jaws and spitting the mangled remnants onto the Nile Street paint depot. When the three of them made it to Denby without once having been hoisted into the sky and chewed to pulp he breathed a sigh of genuine relief.

But it was now after seven (he'd missed *PC49*) and he knew he was in trouble. His tea would be a dried-up mess with the peas lodged in the gravy, and if he was even allowed to eat it before being sent to bed, he would be lucky. He sidled through the gate into the backyard, his eyes glued to the kitchen window for sight of an angry face, so he didn't see the note pinned to the door until his thumb was on the latch. The note read:

> Terry,
> Your dad's gone to pay his Union. Have taken Sylvia to Nanas and Daddy Sams. Your tea is under a plate in the meat safe. Get the key from Mrs Hartley's (Dot, next door). Back about nine. Be a good boy.
> Love, Mam.

(Did she think he didn't know who Mrs Hartley was, and where she lived?)

Terry ate his tea, which wasn't dried-up after all, being a salad with two slices of corned beef, the *Adventure* propped against the Crosse & Blackwell salad cream bottle. Every so often the image of King Kong would loom in his imagination, eyes flashing, teeth gleaming, disrupting the story he was trying to read, 'Keepers of the Scarlet Hand,' and he found he was holding his breath, just waiting for the roof to be peeled away and a set of fingernails as big as car bonnets to descend into the kitchen and squash him like a gnat. So vivid was the vision that he went to the window and looked anxiously towards the ash-tips, convinced that even now the monster was bestriding the river and beating his chest, felling the Arches with a single swipe before turning his gaze directly and malevolently on number 77 Cayley Street.

To divert his fear he ate two pieces of currant flat (he loved his mam's baking) and drank half a pint of milk, then went out into the peaceful still evening. Dusk was infiltrating stealthily, soft blue shadows deepening beneath the eaves of the houses and gathering in the alleyways. Denby lay becalmed in the summer twilight, the smoke from the chimneys rising vertically and winding itself in gentle spirals before forming hazy streamers above the steeple of Good Shepherd Church. The traffic on Entwisle Road was a distant background hum.

The Gang was out in force. They were hanging about outside the allotments on the Bottom Track, leaning against the fence and scuffing their shoes in the dirt; some girls were there as well: Sandra Weeks, Doreen Hartley, Fat Pat Sidebottom, and Laura Parfitt.

Laura Parfitt was thirteen and lived in a detached house (with garage attached) on the corner of Hovingham Street. Her father had his own business, had a van *and* a car – a red two-seater MG whose shattering exhaust could be heard two streets away. She was a tall slender girl with an aloof expression that Terry found sexually stimulating. She didn't usually fraternise with the Gang and for that reason was regarded as a snob, though she was always friendly when you spoke to her and had a lovely pair of knockers. Terry liked her. On the few occasions they had exchanged more than a couple of words he had been surprised to discover an intelligent girl with an independent mind. Girls with both brains and spirit – whenever he encountered them – never failed to astonish him.

Spenner was holding everyone transfixed, acting out King Kong's battle in the jungle with the prehistoric monster and demonstrating how Kong had twisted the monster's neck and tied it in knots as though it were a bicycle inner-tube. He said to Terry, seeking his support: 'Weren't it great?'

'Yeh, smashing,' Terry confirmed. 'And he had teeth, I'm not kidding, this big' – extending his arms to full stretch. (He hoped that Kong wasn't lurking behind the church listening to all this.)

'We'll have to go and see it,' Kevin Hartley said.

'Where's it on at, the Regal?' Billy Mitchell asked.

Alec Bland said excitedly, 'And guess what – we got in by the back——' and yelped when Spenner kicked him on the shinbone.

'Did what?' Roy Pickup said.

'It were nearly full and we had to queue right round the back,' Spenner said glibly. 'There was this long queue so you'd be better off going early. Right, eh, Terry?'

'Yeh.' Terry guessed what Spenner was up to. He didn't want the others to know about the secret way in through the fire exit because the more people that knew, the greater the risk of the Regal's manager tumbling to it: were he to find the first ten rows crammed with boys who hadn't been through the box-office, his suspicions would doubtless be aroused. 'We had to queue for ages.'

Terry saw Spenner's almost imperceptible nod of approval, which swelled him with pride to be trusted by the older lad, and in his confidence.

'I went to see *Copper Canyon* last night at the Victory,' Malc said, which provoked a long yawning silence. 'Ray Milland was in it.'

'Fan-bloody-tastic,' Spenner said, bending at the waist and without any warning charging head-first into Terry's stomach. It was the ultimate seal of his approval. They wrestled in the grass, giving it everything even while mindful of the dog muck, each trying to stab the other with imaginary Bowie knives. Terry received three wounds in the chest and stomach before getting in a fatal thrust between Spenner's shoulder blades. He died spectacularly, straightening up on the tips of his toes, clawed hands clutching the air, screaming *Aaaaaaiiiiieeee!!!* as he fell backwards down the grassy slope to lie spreadeagled, mouth gaping horribly, eyes crossed, fingers twitching, with convincing flecks of foam on his lips.

'Mad,' Laura Parfitt said, shaking her head. 'A total loony.'

'You wouldn't say that if I was King Kong coming to get you,' Spenner said, jumping up and shambling towards her with his hands trailing in the dust. The girls squealed (even Laura Parfitt

stiffened and backed away) and ran off with Spenner, doubled over and growling, chasing after them. Terry said to Laura Parfitt:

'You favour the girl in the film a bit.' In fact she looked nothing like the girl in the film, but Terry could precisely visualise a semi-nude Laura Parfitt lying helpless in the monster's hairy paw.

'Who was it?' Laura Parfitt asked.

'Dunno. Forgotten her name.'

'Somebody well known?' She was clearly flattered to be likened to a film star, especially if it was Linda Darnell or Hedy Lamarr or somebody else with a beauty spot.

'Never heard of her before,' Terry was forced to admit, which was a disappointment to Laura Parfitt and also to Terry, because it brought the promising exchange to an end.

Spenner appeared carrying Sandra Weeks in his arms and slobbering over her, trying to sink his large yellow teeth into her neck. She was screaming and threshing her legs.

'I am Dracula,' Spenner intoned, in a change of dramatic persona, 'and tonight is the night of the full moon. This night I shall drink virgin's blood . . .'

Terry waited, and sure enough Alec Bland piped up with, 'What's a virgin?'

'A girl who doesn't have any elastic in her knicker-legs,' Terry said. Roy Pickup laughed, strings of spittle hanging from his buck teeth, and glanced at Terry as if making a new appraisal of this 'kid'. Terry grinned, aware of his own quick-witted cleverness, and began to show off. He adopted the posture of an ape and went after Doreen Hartley, chasing her past the rickety fences and wooden sheds covered in tarpaulin, and eventually cornered her (it seemed she had deliberately run into a cul-de-sac) against the wall of a garage. Now that they were alone, without an audience, he didn't quite know what to do. Before he could make up his mind, Doreen said – her shoulders flat against the garage wall, her eyes large and round with the whites showing – 'What was it you said to me last week?'

'Eh?' Terry said, straightening up. 'When?'

'Last Thursday. In our back. You said summat.'

'I don't remember.'

'You *know*: you ran past and said something.'

From the corner of his eye Terry could see her pale hands, fingers spread, pressing against the black oily wood, and it seemed as though a blast of hot air had entered his lungs. He fixed his eyes on her and said deliberately:

'I said I wasn't going to stuff you.'

'What does it mean?' Doreen said. Her lips were parted. 'What does "stuff you" mean?'

'You know. "Do" you.'

'"Do" me? I don't know what that means,' Doreen said, the breath whispering in her nostrils.

'You do know,' Terry said. He let the moment drag itself out. 'It means pull your knickers off and shag you.' He put out his hand and looked into her eyes. 'But first,' he said mercilessly, 'I want to feel your tits.'

Doreen lay against the garage wall, her chest moving, as Terry, arms at full stretch, covered both her breasts with his hands. She submitted to him as in a trance, her mouth open and dry. It was like a ritual. No words were spoken. His hands moved over her, not mechanically, but almost perfunctorily, as if this were a function that required a prescribed methodical approach. He felt no desire, and it was only when Doreen made an effort to resist, pushing his hands away, that drove him to grasp her wrists, his mouth coming down onto hers in a kiss that jarred the breath from her body.

'I thought you didn't like playing with girls' titties?' said a voice behind him.

It was Colin Purvis, standing a yard or so away with his hands in his pockets and a smirk on his face.

Down the Figure 7

*

BY HALF-PAST NINE DARKNESS HAD ALMOST TAKEN over and the gaslamps spluttered into life. The sky was clear, shading imperceptibly from deepest black to pale translucent pink in the west, a few faint stars winking on overhead.

Some of the Gang had melted away, but Terry, Alec, Spenner, Kevin Hartley and Billy Mitchell were still there, the girls too; and so was Colin Purvis. He had the lads in stitches, the girls outraged yet agog, with a non-stop flow of dirty jokes and limericks he knew by heart. He never flagged, his memory never failed him, able to relate a dirty joke on any subject you cared to name, from skinny spinsters living alone to hunchbacks with deformed organs.

Terry was fascinated by the performance, and strangely unsettled: it was a side to Colin Purvis he had never seen before. At first Terry had steeled himself for the worst, because the butcher's son still haunted his dreams and turned them into sweating nightmares; but this Colin Purvis – the genial jokester, the life and soul of the party – just dismissed everything that had gone before as so much good-humoured tomfoolery, remarking at one point: 'That night we pinched your bike on Oswald Street and hid it behind't fence. D'you remember? We had a good laugh that night.'

Terry nodded and discovered himself to be smiling. The big lad wasn't so bad after all, once you got to know him; he didn't mean any real harm. Even Laura Parfitt, the snooty one, couldn't tear herself away, listening mesmerised as the jokes got filthier and the language more crude.

'Do you know the one about the nun who ordered a gross of candles for Christmas?' Colin Purvis said, not bothering to wait for an answer before telling the story, which relied for its point on the extraordinary masturbatory prowess of the abbess.

'Where do you get 'em all from?' asked Alec, goggle-eyed.

'All over't shop, but mostly from the van drivers who deliver me dad's meat. One of them's a right randy little fart, not as big as me,' which wasn't hard to believe, Colin Purvis being gargantuan for a boy of fourteen. Somehow, in a way that Terry couldn't fathom, he had a magnetic quality that compelled you to look at him and listen to him. It was partly to do with his bigness, his *grossness*; he was everything to excess, in manner and speech and gesture, the kind of person you had to dislike yet couldn't keep your eyes off.

The evening had now advanced into night, with only a glow on the horizon, fast fading, to mark the sunset. The fences enclosing the pens and allotments poked like sharpened staves into the dying streak of sky, and away towards the river the baying of a dozen hounds, kept for breeding purposes in a crude stockade of wire-netting, sounded sharp and clear on the still air. Terry knew that it was getting late but he didn't want to leave just yet. He said:

'Where are your pals tonight, Colin?' It was amazing, and he realised it, that he could inquire after Eddie and Shaz as though they were old friends of his.

The big lad said, 'Them dozy getts. They've gone to the flicks.'

'We went this aft,' Spenner said, and told him all about *King Kong*, which didn't seem to interest Colin Purvis at all; nothing seemed to interest him unless he had done it or seen it or was talking about it. He asked the girls their names and they told him, giggling.

'Bet you've never played Postman's Knock.'

'Course we have,' they said.

'How do you play it?' he asked with sly cunning.

'We're not that thick,' Laura Parfitt said, giving him a level stare. Yet she could have gone in, it was late, and didn't. His manner was strangely hypnotic, even to her.

'Ever played Strip Jack Naked?'

The word 'strip' was like a stick of gelignite in mixed company. The younger girls blushed and some of the lads laughed in a nervous, embarrassed way.

'No,' Laura said, her tone ironic. 'But I bet you could show us.'

'I could that,' Colin Purvis said, lounging against the fence, the distant lamp near Wellens's shop making craters of his bad complexion. When he grinned with his large loose mouth he was fascinating in his ugliness. Terry wondered what Carol – or any girl for that matter – could possibly see in him. Then reminded himself savagely that all girls were stupid, fickle, addle-headed creatures whose behaviour was as infuriating as it was mystifying. Far better to stay with the Gang than be pissed about by girls and their wiles and snares.

Mitch said, 'I know Sandra Weeks does a bit.'

'I do not,' Sandra Weeks said, putting her hands on her hips. She gave him a look that could kill.

'That's not what I've heard.'

'You haven't heard nothing. What have you heard? Nothing, I bet.'

'Come on, Sandra, don't be shy,' Colin Purvis said in a coaxing, teasing voice. 'If you've done a bit tell us about it.'

'He's a damn pigging liar,' Sandra Weeks said, flushing and glaring at Billy Mitchell, who looked a bit abashed, Terry thought, as though he might have been guilty of betraying a confidence. He wondered what Mitch and Sandra Weeks had been up to, particularly as their bedroom windows faced each other across the back alley.

'Nowt to be ashamed of – eh, Laura?' Colin Purvis said, draping his arm across her shoulders. It struck Terry that, in spite of herself, Laura was attracted to him. He felt baffled and lost.

Kevin Hartley said he was going in and told their Doreen that she'd better come too. Fat Pat Sidebottom went with them. Spenner suggested that the rest of them go to the churchyard and tell ghost stories but nobody seemed keen on the idea: instead they wandered deeper into the maze of pens, known as the Figure 7, because it was a long straight track that turned a right-angle to form a 7, and eventually a dead end, finishing in a semi-circle of huts round a dirt clearing, bordered by hummocks of grass.

It was dark, not a light anywhere, faces and hands pale ghost-like blurs, black sockets for eyes.

Somehow or other (Terry had missed the start of it in the darkness) Colin Purvis was kissing Laura Parfitt, standing in front of her with his legs braced, pressing her against one of the creosoted huts. The others stood round in an awkward, self-conscious group as though they might have been waiting for a bus. Wet smacking sounds, unnaturally loud in the quietness, issued from the huddled pair. Colin Purvis broke away to say:

'There's a spare 'un, you know.'

Terry was about to reach for Sandra Weeks, delayed a fatal indecisive half-second, and, surprisingly, Alec beat him to it, pushing Sandra against the side of the hut and sliding his hands around her waist. This left Terry, Spenner and Mitch with nothing better to do than to stare unseeingly into the darkness and shuffle their feet in the dirt whenever the silence became too oppressive.

The scene suddenly brightened. A wash of light illuminated the pens, the waiting lads, the necking couples as a huge full moon, its topographical contours plainly visible, rose in state above the rooftops of Cayley Street; even as they watched, it cleared the slates and chimney-pots and rose into the sky, flooding the landscape with a hard white light.

'The night of the full moon,' Spenner growled in his throat.

Terry shivered and stared, bewitched. He felt as if his brain was lifting out of his head, his mind drifting away from his body.

'No—' Laura said in a muffled voice. '*No*.' There was a brief struggle.

'All right,' Colin Purvis said easily, 'don't get in a sweat. I'm not going to force you.'

'Don't do it then.'

'Okay, keep your knickers on.'

'I will,' Laura Parfitt said defiantly.

Now that the lads could see clearly what was going on, how the couples were making out, they could also see the bulge in Colin Purvis's trousers. Mitch nudged Terry, Terry nudged Spenner, and all three held their silent laughter in their stomachs, quivering and shaking in an effort to contain it. Spenner said, 'Let's have a go with Sandra,' and Alec Bland stood aside to let him in.

Colin Purvis looked over his shoulder, his face broad and thick-lipped in the moonlight, and said in a matter-of-fact voice, 'D'you fancy having a go with Laura?'

'I don't mind,' Terry said, trembling.

'He's a randy little bugger on the quiet,' Colin Purvis murmured to Laura Parfitt. 'I caught him earlier on touching up that other tart – who is it, Doreen?' He stepped back and Terry took his place. The trouble was that Laura Parfitt's mouth was level with his forehead. When he put his arms round her they encircled her buttocks. She lowered her head and he stood on his toes but it wasn't very satisfactory.

'Stand on something,' Laura said, looking round for a suitable stone or house brick. She spotted one and they manoeuvred towards it, Terry raising himself up so that their faces were level. He couldn't meet her eyes, he was too embarrassed, but in one quick movement inclined his head and kissed her on the lips. She was expert, no doubt about it, and Terry thought he detected a keener urging in her kiss than with Colin Purvis. And Laura was enjoying it: the way she snuggled deeper into the embrace, soft little sounds at the back of her throat.

'The randy little bugger's making a right meal of it,' observed Colin Purvis to nobody in particular. 'Save some for the rest of us.' His laugh was forced.

Terry didn't want to let her go, and to savour the full magic of his triumph he opened his eyes so that he could see as well as feel that he was actually kissing Laura Parfitt in the moonlight, standing on a stone at the bottom of the Figure 7 in Denby, Lancashire, Great Britain, the World, the Solar System, the Universe.

Laura too had opened her eyes, and for the tiniest fragment of time they looked, eye to eye, beyond the superficial glassy stare into the depths of the thing called Laura Parfitt and the lump of stuff labelled Terry Webb: thrilled, fascinated, frightened, shocked even by the naked contact, fierce as electricity.

It was soon over, in less than a moment, their two bodies tensing momentarily before yielding once again to the passive embrace. He was astonished; that this girl who had always seemed to him so distant and aloof should be so warm and alive. And so *near*. It was like encountering a Martian only to discover beneath the alien outer layer a real live human being lurking inside. And it was eerie with the moonlight washing over everything, a flat bland illumination making the pointed fences throw corrugated shadows across the rutted track and hummocks of coarse grass.

The faint cry of somebody calling 'Alec!' came from the direction of Kellett Street and Alec Bland said, 'I'll have to go, that's me dad.' When he had gone Colin Purvis said: 'Four against two now.'

Terry's heart lurched in his chest; for a nasty moment he had the wild notion that Eddie and Shaz were concealed somewhere nearby, waiting for the signal to pounce. And then realised that Colin Purvis meant four lads against two girls. Fluid gurgled somewhere inside him and his legs on the flat stone went weak with relief.

'Laura,' Sandra Weeks said, 'I'll have to be going in soon,' and pulled away from Spenner's embrace.

'Not yet,' Colin Purvis said. 'Not till you've paid your forfeit.'

'What?' Laura said, stiffening.

Terry stepped down off the flat stone as Colin Purvis moved in.

'You've got to pay a forfeit before you can go.'

'Who says?'

'Four against two.'

'Oh really?' Laura Parfitt looked at him in the moonlight with perfect cool detachment.

Mitch said, 'Sandra's got to pay one too.'

Colin Purvis grinned and placed his large heavy hand on Laura's shoulder, and when she didn't immediately shake him off Terry was inspired by the sudden realisation that girls not only required but actually desired an element of force: he could see it in Laura Parfitt's eyes, the conflicting emotions of rejection and submission, fear and desire, and he was seized by a dreadful gathering excitement.

'What they gonna do for a forfeit?' Colin Purvis mused to no one in particular.

'We're not doing anything,' Laura said.

'Come on, don't be chicken.' Colin Purvis's hand slid from her shoulder to just above her right breast, his broad flat thumb stroking the material. He said softly, 'Take your blouse off, let's see how big they are.'

Laura stared at him.

'We're not going to hurt you. We just want to have a look.'

'I've got to go now,' Sandra said.

'I said not yet.'

'I've got to go, honest.'

'You,' Colin Purvis said, 'have got to take your knickers off before you go anywhere.'

'I won't,' Sandra said. 'I won't.' It was beginning to dawn on her the predicament she was in. 'I have to go. Me dad'll be out looking for me.'

'Take your knickers off first, then you can go.'

Terry said, 'Or we can always take them off for you.'

Colin Purvis said silkily, 'Or we can do what Terry says.' His hand was touching Laura Parfitt's breast. She was standing very still, breathing the lightest of breaths. Was it fear that held her, or temptation, or a slow boiling anger that would suddenly spill over into flying fists and stinging blows?

Terry watched and waited, his throat dry, the sweat gathering in the palms of his hands. He felt just as he had done that afternoon in Doreen Hartley's kitchen when there seemed to be a giant pulse beating in his head, jarring his skull. The air seemed to have in it a peculiar kind of intensity as though a high-pitched sound beyond the range of human hearing was vibrating the molecules to a frenzy.

Another sound – a real one – infiltrated the silence: Sandra Weeks's muffled sniffling sobs, like the noise a mouse or a small timid creature might make, caught in a trap. Terry experienced the warm enveloping glow of deepest satisfaction.

Laura Parfitt said, 'Don't let them scare you, Sandra. They won't do anything.'

'I have to go,' Sandra wailed. 'I have to, I have to.'

'You go then,' Laura said. 'They can't stop you.' She was staring levelly into Colin Purvis's eyes; it was an attitude finely balanced between defiance and an outright challenge; they were an even match, her stare said so, and they both knew it.

'Are you staying if she goes?' His hand hadn't moved from her breast.

'No I'm not,' Laura said, and coolly, 'Not with you here.'

Terry expected Colin Purvis to react violently to this: what he did in fact was to drop his hand and turn away with a contemptuous shrug, muttering in a low voice, 'Piss off then. I've kicked better slags than you into touch.'

Laura tucked her blouse back into her skirt. She took hold of Sandra's arm and pulled her up the Figure 7. Terry watched them go. They were gone in a trice, even before his disappointment could register itself. Mitch said:

'Bloody Nora, I could've poked Sandra Weeks tonight.'

Colin Purvis laughed harshly. 'What with, your little finger?'

'I could do it as well as you, any road,' Billy said heatedly, and rather unwisely. He was six inches smaller than Colin Purvis, which should have been warning enough.

'Let's have a look then,' Colin Purvis said, encircling Mitch's shoulders from behind so that he was held captive. 'Get the bugger out and let's see it.'

Mitch struggled but Colin Purvis held him powerfully, without undue strain. They scuffled this way and that in the dirt, tripping over each other's feet.

'Get off,' Mitch said irritably. 'Bloody get off.'

'Not till we see this ten-inch prick of yours.' Colin Purvis increased the pressure, crushing Mitch to the point where it began to hurt.

'Don't,' Mitch said in a whining voice. 'Stop it, please, Colin.'

With a fury and savagery that took Terry's breath away, Colin Purvis flung Mitch across the track and into the fence. Mitch rebounded and lay in the grass. Terry didn't say anything. He didn't dare approach Billy to see if he was hurt or not.

'This is what you call a *dick*,' Colin Purvis said, opening his trousers and pulling it out into the open. The long thick shape was plainly to be seen in the moonlight, standing up from his trousers. He stood with his legs splayed and masturbated. There was the sound of sucking flesh.

'Come on,' Colin Purvis said, breathing heavily.

Terry undid the buttons on his trousers and felt a surge of

release as the cool night air touched him. He was already hard. Spenner did the same; the three of them stood in a circle.

'Let's swap round,' Colin Purvis said to Terry. 'You do mine and I'll do his and he can do yours.'

They grasped each other in a chain and worked them back and forth, panting, with intense concentration, lost to everything. Colin Purvis felt enormous, and burning hot: the flesh was hard and yet pliable in Terry's hand. They worked on each other for a while, no other sound but steady breathing, and Terry knew he was getting nearer. The feel of Colin Purvis shocked him: such bigness, rock solid: he had never imagined an experience like it in his life before.

As he was doing it to Colin Purvis another hand was doing it to him so that he thought he would explode if nothing happened soon.

'What's her name, that girl?' Colin Purvis said, his voice slurred.

'Laura Parfitt.'

'Laura fucking Parfitt,' Colin Purvis said, his breath rasping. 'Laura, I could fuck fuck fuck you. Oh yes.' He said, 'I could rip your blouse off and feel your tits. Oh yes.' He said, 'Laura, I could open your legs and push it in and shoot up you. Oh yes. Oh yes.' He said, 'If she was here now I'd get her on't grass and shag her till green sparks flew from her arsehole. I would. I would. Oh yes. Oh yes. Oh yes. Oh yes. Oh fuck—'

He jerked, groaned and pulled away, quivering.

Terry felt himself go in the next moment, the sweet pain rushing through his thighs to be swept clean out of him and lost in the dirt at the bottom of the Figure 7, the bright-as-day moonlight washing over everything. He was weary and content and not afraid of Colin Purvis any more.

When he had buttoned his trousers he went to see if Mitch was all right, lying motionless in the grass. His trousers were open; he had tried and failed.

The four of them walked through the pens towards the gaslamp on the corner near Wellens's shop. Terry was scared at the thought of what time it was. If it was gone ten – and it must be at least that if not later – he would get pasted. Spenner turned off to go down the back-entry, saying, 'See you,' and Terry walked on with Mitch and Colin Purvis. Dolly Bland went clacking by in her high-heels, giving the three of them an old-fashioned look for being out on the streets at this time of night.

As he left them to go along Hovingham Street, Colin Purvis said, 'Be seeing you. Next time we'll get Laura Parfitt on her own and we'll all shag her one after the other.'

Terry went on to number 77, shivering, despite the warmth of the night, with thrilling anticipation.

The next morning he came to the tiny square landing at the top of the stairs in response to his mother's call and she threw the brown envelope up to him. It landed on the second step from the top. Terry stood in his short vest on the landing and squinted in the poor light at the printed form – with his name typed above the dotted line – which informed him that on the basis of examination he had been selected for the High School for Boys, and that if his parents wished him to attend they should confirm acceptance in writing to the Education Offices, Fleece Street within fourteen days.

Terry ran into the street in his vest and short trousers and met Malc Smith (also wearing vest and trousers) pelting out of his front door followed by Bessie. The two lads held one another and danced in their socks in the dirt while Barbara went to stand with Bessie, their arms folded across their pinnies, discussing the cost of uniforms, satchels and sports equipment.

'I'm dead glad you've passed for the Tech, Malc.'

'I'm glad you've passed as well, Terry.'

They began to realise they'd passed, dancing in the dirt, singing a song to the tune of *D'ye Ken John Peel* about passing for the High School and the Tech.

More than half of the class hadn't passed for anything. Terry considered feeling sorry for them, even a bit sad, but that didn't last long, because in all honesty it didn't matter; he wasn't staying on at Heybrook in the Seniors and he wasn't going to the Tech where they made joiners and plumbers and sheet metal workers. Terry Webb was going to the High School, as he'd always known he would: he was one of the cream of the cream, as he'd always known he was.

Part 3

First Term

*

TERM STARTED ON SEPTEMBER 3RD. TERRY HAD arranged to meet Roy Pickup on the corner of Good Shepherd Church and they walked together to the town centre where the High School was scattered about several buildings, sharing premises with the Technical College. Roy was in the Third Year, and starting today he wore long trousers over his lanky legs. Terry felt proud to be walking beside him: the only two lads from Denby who went to the High School.

Terry was a brand-new boy, with his new green blazer and cap, new striped tie, white shirt and grey pullover, new black shoes, new brown leather satchel, new short haircut and new scrubbed face. He looked like a little cherub.

In the assembly hall the First Year were divided into three forms, 1A, 1B, 1C, and to his shock and disappointment Terry was put in 1C. He simply couldn't understand this. He had never been bottom of the class in anything, except sums. He felt insulted, and thought to himself: just wait till the first lot of exams at Christmas (when the top and bottom half-dozen in each form were re-allocated) and then we'll see.

The neat green line of boys with gleaming satchels was led across the road and past Ivesons' furniture warehouse to the rear of the Champness Hall, an old building used by the town for choir concerts and speech days. It was a dreary, draughty barn of a place with grey-washed walls and stone floors. The windows were of coloured glass in abstract patterns with wire screens to protect them. The classrooms were featureless square boxes, thirty-odd desks in 1C, marooned and forlorn in the middle of the vast room. It always felt cold, even in summer.

The first couple of weeks were strange and a bit daunting for all of them. Terry expected this and was prepared to put up with the strangeness, the new regime, the inexplicable customs because everybody else, he realised, was just as lost and at sea as himself. But it didn't take long for him to begin to hate the High School. It wasn't just that the lessons were hard and required painful and sustained effort, nor that he had to grapple with the mumbo-jumbo of Latin and the weird logic of Algebra, nor even that the masters in their billowing chalk-smeared gowns frightened him with their harsh standards of discipline. All this did have its effect, it was true – but really it was the feudal hierarchy of the class that shrank his soul and put fear in his heart. Within a few days this had established itself as a regime of two or three boys and their lickspittle cronies who terrorised everyone who didn't belong with them or were physically smaller, or could be intimidated.

By the end of the third week Terry, along with a dozen others, was being victimised daily. Arriving in the mornings was torture: edging nervously into the classroom, his eyes everywhere at once, expecting somebody to be lurking behind the door, or that when he reached his desk in the second row to find the pencil box his Auntie Martha had bought him filled with ink or smashed to pieces on the floor.

And it was no good complaining to the masters, who it seemed were themselves staunch advocates of the law of the jungle and the survival of the fittest. It was not only useless but fatal ever to complain to authority, because if Leach and his pack got to hear about it, or even faintly suspected, they would show no mercy, making an example of the informant by means of a cunningly-planned ambush and fiendishly-executed torture. No one ever complained.

Terry was thankful, in his more reflective moments, that he wasn't the prime victim. Hilton was the name of the unfortunate boy who hardly managed to get through the day – any day – without being kicked, punched, jostled or 'scragged' – held spreadeagled by the arms and legs and beaten like a carpet against the ground. Terry had undergone this treatment once (as had most of the others in the class) which had been devised by Leach and his associates as an initiation ceremony. Initiated into what exactly, no one knew; it was merely an excuse for sadistic highjinks.

Leach himself had a trademark that seemed common to all bullies: he had big teeth. In a way he was a good-looking lad, with a broad open smile and thick dark hair that rose up in a tidal wave at the front and tapered to a neat trim at the back. But it was this openness, this bright-toothed smile, that was the chilling thing about him. The smile was empty, without human warmth, as chill and bare as the classroom they inhabited inside this dank, echoing shell of a building. He took over in Terry's imagination the role that Colin Purvis had once had, which had been mercifully vacant until Leach came along and filled it like a looming evil shadow. Now Terry woke in the middle of the night with a wide bright smile lodged in his brain instead of a pock-marked crater-face.

When in class, facing Mr Short, who taught French, or Mr Bulmar-Todd who took them for Physics, it seemed to Terry that Denby was a land he had read about in a storybook, as a small child a long time ago. There was nothing to link this world of grim-faced masters and schedules and homework and detention periods, where everyone was a curt surname, to the unpaved streets and flickering gaslamps, or to the Common where the Gang played cricket and football, or the pens and allotments, the Ginnel, the Figure 7. Sometimes he felt so cold – right to the core – that it seemed all the joy and warmth had been drained out of him. What had Trigonometry to do with swaling on the

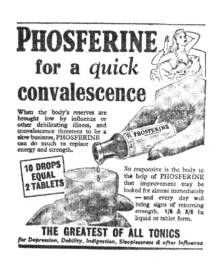

railway embankment? Or Mr Short's 'Preceding Direct Object' or Mr Bulmar-Todd's 'Coefficient of Friction' to do with anything? These were abstract concepts that chilled the blood because they were the meaningless language of a new doctrine he couldn't grasp. And looking back on it now, class 4A at Heybrook and patient, kindly Mrs Butterworth existed only as figments of his imagination; he might have dreamt them, and Denby too.

Yet in a curious way, his present existence also had a dreamy quality about it. As he sat listening to the master's drone, a section of his mind became detached and floated away, flitted along the bleak corridors and over the draughty open stairwell. It was as if his spirit was searching, hopelessly and randomly, for a meaningful sign, a familiar landmark. He felt abandoned and forsaken. As though he had been dressed in uncomfortably stiff, ill-fitting clothes, then dumped here and forgotten, expected to cram his head with gibberish, with nowhere to turn to for help, not a friendly or sympathetic face to be seen.

But he did make one close friend in 1C, John Tidmarsh, whose father owned a large hardware store in the centre of town. John was a neat, tidy boy who wore a clean white shirt every day of the week, whose tie was always pressed, shoes polished, fingernails trimmed. It was obvious, without John having to say so or boast about it, that his family was well-off: his appearance, his expensive leather satchel, his polite manner told you that he lived in a house with a bathroom, somewhere posh probably, near Falinge Park or up Bamford.

They became friends by the accident of sitting next to one another and through their shared hatred of Leach and his toadying henchmen – in particular a boy with frizzy yellow hair called Martin Jackson. By a quirk of the system, Jackson was nearly a year older than anyone else in 1C, which gave him an unassailable advantage. He had passed the eleven-plus at the second attempt during his first year in Brimrod Seniors, in an exam designed to catch potential High School material that had slipped through the net. He and Leach were natural allies in the domination of those such as Hilton, John Tidmarsh, Terry Webb and a dozen or so others, taking real relish in making their lives a misery; and the trouble was, there was nothing to be done about it.

Apart from the bullying, there was something else that scared Terry witless; if anything it was even worse, sinking his mind into a stupor. Whereas at Heybrook he had accepted his quickness at learning as natural, an innate gift, here he had to sweat and struggle just to keep up. It was a new and terrifying experience, and this, he reminded himself, was the lowly C form. He could barely imagine the impossible standards demanded by the A and B forms above him. They seemed so far out of his reach that he began to think of himself as actually thick. Latin and French were impenetrable; Mathematics and Physics (the latter taught by the Bull, as Bulmar-Todd was universally known) just plain baffling, a million random facts rattling aimlessly around Terry's numbed brain. It was pointless to look to the masters for sympathy or understanding. Their attitude implied that the privilege of being selected to receive this superior education carried with it the responsibility of behaving as an adult and possessing sufficient intelligence to cope with the work they were asked to do. But! Terry wanted to protest, it's too soon, I'm not ready, I'm not good enough! He never said any of this to anyone, of course, and they wouldn't have listened if he had.

On his morning walks to town he was tempted once or twice to ask Roy Pickup for the secret. There had to be a secret, no question about it. Because looking up at Roy as they walked along, trotting to keep up, Terry saw nothing that marked Roy Pickup out as in any way special or more brainy or cleverer than himself. He was quite ordinary, in fact, perfectly unexceptional. Yet Roy had survived two years of High School and was now in the B form of the Third Year. So there had to be (Terry reasoned) a magic key, a secret code, a password, that would enable him to survive in this strange, hostile environment. But he never raised the subject or sought advice; it would have been an admission of failure and defeat.

The day the Latin master was late in arriving for the lesson Terry had already suffered the indignity of a mushy gob of paper, stewed in Leach's warm spittle, splattering his right ear, which had to be cleaned out with a corner of his handkerchief. Being left unattended, there was pandemonium among the desks. Hilton got a paper dart topped by a sharpened pen-nib which drew blood from his calf, while Jackson and an associate set about little Jimmy Oldham with rulers, twanging them against the back of his head and rapping his knuckles when he sought to protect himself. Amidst all this noise and chaos Terry and John Tidmarsh were trying to have a quiet discussion, and it was only when silence fell with dramatic abruptness that they looked up to see the bulk of Mr Bulmar-Todd filling the doorway. He was taking 1B, the class next door, for RE, one of his alternative subjects.

The Bull stood in the doorway with his hands on his hips, gown draping his broad shoulders, rocking backwards and forwards on the balls of his feet. Very slowly he straightened his arm and pointed his finger, squinting along it as through a gunsight. 'You boy. Come here.'

Terry climbed out of his desk and walked across the stone floor until he was standing in front of Mr Bulmar-Todd. The eyes of the Bull were flat, grey, and Terry had no option but to stare back, transfixed as a rabbit by a snake.

The Bull spread his meaty hands on Terry's shoulders, placing his thumbs on the collar-bones with the lightest of pressure. This by itself was an oddly threatening gesture, which the class observed in total glazed silence. A new form of torture learned in a Japanese POW camp? Unarmed combat, Commando-style?

Very quietly, so that only Terry could hear, the Bull said:

'When I tighten my fingers you will slowly rise on your toes. You will remain on your toes until I relax my fingers.'

He looked into Terry's eyes to make sure the boy understood, then increased the pressure of his thumbs, and Terry rose up on his toes as instructed and hung there, so it seemed, for a long time. To the watching class the Bull's strength must have seemed prodigious – lifting a boy by the shoulders without, apparently, the slightest exertion. And Terry played his part well, teetering on tiptoe until the Bull released the pressure and he could sink back to the floor. The Bull said:

'Return to your seat,' and Terry turned and walked back to his desk under the full gaze of the class, his ears burning and his cheeks aflame. He couldn't fathom what the incident meant, except perhaps that he had been the victim of an experiment: he had been used (as the Bull might have used a magnet and iron filings or an ebonite rod) to demonstrate an important physical law; moreover sitting at his desk he felt squashed to mere noth-ingness, an object of ridicule. From that moment on his respect for Mr Bulmar-Todd was diminished to zero.

Another incident reinforced his hatred of the school. The class straggled up from the chemistry lab, situated in the basement, after a morning double period with Mr Haggerby, a large, ugly, pear-shaped man known with detestation throughout the school as the Hag, and who everyone agreed was the most boring teacher on the staff.

The next period was PE with Mr 'Monkey' Baker. There were a couple of minutes to spare, just time enough to go for a pee. Terry and John Tidmarsh were amongst a group of other first-formers queuing for a place at the urinals when some sixth year boys charged in and muscled their way to the front. They stepped forward and took their places, leaving, Terry saw, the central urinal vacant. Feeling annoyed at the sixth formers pushing in, and before John could stop him, Terry defiantly moved forward and filled the vacant stall, a moment later to be crushed by four hulking bodies against the wet and steaming pot surface, his arms trapped at his sides, his blazer and short trousers soaked, his shoes wedged in the trough of urine.

When they'd gone off, whooping and yelling, and Terry had trailed dismally to the washbasins, holding back his tears, John told him that it was an unspoken ritual of the school never to use the central urinal, and that green first formers were targets of the ceremony. Terry thought the whole thing stupid and child-ish. His uniform was wet and stinking, his shoes were flooded, and he didn't know what to do.

'You'll have to get a move on,' Hilton said from the door. 'Monkey Baker's waiting in the hall.'

'Put your kit on in here,' John Tidmarsh said. 'After PE you can wash your clothes in the sink.'

'I'm not coming.'

'You'll have to, you'll get done.'

'I can't do PE like this!' Terry shouted, staring at the rows of taps, his throat tight and dry. But he wasn't going to break down in front of them; he hadn't cried openly at the High School yet, not even when Leach and his mob had scragged him.

'Come on,' said Hilton anxiously. 'We'll be late.'

'What if Monkey Baker sees you're not there?' John said. He was concerned, bound by a sense of loyalty and comradeship.

Terry said, 'He won't notice I'm not there if nobody splits on me. Go on, see you later.'

But Monkey Baker did notice, or somebody told him, and he came to look for Terry in the lavatories. He poked his wizened inquisitive face round the door and then came in: he was wearing a red track-suit and proper running shoes with thick ribbed soles.

'Webb, isn't it?'

'Yes sir.'

'What are you doing here when you should be in the hall?'

'I got shoved in the —'

'Have you got your kit with you?'

'Yes sir. But I got —'

'Right. Get changed. I'll give you a count to one hundred.'

'But sir!' Terry said, his eyes filling with tears.

'Don't argue with me, boy. You should have been changed and in the hall five minutes ago.' He seemed oblivious to the state Terry was in. He turned to go. Terry stood mutely by the washbasins. When he showed no sign of moving, Monkey Baker said:

'Report to C7 detention on Thursday. And if you're not changed and in the hall inside two minutes you'll be on your way to see the Head.'

C7 was the more serious of the two detentions: unlike C5, which was for minor offences, it went on your end-of-term report. When school was over on Thursday Terry stood in the line of other offenders in the corridor outside Room C7, waiting for the prefect in charge to arrive. It turned out to be a hulking sixth-former with close-cropped red hair, known throughout the school as Trog, one of the boys who had pushed Terry into the urinal.

At the Baths

*

ON WEDNESDAY AFTERNOONS MONKEY BAKER took 1C to the Municipal Baths. It was an enjoyable double period for Terry, because being a decent swimmer he was allowed into the deep end instead of being under constant supervision and having to practise the breast-stroke with the learners.

On the afternoon he saved Jimmy Oldham from drowning he had been diving for the block with John Tidmarsh and Frank Taylor. They took it in turns to plop the weighted rubber block into the 8 Feet and pretend it was an underwater mine they were defusing. After a few dives Terry got fed-up and swam leisurely towards the shallow end. Somebody came swimming by, face down, as if searching the bottom, and kicked Terry in the stomach. It wasn't much of a kick, more a feeble twitch, and Terry stood up to watch the swimmer wallow and lurch through the water. Whoever it was, he had remarkable lung power. When he carried on and on, circling aimlessly and not bothering to surface, Terry waded across and jerked him upright out of the water. He was a dead weight, arms like floppy rubber tubes, eyes wide open in a zombie's stare with faint white haloes round the irises.

Monkey Baker came in response to Terry's shout and they laid Jimmy Oldham's pallid figure, limp as a rag doll's, on the tiles at the side of the pool. He puked up some warm green water and froth, Monkey Baker kneading his rib-cage with a firm even pressure and working his arms up and down like pumps.

'Shouldn't he be face down?' Terry said.

'Thank you for the advice, Captain Webb,' said Monkey Baker, making a joke Terry didn't understand. 'This is the Swedish method; you'll learn about it when you go in for your bronze medallion.'

Jimmy Oldham returned to the world of the living, his eyes as big and blank as saucers. His lips were the same colour as the rest of his face and he had blue puckered fingertips. He didn't say 'Where am I?' or anything else for that matter, but sat quietly in a canvas chair sipping milky tea brought by the pool attendant.

'Would he have drowned, sir?' John Tidmarsh asked Monkey Baker.

'Doubt it. I'd have spotted him in time,' which Terry knew was a bloody pigging lie. True, he himself had never personally seen anyone drown but he guessed that Jimmy Oldham hadn't had long to go when by pure chance he had kicked Terry in the stomach. Terry wasn't seeking to be made a hero, but all the same a 'Well done, Webb' wouldn't have been out of place.

In the cubicles afterwards, as Terry sat drying his feet, Frank Taylor's gap-toothed grin appeared over the dividing wall. Taylor always slavered when he spoke, his tongue lolling about as though too big to be tucked tidily away inside his mouth. Still grinning, he said in a low voice, 'How about this then?' and straddled the wall, naked, a thunderous erection straining upwards at forty-five degrees. He hunched his shoulders, gripped himself, and grunted in a parody of an ape playing with itself.

'Urg, urg, urg,' Taylor grunted, working himself. He dropped down into Terry's cubicle, large and white, body hard, and it almost seemed as if there were three of them in the confined space.

'Let's have a look at yours,' Taylor said in a spirit of good-natured interest.

There wasn't much to see, except for a slight unbending.

Taylor flipped it with his finger, his own upright and magnifi-

HEALTH

ON LEAVING THE LAVATORY
PLEASE SEE SAME IS AS CLEAN
AS YOU WOULD WISH TO FIND
IT YOURSELF ON ENTERING.

THANK YOU!

cent, standing apart in a superior fashion, and said, 'You haven't got much, have you?'

Terry didn't say anything. He was fascinated because Taylor was circumcised, the smooth polished purple crown curiously naked and vulnerable. He wondered, not for the first time, whether there was something wrong with him. His was covered by a layer of skin that was painful to pull back. Now looking at Taylor he was envious and unhappy: perhaps without the flap of loose skin his would be as large and proud.

When it became apparent that he wasn't fully responding, Taylor said, 'Watch me,' and masturbated himself fiercely, leaning back from the hips and aiming at the wall. The stuff came out – an incredible amount of it – spitting from the blunt end and dribbling over his fingers.

'Bloody Nora,' Terry said involuntarily.

Taylor shook his hand towards the floor to get rid of the excess and wiped the rest on Terry's towel. He looked down and lifted the now flaccid protuberance with his forefinger with an air of modest satisfaction ...

'Bet you wish you had a dick like that,' he said, and went off swinging his arms, going, 'Urg, urg, urg.'

As Terry was combing his hair in front of the mirror Monkey Baker came up in his red track-suit and put a penny in the Brylcreem dispenser. He stood behind Terry briskly lacing his fingers through his hair and humming a tune; he caught Terry's eye, smiled and winked at him in the mirror. That was all – he went away – and Terry was left feeling wonderful, thinking Monkey Baker the best master in the school. It had never occurred to him before that masters were actual human beings.

When he went up to the cafe he found that John Tidmarsh had ordered Oxo and toast for him and brought it to the table, which Terry thought was a nice gesture. They sat on tubular metal chairs with Tom Sorenson, three pale and unnaturally clean-looking boys with damp hair stuck to their heads.

'Chemistry test tomorrow,' said Tom.

'Yeh,' Terry said, unconcerned for once.

'The Hag hates your guts,' John said.

'He's a prick,' Terry said succinctly.

'It's a wonder you didn't get C7.'

For once Terry had been accused of and punished for a crime he had actually committed: he had been passing laxative chewing gum round the class and trying to persuade Tony Hilton that it was Spearmint, and Haggerby's square grey-jowled face (like a badly preserved Easter Island statue) had revolved ponderously from the formulae on the blackboard and caught him in the act.

Oddly, this incident raised Terry's prestige in the class, for he was one of a small select group of boys who had received both C5 and the more serious C7 detentions in their first month at High School. Leach and Jackson stopped picking on him, and amongst his classmates he came to be regarded as somebody prepared to accept a dare.

'It is nowt anyway,' Terry said, dipping a finger of toast into the Oxo. 'You just have to sit there for an hour, that's all.'

'If you get three in a term you have to see the Head,' John said.
'So what?'

'You get the cane and it goes on your report.'

Terry doubted whether anything that appeared in his report —
that he'd peed in the inkwells or set fire to the school — would
affect his parents in the slightest. If they took the trouble to read
it he would be surprised, and if they read it and understood it he
would be amazed. Since he started at the High School his dad
hadn't asked him a single question about the work or whether he
liked it there; as a subject for discussion it was non-existent.

At another table Taylor was being tormented by Leach and a
couple of cronies. Even though big for his age, and not skinny,
Taylor was one of their favourite victims because he never, under
any circumstances, retaliated. He just sat there with his tongue
hanging out like a drooling idiot, never seeming to realise that he
had the size and strength to hit back.

Leach had pinched Taylor's rolled-up towel and was using it as
a rugby ball, making low passes to Martin Jackson over Taylor's
head. When Taylor swivelled in his chair to intercept it, Leach
crept up behind him and clapped his hands with terrible ferocity over Taylor's ears. Jackson then completed the manoeuvre by
returning the pass and waiting for Taylor to swivel the other way
before thumping him between the shoulder-blades.

Terry said, 'He doesn't want to stand for that, the daft sod.'

'Too mard,' Tom Sorenson said, who though small was stocky
and sturdily built, and had the kind of square jaw that made you
think twice before picking on him.

'Nowt to do with us,' John said.

'No,' Terry said. 'But one of these days somebody's going to
hammer Leach.'

'Go on then,' Tom Sorenson said humorously, which was all
Terry's outraged sense of injustice needed to shut it up.

*

A bonus of having a double swimming period in the afternoon was that it was only a short walk for Terry from the Baths at the bottom of Entwisle Road, so he was home twenty minutes earlier than usual. As he came in through the back door he knew there was something wrong, and stopped dead with panic crawling up his throat. There was a battered brown suitcase at the top of the cellar steps. His first thought was that his mam had had enough and was finally off, taking Sylvia with her and leaving Terry behind with his dad. Where was she going, to stay with Auntie Hylda in North Wales? Then from the front room he heard a warm, full-throated man's laugh that was a rarity in the Webb household.

Suddenly it was like Christmas. There was a fire in the grate (on a Wednesday!) and standing with his back to it, big as life, was Uncle Jack. Terry felt weak in the knees from relief. His mam was sitting on the sofa with Sylvia on her lap; she looked watery-eyed, whether from laughing or crying Terry couldn't tell.

'Watch out! Here he comes! The boy from the Brains Trust!'

Jack grabbed Terry and wrestled him to the floor.

'Not so tough, these High School swots, sis,' Jack said, tying him in knots. 'Soft as pig muck.' His roar of laughter was infectious, and Terry was soon helpless, rolling on the carpet, feeling happier than he had in weeks.

Even Joe's arrival from work didn't completely dampen the mood. As a special treat they had their tea (liver and onions and chips) on the extended dining table, and Barbara sent Terry up to Wellens's for some Kunzle cakes and a packet of Cadbury's Chocolate Fingers. The curtains were drawn and it was snug in the front room, the firelight making patterns on the wallpaper, soft music on the radio coming from a posh hotel in Mayfair with a singer called Hutch. It seemed to Terry a lifetime ago since he'd seen Uncle Jack. He remembered him in his army uniform, wearing boots with toe-caps like mirrors. He'd just come back from Egypt, and with his tanned skin and black glossy hair and dazzling smile he'd seemed like somebody out of a film. His hair was more unruly now, flopping over his dark brown eyes – eyes that were the same as Barbara's, which Terry had inherited too.

'Started collecting bommie wood yet?' Jack asked, lighting up.

'Next week probably.'

'What about the Denby gang? How many are in it?'

'Er, nine I think ... ' Terry did a quick calculation. 'Ten of us.'

'Who's yer main rivals?'

'The worst lot? South Street.'

'South Street! By heck, we had some rare battles with them. What was he called, now, their leader ... Arthur Jessop! We used to call him Jessie. By heck, they used to threaten to stick us in dustbins, slap the lid on and set a fire going underneath. Chased us for miles one year along th' Arches and the top embankment. I nearly cacked me britches.'

Terry snorted and covered his face. Barbara said, 'Jack ... please.'

'So who's your leader now?'

'Spenner. Dave Spencer.'

'Who's theirs?'

'Brian Creegan.'

'Don't remember him.'

'Well you won't, Jack,' Barbara said. 'He's only twelve.'

'Thirteen,' Terry corrected her. 'Nearly fourteen.'

Jack puffed on his Park Drive. 'I wonder where he is now?'

'Who?' Barbara said.

'Jessie Jessop. Right bloody tearaway he was. I used to have nightmares about him chasing me over the railway embankment, cobbing half house bricks at us. I'll have to buy him a pint for old time's sake.'

'He was lost at sea,' Joe said.

'On one of them Arctic convoys,' Barbara said sadly.

'Atlantic,' Joe said.

'Atlantic conveyors.'

'As you were,' Joe said. 'Convoys.'

'They had a service for him at the Good Shepherd. No body of course. They gave him a medal.'

'Well they would, wouldn't they,' Jack said, grinding out his cigarette in the saucer. 'Bloody nice of 'em, I don't think.'

Terry said, 'Did you get any medals, Uncle Jack?'

'Aye, the DSO.'

'Did you, Jack?' Barbara's eyes lit up. 'You never told us. What's that stand for?'

'Deputy Shithouse Orderly.'

'Jack, really ...' She frowned in Terry's direction. 'The lad.'

'You think he hasn't heard worse than that in the school playground, sis? Here – hang on.' He went into the kitchen and came back a minute later with an object wrapped in greaseproof paper. 'What do you reckon to this, then, eh Terry?'

Jack unwrapped it and held the weapon in the flat of his hand. 'Bloody Nora ...'

'Hey, watch that bloody tongue of yours,' Joe said.

'Real Luger, nine millimetre, 8-round magazine, as issued to German officers. Swapped it for two hundred Capstan Full Strength from a squaddie in Bengazi.'

It looked practically new to Terry, a dull machined shine under a coating of oil. The handle was moulded plastic with deep slanting ridges for a better grip.

Jack held it out. 'It's been fired. Smell.' Terry bent forward and there was a faint acrid whiff. His mam said: 'You won't get into trouble, will you, Jack, carrying a gun round with you?'

'Not if you keep quiet, sis.'

'Is it loaded?' Terry asked.

'Never wave around a loaded weapon,' Jack said. 'First rule of soldiering. Keep the bullets separate for safety.'

'I'd have thought you'd had enough of such items,' Joe said. 'Not as if you can go out shooting rabbits with the damn thing.'

'It's just a souvenir,' Jack said. 'Like them Nazzy spoons I brought you.'

'Spoons with swastikas on is one thing,' Joe said. 'Guns is another.'

Barbara started stacking the plates. 'You'll stay with us, won't you Jack?'

'I will if you'll have me. Till I find a place.'

'Course we'll have you – won't we Joe? I'll move Sylvia in with us and you can have the back room with Terry.'

'Oh yeh! Great!' Terry punched the air.

'You planning on finding work up here?' Joe said. 'Some mills are on short time as it is.'

'Same in the Midlands. I had a decent job driving a lorry for a haulage firm till it went kaput. Thought I'd try my luck up here.'

'You'll need plenty of that,' Joe said.

Ambush

*

I T WAS QUITE A PRIVILEGE TO BE ALLOWED PEACE
and quiet in the front room to do his homework, for it meant
that an extra bulb was burning beneath the tasselled shade of
the chrome lampstand in the corner. The lamp threw a circular
orange glow over the linoleum and the edge of the carpet,
marked the wallpaper in parabolic curves of light and shade,
and faded away to shadow behind the leatherette armchairs and
underneath the dark-stained sideboard. There must have been
all of sixty watts pounding into the room.

Terry was writing an essay on Sir Francis Drake and the voy-
ages of the *Golden Hind*. He was cribbing most of it from *100
Daring Sea Adventures*, relying on the fact that Mr Redfern, the
History master, would never know.

From the street he could hear Doreen Hartley's voice calling
to someone out of earshot; the activity of the night was just
beginning. He closed his mind to the temptation and pressed the
nib of his Platignum pen into the paper. He wrote steadily, filling the pages with curling blue words. It was very satisfying. He
felt rather smug and self-righteous, working so diligently when
most of the other lads would be out on the streets, roaming the
pens, generally messing about and wasting time. Perhaps if he
got a move on and cut it short he might even take a ride over to
Gowers Street.

Terry still saw Margaret Parry, most afternoons in fact. Both
she and Betty Wheatcroft had passed for the Girls' High School,

and often were in the same bus queue as Terry on the way home from school or sitting a few rows in front of him on the upper deck. Margaret didn't so much ignore Terry as somehow arrange it so that she was never looking in his direction when he happened to be looking in hers. He could have been wrong, it might not have been calculated, but all the same their eyes never met. Yet how to approach her, how to recapture the magic of that blissful summer day defeated him.

For a moment the page slid away and he was gripped by a raging frustration. In one sense it was revenge he was after: he wanted to break through Margaret's defences in a wild rush, behaving callously, oblivious to her feelings. Yet in another sense, which was quite the opposite, the desire to be forgiven stirred within him, to be taken back and comforted. Both impulses squabbled like spoilt toddlers, the yearning to be accepted once again, and the malice of spiteful jealousy.

How easy and simple life had been at Heybrook! Terry recalled with a kind of baffled wonderment how much he'd looked forward to going to the High School. A bright new world in which kindly masters in gowns revealed the mysteries of exotic subjects like Latin and French, Physics and Geometry. Instead he was lost and floundering, scared because he couldn't cope with the work, hating the class he was in, the classroom itself, the building, the fabric of the school and everything it stood for. It was like being caught in a trap. It *was* a trap. He was trapped.

He didn't have the patience or willpower to complete the essay properly and scribbled the last page, making the words bigger to fill more space, capped his pen and bunged the lot in his satchel.

Alec Bland said, 'We could chuck him in't river.'

'No, summat worse that that,' Terry said.

'What if he's got his gang with him?'

'What if he has?'

'Chicken shit,' Colin Purvis said.

The three of them were loitering in the doorway of the disused shop on the corner of Hovingham Street discussing how best to get Shap and what to do with him once they'd got him. Although this was Terry's idea, he hadn't explained why they were doing it; Colin Purvis didn't seem to need a reason.

'He hangs round his pigeon loft a lot,' Terry said.

'We could burn it down,' Colin Purvis said.

Terry didn't know whether or not to take him seriously. You never could with Colin Purvis.

'Roasted piddies,' said the big lad, smacking his fleshy lips. 'Yum-yum.'

'No use taking it out on his piddies,' Terry said, thinking of his own birds. 'It's Shap we want.' He snuggled deeper inside his jacket, staring unseeingly from the shadow of the doorway.

A steady fine drizzle floated down, making everything slick-wet. It was the first of the depressing autumnal evenings when the sky seemed to close over like a grey eyelid, shutting out the night and stars. The people of Denby were comfortably locked away in parlours and kitchens listening to *Radio Newsreel*, looking forward a little later on to a variety programme featuring Ivy Benson and her Band, with top of the bill Lester Ferguson.

The three of them set off along Entwisle Road, staying close to the stone-fronted houses in a forlorn attempt to keep dry. They sidled behind the hoardings and nipped across the empty Common, climbed the gate decorated with barbed-wire and ran into the draughty shelter of the Arches. The brook made a fast rushing sound in the darkness, the level having risen several inches after the recent rains. The odour was wafted downstream.

Terry felt secure in the night: he knew the Arches like an old friend, every mark and dispoilment on the crumbling brickwork; the way the light from the lamps across the stream was reflected wetly in long diagonal gleams – even the smell of dampness and decay that entered his nostrils like incense. 'Come on,' he said, leading the way, his voice hollow under the vault of brick, and they moved in single file up the cindery slope towards the pigeon hut, the black and white stripes painted in tar and white-wash discernible in the gloom.

'There's nobody here,' Alec said, with what sounded to Terry suspiciously like a short nervous laugh of relief.

They approached Gowers Street, dodging from garage to garage in the manner of an Indian raiding party stalking a wagon train. Terry felt no fear – not with Colin Purvis on his side; the stealth was merely an added refinement in order to generate a pulsebeat of excitement.

But Gowers Street was empty. Nothing stirred, not a human soul, dog or cat.

'I'm getting soaked,' Alec Bland complained. 'Can't we find somewhere to shelter?'

'Bloody soft cock,' Colin Purvis said shortly.

'It's all right for you,' Alec said. 'You've got wellies on. My feet are sopping.'

'Give it a bleeding rest,' Terry said.

They walked along the dead street towards the main road and stood in the doorway of a shop that sold and exchanged paperback books. There was a row of Hank Jansons fastened by bulldog clips to a sagging wire. The covers showed men with hats shadowing hawklike features, wearing belted raincoats with square shoulders, and screaming red-lipped women clutching torn nighties to their bosoms.

'I've read that one,' Colin Purvis said, pointing to *Moan Softly As You Die*. 'There's a great bit where they shoot a bloke's knee-caps off, blood and bits of bone splattered all over the ceiling.'

Alec said excitedly, 'Have you seen what's on at the Ceylon, Thursday, Friday and Saturday? *Spider Woman Strikes Back*.'

'What use is that?' Terry said. 'You've got to be seventeen or eighteen to get in an H film.'

'You'd get in't Ceylon,' Colin Purvis said. 'Dead easy. Wear

long pants and go in round the back in't ninepennies. There's only an old crone there, seventy-odd, with a deaf-aid.'

'Have you ever seen an H film?' Alec asked.

'Loads. I saw *Devil Doll* at the Palace. All about this mad scientist who gets these dolls to kill people. And I've seen *Frankenstein* with Boris Karloff.'

'What time do you reckon it is?' Alec said.

'Eightish,' Colin Purvis said. He added, 'I've got an Everite watch but it's being repaired. I went to the baths on Saturday and forgot to take the bugger off. Me dad said he'd get me a new 'un but I said don't bother, I'd have it repaired instead.'

This reminded Terry – uncomfortably – of the payments still owing on the 17-jewel Swiss-movement Cocktail Watch he'd bought for his mam's birthday. After he'd started at his new school the paper round hadn't lasted long and since then he'd been struggling to meet the payments out of his spence. The struggle hadn't been too successful: there were two monthly instalments overdue and October's fast approaching.

Alec said, 'I'd rather go back to Denby, see if any of the gang's out.'

'Nobody's stopping you.'

Alec wavered, stepping on and off the step in his damp shoes, glancing up and down Entwisle Road, all of a fidget. Before he had time to make up his mind, two girls came down Oswald Street and crossed the main road, linking arms. One of them was Margaret Parry, the other, as Terry recalled, was called Muriel. They had been up to Hamer Youth Club in the basement of Heybrook School. Terry had been once or twice, but it hadn't much to offer except table-tennis, a threadbare billiards table, crisps and soft drinks.

'Seen Shap?' Colin Purvis asked bluntly, which made the girls pause.

'No,' Margaret said, looking at Colin Purvis and not at Terry.

'I saw him on his bike earlier on,' Muriel said.

'You girls are getting wet,' Colin Purvis said. 'Come in here with us.'

Muriel took a half-step.

'No thank you,' Margaret said.

'What's up, scared?'

'Definitely,' Margaret said. 'Shaking in our shoes.'

She was so lovely Terry could have killed her. He said, addressing himself to Muriel:

'Anybody at the club?'

'Not many. Rod Callaghan was there. Jean Ashmore. Margaret Sutcliffe. Iris Butterworth.'

Terry regretted not having gone to Hamer Youth Club. It would have been one further opportunity to snub Margaret Parry. He could have been near to her and ignored her at the same time.

'What do you want Shap for?' asked Muriel.

Colin Purvis smashed his meaty fist into the palm of his hand.

'Why,' Muriel said, 'what's he done to you?'

'Nothing at all,' Colin Purvis said, a fat grin spread across his face.

'What for then?' Margaret said. Her face had become sour and ugly with repugnance.

'Be-Cause,' Colin Purvis said softly from the shadow of the doorway, 'he's got it coming. That's what for.'

'I thought you'd have more sense,' Margaret said to Terry, and his heart leapt because she'd spoken to him directly. She said, 'If I see him I'm going to tell him.'

'Tell him then,' Terry said, knowing with a kind of sickly pleasure the expression that must be disfiguring his face. He didn't care; he revelled in his depravity.

'I'm not going with him, you know.'

'What if you are?'

'I'm not though.'

From the depths of the doorway Colin Purvis said, 'Who does she think she is, bleedin' Lana Turner?'

'Nobody asked you,' Margaret flared up.

'Chicken shit,' said Colin Purvis, his latest catchphrase.

'I think you're rotten, the lot of you,' Muriel said. 'Three onto one isn't fair. You wouldn't like it if a load of lads set on you. What if the South Street gang came down now and beat you up?'

Colin Purvis let go a deep rasping fart. 'I'd batter their faces in.'

'You're a load of pigs,' Margaret said.

'If you're not going with him why are you so bothered?' Terry felt compelled to ask.

'She fancies him,' Alec Bland said. 'He used to stuff her,' which pierced Terry's heart like the point of a knife. He didn't want to hear this: he wished it had never been said. Roll back time, erase everything, start again.

'I know I wouldn't let *you* touch me,' Margaret Parry said, flaring up fiercely and thrusting her face at Alec Bland. 'Nor any of you. And you — ' Margaret said, looking him full in the face. 'You, Terry Webb. I'm really disappointed in you. A boy who goes to the High School behaving like – like a pig and a bully. You think you're clever but you're lousy, rotten, a bloody stinking sod.'

'Yeh,' Terry said with grim, gloating satisfaction. 'I am.'

When the two girls had gone off in the drizzle they left a silence, almost a vacuum, behind them, which didn't last long – less than a couple of minutes – because just then a lad in a windjammer came pedalling along Entwisle Road and pulled over to the kerb when he saw them. It had to be Shap of course, and it was.

A Blazing Row

*

TERRY WENT THROUGH THE BACKYARD WITH A slight ache in his jaw, like nagging toothache. He touched his chin, wondering if there was a bruise. Before he'd reached the back door he could clearly hear the row going on in the kitchen, the by-now familiar interplay of his mother's high cracked voice and his father's guttural bass. He stopped with his hand on the latch and listened. It didn't take long to pick up the gist of it, which was to do with Barbara going out on her own one night a week (even though Joe refused to take her out for a drink, dancing, or to the pictures); with the state of Barbara's nerves, which had reduced her to 'a nervous wreck'; with the cause of that situation, which amounted to his total inability to show her any real affection or love, apart from the once-a-week ritual (Terry guessed what this meant); with his mean-fisted obsession with money – or rather the lack of it – which was driving her into an early grave; with the fact that she had again been to see Dr Charles, who had advised a course of ECT treatment at Sparthfield Clinic; with the crying need to get out of 'this bloody rabbit hutch' into a place big enough for a growing family; with the fact that Dr Charles had agreed to write to the Housing Department and recommend that due to her health they be given priority on the waiting list, and with lots of petty everyday irritations that Barbara rhymed off as though she'd been rehearsing them for months.

Terry waited, his thumb on the latch, for a suitable moment to interpose himself on this scene. He prayed, his heart thudding in his chest, that Joe wouldn't resort to violence, as had happened in the past. Even the thought of it made Terry's stomach churn and his hands tremble. The notion that his parents might separate had, on a holiday in Wales three years before, transfixed him with terror. Now he pretended to believe (or convince himself) that they rowed no more, or any less, than Malc Smith's mam and dad, or Alec Bland's, or Spenner's. All parents had rows; it was only to be expected.

Eventually there was a lull in the hostilities and Terry made a show of clearing his throat, kicking the dirt off his shoes on the step, pressing the latch and opening the door. The air was charged with static. You got the feeling that if anyone struck a match there would be a mighty explosion, ripping number 77 Cayley Street asunder.

Barbara wouldn't look at him directly as he came in. 'Get your supper, love,' she said, gazing at his left shoulder.

Terry put a bowl and spoon on the table and stood on a chair to get the Shredded Wheat. He poured milk from the bottle, sprinkled two heaped spoonfuls of sugar, and sat down to eat, all to a background of silence that seemed to set the molecules vibrating in his ears.

The milk dripped from the spoon. The Shredded Wheat crackled between his teeth. The soreness in his jaw made it difficult to chew properly.

'Where've you bin?' Joe said. He sat motionless in the rocking-chair.

'Gowers Street.'

'Who with?'

'Alec Bland and Colin Purvis.'

'Did you get your head wet?' Barbara asked.

'No, we sheltered.'

'Whereabouts?' Joe said.

'In a shop doorway.'

Terry suddenly remembered that he had to ask for four shillings to pay for a trip to York Museum organised by Mr Redfern. He opened his mouth and put some Shredded Wheat inside it.

'How would you like to live in a new house?' Barbara said.

'Where?'

'Kirkholt Estate. You'd have your own bedroom. And there'd be a proper bathroom, like your Auntie Martha's, and an inside lavatory. There'd be a garden as well.'

'You'd have to get rid of your pigeons,' Joe said. 'They don't allow animals on council estates.'

'He could have a shed, couldn't he? Somewhere?'

'No. I've just said. They don't allow pets.'

'You'd have your own bedroom though, Terry. Just think: you could hang your model aeroplanes up and have pictures on the walls. There'd be cupboards and drawers for all your things.'

'When are we moving?'

Barbara gave a little dry laugh, more like a croak. 'Oh, it isn't fixed up yet. It'll be ages, next year probably. I've got to go and see the Housing Manager and arrange everything.'

'I thought you said Dr Charles was writing to them?' Joe said.

'He is, he is writing to them, but we've got to get our name down haven't we? How do you expect to get a house if your name isn't even on the list? Talk sense.'

'I am talking sense, woman. It's you, you can't tell a proper tale. One minute you're saying one thing—'

'If you showed a bit of consideration – understanding – a bit of gumption – you'd offer to go down there yourself and talk to them. But oh no, sit back, let muggins do it. I've been on at you for six months to write or go and see them but you won't bloody budge your big fat arse off that chair. You'll go and pay your Union, you'll traipse off to watch bloody 'Dale in all weathers quick enough, but when it's something for other folk you sit back and do nowt.'

'When have you asked?' Joe said. 'When did you ask me?'

'Umpteen times.'

'When – that's all I'm asking – When? That's what I mean about you. You never come out with a proper tale. You invent things to suit yourself.'

'*I do not!*' Barbara screamed at the top of her voice. She jabbed her finger, her face white and strained:

'You twist every little thing I say. You've never shown me *that* much' (she snapped her fingers feebly) 'consideration all the years we've been married. Not once. You've never ever thought, have you Joe, "I wonder if Barbara would like me to do something for her"? Not once all these years.'

'Do what for you?' Joe said, his face crinkling grotesquely. He was fractious, non-comprehending, on the edge of real anger.

'You see, you don't even know.'

'Don't know what?'

'What I'm on about.'

'Of course I don't know, woman, if you won't bloody tell me!' His voice had risen to the level of hers. His normal high colour had faded, his face ashen.

'All these years,' Barbara said, beginning to weep. 'A complete total waste.'

'What you on about now?' Joe said. 'What are you on about?' He heaved himself out of the rocking-chair. She was leaning over the sink. He poked her in the back. 'Tell me what you're on about now I'm asking you.'

Joe's eyes were wide: there was fear as well as anger in them.

'I said What You On About Now? Answer me. Will you answer me?'

'If you don't know now you never will.'

'Know – *what?*'

The argument was like a locomotive with a full head of steam that couldn't get started because the wheels kept spinning on the track.

Barbara was standing at the sink crying freely. Terry was crying silently, the tears dripping onto the pieces of Shredded Wheat he was unable to swallow.

'I'm losing me mind,' Barbara said, holding onto the sink. 'No wonder me periods keep being late. I'm losing control of me own mind.'

'Rubbish, woman,' Joe said.

'You ask Dr Charles; why do you think he's put me down for shock treatment at Sparthfield?'

'It's just nerves, I keep on telling you,' Joe said. 'Nerves.'

'Aye, what's left of them.' Barbara shakily blew her nose. She turned from the sink and said, 'It's past your bedtime, our Terry. Get off upstairs.' She saw he was crying and said, 'Oh *love*.'

'Don't mard him,' Joe said. 'Go on, do as your mother says.' He gestured with his thumb and made as if to move forward, only half a step (if that) towards the table, and Terry said:

'Keep your filthy hands off me.'

Joe knocked him off the chair and the momentum carried him head-first into the cellar door. Things went muffled and distant for several moments after that, but at least he had enough sense left to stay down on the coconut matting. In a weird kind of way (because he believed in the justice of the jungle and the workings of fate) Terry supposed it was only what he had coming to him: fair and just retribution for what they'd done to Shap.

The crash must have wakened Sylvia, because from above came a wailing cry.

There were footsteps on the flagstones and a wicked draught swirled everywhere as Jack came in through the back door cradling a tiny brown puppy inside the wide lapel of his overcoat. 'Got this little chap for fifteen bob from a fella in the Cloverdale.' Jack nuzzled the puppy's nose with his own. 'Swore he was a pedigree. I'm going to call him Champ.'

Just a Black Eye

*

I N FACT LEACH GOT HAMMERED SOONER THAN anyone expected. It had been growing all morning, starting during Physics with the Bull, when Leach – out of sheer obnoxious perversity – kept taunting Taylor about his stupid tongue-lolling appearance and calling him 'the village idiot'. It continued after the break and right through Latin with Mr Neddiman, Leach saying such things as: 'If I looked like Taylor I'd commit suicide' and 'The reason Taylor can't run is because he keeps tripping over his tongue'. Jackson abetted him in this constant barrage of taunts and jibes, adding his feeble wit whenever the pace started to flag.

Terry understood perfectly why Taylor was such an irresistible target. Partly it was that he never put up any defence, but mainly it was his reactions, which were so comic: he would drool and roll his eyes helplessly, wincing whenever Leach or Jackson made a mock assault, cowering behind his gangling arms. It was this display that spurred them on to devise other more fiendish methods of mental and physical torture.

Mr Neddiman departed, having spent an abortive forty-five minutes trying to teach the class *Gaudeamus*, the school song, which everyone was required to bellow out on Speech Day at the Champness Hall. There were two lines in it that convulsed them:

Vivat nostra civitas
Maecenatum caritas

– the last word of each line, as sung by 1C, coming out as 'kiwit-arse' and 'carrot-arse'.

Mr Neddiman watched, hawk-eyed, for any smirking (having taught *Gaudeamus* to innumerable First Years) but always managed on his lightning sweeps of the class to miss the smirks by one-tenth of a second.

After he had gone the rhyming couplets involving kiwit-arses and carrot-arses went on, amid much chatter and screaming laughter. And when Reggie Short still hadn't arrived to take them for French, Leach and Jackson turned once more on Taylor. He was Prize of the Day, imbecilic, defenceless, inviting their scorn.

'Hey, Taylor, is your prick as big as your tongue?' called Leach across the class, grinning with all his large teeth.

'He dun't know,' a crony chimed in. 'He can't tell the difference.'

Leach flicked an ink-soaked pellet with his ruler which skidded along several desks, leaving an inky trail. The class was resentful but there were no complaints. Terry would have bet a month's spence that Leach was the type who as a kid cut worms into little pieces and inflated frogs with a straw till they exploded.

'Hey, Leachie,' Jackson shouted, 'let's see if it is as big as his tongue.'

'What?'

'His prick.'

They closed in on Taylor, both of them with anticipatory grins on their faces, and made a sudden grab, Jackson pinning Taylor's arms behind his back while Leach stamped on his feet to keep them still and started rummaging at his flies. Nobody interfered. Leach had unfastened the buttons and put his hand inside when Taylor got one of his arms free and hit Leach in the teeth with his fist. Leach fell back, already bleeding from the mouth, cross-eyed with stupefaction, and somebody from the back of the class said faintly but urgently, 'Get him, Taylor!'

It was like a story in the *Rover* when at last the tables are turned and the timid trembling underdog suddenly rebels and thrashes the bully and braggart to within an inch of his life. Everybody crowded round in a circle, jumping on desks and banging their feet, cheering as Taylor stood face-to-face with Leach and lammed into him. The stored anger was like high-octane fuel, feeding Taylor's aggression so that he was nearly insensible to what he was doing, and even when it became apparent that Leach had had enough (which didn't take long), Taylor still went on hitting him, sometimes to the body but mostly in the face.

Terry was behind every blow, fists clenched, lending his impotent strength and cheering along with everybody else, urging Taylor on with shouts of encouragement. He exulted in seeing the large white teeth ringed with blood and Leach's sick, frightened, defeated face and hearing him say again and again, 'Enough, all right, that's enough, that's enough, that's enough.'

It wasn't enough, however, until Taylor had exhausted himself and Leach was lying between the desks, blubbering softly and rather pathetically, his chin covered in blood, his collar and tie soaked through.

Tom Sorenson put his arms round Terry's and John Tidmarsh's shoulders and all three grinned at one another and hugged one another.

'I'm right glad!' Tom Sorenson said fiercely. 'It were great! I'm right bloody glad!'

It was a good moment, the best Terry had known since coming to the High School five weeks and several lifetimes ago.

He was surprised on his way home that same afternoon when Margaret Parry came up to him in the bus queue and said quietly, 'Do you mind if I stand next to you?'

Terry shook his head. It struck him that her face looked rather pale, but he said nothing. There was something different about her, even rather odd, the dark eyes withdrawn and inward-looking.

The bus arrived and they went upstairs. Margaret sat near the window. The town centre was busy with schoolchildren, shoppers and a few office workers on their way home. It was the time of year when people were beginning to think of wearing scarves and overcoats. In less than a month, Terry thought, it would be bonfire time. He said:

'I'm sorry for acting so daft.'

'It doesn't matter.'

'Honest?'

She didn't respond.

'Will you go with me again?'

Margaret nodded, looking through the window, and started to cry.

Terry was moved. A girl had never cried over him before. He felt a lump in his own throat. What an idiot he had been. The summer had been wasted through his jealousy and stupidity and spite. He felt deeply ashamed of what he had done to Shap. Even though Margaret knew, of course, what he had done, Terry wanted to confess to her, to unburden himself, purge his guilt. He tried to summon up the nerve, and just when he thought he had, Margaret said, 'Betty Wheatcroft died today in school.'

The bus started and jerked all the heads back in unison; the town centre slid away outside the windows as the bus laboured up the shallow incline of Smith Street. It stopped at the lights.

In place of thought or emotion Terry felt an urge to say something frivolous like, 'What did she die of, short of breath?' but he knew he couldn't say that and yet couldn't think what else to say. The bus set off again, grinding its gears.

'They took her to the Infirmary at dinnertime with a black eye.'

Terry rotated his head to stare at her.

'She fell in the yard and banged her forehead. She was all right at first, she just had a black eye. We all thought it was funny. Then she started to go dizzy and kept falling down and Miss Brookes took her up to the Infirmary in her car. She had a clot of blood in her brain and they tried to operate on her but she died.'

'All she had was a black eye?'

'There was no cut or lump or anything. But when she fell it must have ...' she didn't know how to express it '... shaken a clot of blood loose or made it form or something. Miss Brookes came into Biology this afternoon and told us all.' Margaret's face suddenly screwed itself up into vertical and horizontal lines. 'Miss Brookes was crying herself.' She made a noise and the people in front turned round.

Terry fiddled with his bus ticket. He noticed an ink stain on the index finger of his right hand, just where he held his pen. It must be leaking, he thought. For the life of him he couldn't remember what Betty Wheatcroft looked like. He remembered her hair, which was brown and worn in long loose ringlets (he used to tie them together when he sat behind her in 4A at Heybrook), but when he thought of her face all that he could see was a white space with a black blob where one of her eyes should have been.

Margaret continued to make embarrassing sounds all the way along Entwisle Road and Terry had to help her off the bus when it stopped at the Arches. She leaned against him, weak, shaking, her cheeks inflamed with the salty moisture. Terry supported her; it was like holding a large helpless doll.

'Do you want me to come home with you?'

'No.'

'It won't take a minute.'

'No.' She straightened up and opened her satchel.

'What are you looking for?'

'Another hankie.'

'Use mine.'

It was clean today, thank goodness, with no chewing gum or crows stuck to it. He gave it to her, thinking what nice hands she had. He himself felt nothing about Betty Wheatcroft's death. He

didn't believe she was dead. He tried to think of how she had been when alive (waving to him on her way to the Co-op with a shopping bag) but that too was unreal, because then she was still living. Perhaps he didn't have any feelings or emotions. Supposing he had to go through the rest of his life not really caring for anybody. But neither was that thought real: thinking about what he should have been thinking was of itself empty, without meaning. He might have been filling in the solutions to a crossword puzzle. Answering an exam paper.

The least he could do was to see Margaret across the road. Then he went home for his tea. He didn't tell his mam about Betty Wheatcroft because he didn't know what kind of expression to put on his face when he told her. The one thing, the only thing, that had any connection with her death and his life was remembering that Margaret or Muriel or somebody had once said that Betty Wheatcroft fancied him. That was the sum of it. Nothing else. It staggered him, this callous indifference – that he could be so utterly devoid of feeling. And therefore he went up to the back bedroom and had a little private weep, squeezing out the tears one by one from beneath dry eyelids like drops of glycerine.

Under Attack

*

FTER TEA ALEC BLAND CAME TO CALL FOR him, and though Terry had some homework he calculated he could do it tomorrow dinnertime, before the French period in the afternoon. Besides, he hated Reggie Short's guts, and he suspected the feeling was mutual. Terry was rather proud of his French accent but he was hopeless at the grammar; he couldn't get the hang of rules like 'Preceding Direct Object' and so Reggie gave him consistently low marks.

There was nothing to keep him in the house, especially since *Dick Barton Special Agent* had finished on the radio a few months ago. Terry still missed it badly, the thrilling music and the knife-edge suspense, the screeching car chases and fists socking jaws, sitting on the cold linoleum with his ear glued to the speaker.

'Hurry up, don't keep Alec waiting at the door,' Barbara said. 'And get well wrapped up, it feels parky.'

'Where's Uncle Jack? Has he got Champ with him?' Terry asked, taking his windjammer from the hook.

'You know very well where Uncle Jack is, he's upstairs,' Barabara said, exasperated.

'Oh yeh,' Terry said, 'I forgot,' content to have reminded Alec who they had living with them. But Alec didn't take the bait right away, which meant Terry had to raise the topic again as they were walking along the Top Track.

'My dad used to build bombers during the war, in Chadderton.'

'My dad was in Burma,' Alec said, 'in't jungle.'

'Is that why he's ill all the time? He's dead thin, in't he, and a funny yellow colour.'

'Me mam says it's murry-earlier or summat.'

'Is he going to die?'

Alec shrugged. 'Dunno. He can't work.' And at long last: 'Your uncle was in the war, weren't he?'

'The Desert Rats. They were in Africa near the pyramids. He fought against Rommel.' Terry nearly corrected himself; weren't the pyramids in Egypt?

'Who was that?'

'German general called Rommel. He was in charge of the Pansies.' He wasn't entirely sure about this either, though that's what it sounded like when Jack told him about the tank battle near somewhere called Tobruk. Before Alec had the chance to doubt him, or even worse, question the truth of the story, Terry went on quickly: 'Yeh, he brought back some spoons with swastikas on them – they're a funny grey colour and you can bend 'em dead easy. And a real Luger gun, weighs a ton, you need both hands to lift it.'

'Does it fire?'

'Course it fires. He fought a German captain for it, in a trench. The Jerry was just going to shoot and Uncle Jack jumped on top of him and kicked it out of his hand, sent the gun spinning.'

'That's what Biggles did to von Stalhein!' Alec said alertly.

A voice called out: '*Halt!* Friend or Foe?'

They made out the dim figure of Dougie standing near the entrance to the air-raid shelter.

'Friend,' Terry said.

'Password?'

Terry sucked his lips. 'What's the password, Alec?'

'Haven't a clue.'

'What's the password, Dougie?'

'I'm not allowed to tell you.'

'How do we get in if you won't tell us?'

Dougie sniffed loudly and stared at them in the gloom. Eventually he said: 'What do paratroopers yell just before they jump out of a plane?'

'Geronimo,' Terry and Alec said together.

'Pass, Friend.'

'Where's the rest of 'em?' Terry asked, poking his head inside the shelter to find Spenner on his own.

'Kevin, Roy and Mitch are coming down later.'

'It's still not going to be enough of us if they attack, is it?'

'Who you scared of – Brian Creegan? He's nowt but a tub of lard.' Spenner was rummaging through the piled-up wood.

'What you doing?'

'Them doors and window-frames'll burn great ... Dougie, where's that candle in the jam-jar? I'm going to make a table out of this door. Get hold of that end, Webbie. If we prop it on them boxes we can put the candle in the middle and sit round ...'

In a few minutes they were sitting facing one another in the wavering beams from the jam-jar.

'Great this, innit?' Terry said. 'Like being underground.'

'In a bunker,' Alec said. 'Hitler was killed in a bunker.'

'Anybody got any cigs?' Dougie asked.

Spenner said, 'I've got a dimp. We'll pass it round.' He lit up and they each took a drag. Sucking in smoke, Dougie said:

'Hitler's not dead, you pie-can. He was captured by the Russkies and they took him to Sibera. He's there now, nobbut a skeleton, chained up in't salt mines.'

'That's all you know,' Spenner said with a harsh laugh. 'He's in South America. He had a U-boat waiting to take him there when the Jerries surrendered.'

'Give us another drag, Spenner.' The dimp went round, scorching their lips.

'Anybody seen *Commanche Territory* at the Ceylon?' Terry asked.

'Who's in it?'

'Randolph Scott.'

Alec kept looking over his shoulder. 'Why don't we start a fire?'

'We don't want to waste all our bommie on a tiddly fire,' Spenner said.

'Well let's keep a look-out then in case they sneak up while we're in here. They might —'

'Ssssshhh!' Dougie said. The shelter went deathly quiet except for the holllow sounds of breathing. Terry couldn't hear anything. Alec was chewing his lips.

'What is it?' Terry whispered.

Then they all heard it – a scuffle of footsteps, low voices, muffled laughter.

Alec jumped up. 'Steaming Nora – it's them! – they're coming! – we're being raided! —'

'Is it buggery, that's Kevin, laughs like a hyena.' Spenner called out, 'We're in here!' Kevin Hartley, Roy Pickup and Billy Mitchell came in, still sniggering at a joke Roy had told them about a bloke whose knob fell off. 'Seen any of the South Street lot?' Spenner asked.

'I saw Brian Creegan near the Co-op,' Mitch said.

'When?'

'Half hour since.'

'Which way was he going?'

'Down here. Anyroad towards Kellett Street.'

'On his own?'

'Yeh.'

Spenner took a final drag and ground the dimp into the concrete floor. 'Could be an advance scout. We'd better post sentries. Terry and Alec – get up on the roof, lie flat, keep your eyes skinned. Roy, Dougie, Kevin – spread out on three sides and get down in't grass. Mitch – you go to the top of the embankment. You can see right to the far end of Kellett Street from there. If any of you spot anybody, shout "Bandits".'

'I'll be on me own,' Mitch complained. 'Why is it allus me on me own? Send Alec or Dougie . . .' He usually got the short end of the stick because he was six months younger than the others.

Spenner said, 'More likely they'll come across the Common and down Ma Rigall's back-entry. Or maybe through the pens. Somebody better keep a watch on the Ginnel as well.'

Kevin said, 'Shit and corruption, it's like the Black Hole of Calcutta down there! There's no gas lamps.'

'What's up, Kevin, chicken?'

'Shut it, Dougie, fart-face.'

'You bloody make me.'

'Think I can't?'

'Will you two belt up!' Spenner yelled. 'Honest, you're worse than kids in th'Infants class. We're supposed to be fighting the South Street gang, not each other. Right, get going . . . spread out and keep quiet!'

Lying flat on the roof of the shelter, it occurred to Terry to wonder what defence they could actually muster if they really were attacked. Cob a few half house bricks he supposed. But would the South Street lot bother traipsing all this way for a few doors and window-frames? He huddled deeper into his wind-jammer. He could hear something rattling; it was Alec's teeth.

'Jesus wept, Terry, I'm bloody frozen. Me feet are like lumps of ice.'

Peering into the darkness, Terry couldn't see any of the others, and it had gone eerily silent. 'Where's Kevin and Roy got to? And what's happened to Spenner?' It was unnerving, with only the wind whispering through the grass.

'I want to go home,' Alec said, clenching his teeth to stop them chattering.

'You can't do. We're supposed to be on guard —'

They both cried out as a bright flash like splinters of light burst overhead, followed a second later by the deafening crack of an explosion. Several more bangers went off, nearer and louder, and they heard whoops and cries in the distance, also getting nearer and louder.

'Hell's bells,' Alec said, 'they're coming. I'm buggering off!'

Terry had started trembling all over. 'I can't see a bloody thing.' He hung his head over the rough edge of the concrete roof and called in a hoarse, strangled whisper: 'Spenner ... Spenner! They're attacking!'

Stones and chunks of brick started raining down on them, bouncing off the roof. 'I bet the yellow sods have scarpered,' Terry said, really scared now.

'They're cobbing dirty great house bricks,' Alec whimpered, curling up in a ball. 'I want me mam.'

Something fizzed through the air in a pretty sparkling arc and the banger went off a few feet over their heads, deafening and blinding them. Alec started crying. 'What's up, are you hurt?' Terry could hardly hear his own voice, it sounded muffled by cotton wool.

'They – they roast you alive,' Alec's voice quavered between sobs, 'in dustbins ... over the fire ... with the lid on ...'

'There's somebody on the roof,' a voice said. 'Boot 'em down, Hoggy.'

A grinning head appeared, crooked teeth in a grimy face. 'There's two up here, Bri – a couple of little squirts.' Terry recognised him, a lad called Harold Hodges. His hair, which looked orange in this light but was, Terry knew, bright red, stuck straight up in spikes. He was one of the ugliest kids this side of Yorkshire Street.

'Don't let 'em escape, Hoggy. They're our prisoners.'

'Looks like your pals have buggered off and left you,' Hoggy said. 'Do you want to get down or be thrown down?'

As a form of greeting, as they reached the ground, and to show them who was boss, Brian Creegan shoved Terry aginst the wall of the air-raid shelter and punched him in the ribs.

'Ow, quit that, Creegan.'

'Who you calling Creegan?' Brian Creegan said, and punched Terry harder, aiming for the kidneys. 'Gone soft all of a sudden, eh? Now yer mates have gone. A minute ago you were cobbing house bricks at us.'

'No we weren't. You were cobbing 'em at us! And bangers as well.'

'I'm a liar am I? Who was cobbing 'em then? Eh? Eh?'

'Don't hit me,' Alec snivelled. 'I've got a weak stomach . . .'

'Oh dear, hecky thump – hear that, Bri? This little squirt's gotta weak stomach.' Hoggy poked Alec with stiff ramrod fingers. 'Where's it weak then? Hereabouts is it? Here?'

'Oh me stomach's hurting . . .'

Hoggy mimicked him in a mincing little girl's voice: 'Oh me stomach oh me stomach oh me bleedin' stomach . . .'

Terry said, 'It's not fair. There's more in your gang than ours. And you two are older than us.'

'What's that got to do with it?' Brian Creegan said, pushing his face into Terry's. 'You're a right cheeky kid, aren't you. What's your name?'

'Terry Webb. You two are thirteen. We're only eleven-and-a-half.'

'Aw, mammy's boy's only eleven-and-a-half, Hoggy. What a shame.' He hit Terry hard with his bunched fist on the upper arm, right on the muscle, which hurt like buggery, and Terry burst out crying.

'You're a bloody big fat bully, Creegan,' Terry sobbed.

'I'm a what? What did you just call me?' Brian Creegan's voice sank to a guttural whisper. 'A bloody what?'

'Nothing.'

'Am I going deaf or am I stupid or what? Right. I've changed my mind. I was going to let you go, let you scram off home to yer mams, but not now. Now you've really had it.'

'I didn't mean owt, honest,' Terry said. 'I'm sorry.'

'Too late, Webbie.' Brian Creegan was enjoying himself.

'What we going to do with 'em, Bri? Chuck 'em in the brook?'

'I've got a better idea.'

'It's not fair, just picking on us.' Tears were running down Terry's face. 'You can have the lousy bommie. Go on, take the lot.'

'I want me mam,' Alec wailed until Hoggy elbowed him in the chest. 'Shut yer gob, you big soft tart. What we gonna do to 'em, Bri?'

'Tell you what we'll do. Take their pants off, build a fire and get some red-hot sticks and —'

Alec's high-pitched scream of terror drowned him out, and then silence fell all of a sudden as an adult voice said, 'Any of you lads seen Terry Webb?'

'It's me, I'm here,' Terry said. 'Am I wanted, Uncle Jack?'

'Wondered if you fancied coming to the flicks. There's a picture on at the Rialto about POWs in a kraut prison camp. Unless you want to stay with your pals . . .'

'No, I'll come. I'll come.'

'I'll come with you.' Alec said, moving past Hoggy.

'Your mam says you have to have a wash first and change your shirt and trousers. Sure you want to come?'

'Yeh, dead sure.'

'Come on then if you're coming.' Jack was halfway up the track. 'It starts at ten past eight.'

'See you, Webbie,' Brian Creegan called after them.

'Not if I see you first, Creegan,' Terry said over his shoulder.

It was nearly half-past ten when they came out of the Rialto, leaving in the nick of time to miss 'God Save the King,' just as the gold lamé curtains came rippling down in overlapping waves. Under normal circumstances Terry would-n't have been allowed out so late in mid-week when there was school the next day; he assumed it was because Jack had offered to take him (and more importantly pay for him) that had swung it with his dad. 'Keep wrapped up,' Jack said, pulling Terry's scarf tighter. 'Your mam'll drop on me like a ton of bricks if your ear-ache starts up again.' They walked down Drake Street, which had all the posh shops – Ivesons the Furnishers, Fashion Corner, Butterworths the Jewellers – towards the town centre, deep in discussion about *The Wooden Horse*, which Terry reckoned was one of the best pictures he'd ever seen. He'd been breathless with excitement when the tunnel collapsed on top of the escaping prisoner, and the other POWs couldn't rescue him because the grim-faced krauts were watching stony-eyed from the guard-tower, itching to spray them with hot lead.

Jack said it was very realistic: the German weapons and uniforms looked genuine to him. They boarded the No. 7 bus and sat downstairs. Terry was about to ask him about the Luger when his uncle gave him kind of a half-grin, one eyebrow raised. 'What was that performance down at the shelter all about?'

Terry was surprised he'd caught on. 'South Street lot were after our bommie.'

'Where was the rest of your gang?'

'Scarpered off somewhere, leaving just Alec and me. And they're older than us as well, Uncle Jack,' Terry said, his voice rising. 'Brian Creegan's thirteen —'

'Age doesn't matter, Terry. Size doesn't really matter either, not if you get yourselves organised. There's enough of you all together in't there? Ten or more? Get yourselves sorted out proper, build up your defensive perimeter, set ambushes, form a pincer movement. Push 'em one way, towards the river, and then block off their retreat.'

'We posted guards to warn us but they vanished, didn't they?' He was still seething about that.

'Posting guards isn't enough on its own,' Jack said. He opened a packet of Park Drive and then realised he was downstairs. 'What's your leader called? Spenner? What's he like?'

'How d'you mean?'

'Do you trust him?'

'I suppose so … he's the oldest anyroad. And he's not mard.'

'Can't be right, South Street nicking your bommie. What you need is a strategic battle-plan. That's the way to knock 'em for six. And that's how Monty did it at El Alamein …'

Jack talked about tactics and strategy all the way up Entwisle Road until they got off the bus at the Arches. Several other people came clattering down the stairs and followed them off. Someone called out Jack's name and he turned, frowning.

'Er … hello?'

'Hiya Terry.'

'Hiya Eileen.' It was Phil Kershaw's sister. She smiled at Jack. He gave a nod of recognition.

'Where've you two been, the pictures?'

'Yeh, the Rialto.'

'Me as well,' Eileen said. 'Not my cup of tea really, all that digging and sweating. I went with Ivy from work. She lives up Syke. I didn't see you in there,' she said, tilting her head sideways to look up at Jack.

'We were upstairs in the one-and-threes,' Terry said grandly.

Eileen pouted and her eyes were like saucers. 'Ooooooooohhh!'

'And I had a choc ice.'

'Pigs in muck! I heard you'd come back and were living with Terry's mam and dad, Jack. I thought you might have called round. You know, for a natter. How've you been getting on?'

'This and that. Job hunting mainly.'

'Any luck?'

'Not so far.'

'Where've you been living since you left the Forces?'

'All over't place. Leicester for a while, the north-east near

244

Gateshead, then a driving job in Walsall. Ended up tramping round for six months. It was all short-term stuff, a week here, a week there. Nowt solid.'

Eileen was shaking her head, making her kiss-curls swing to and fro. 'It's shocking I think, after what you did in the war. There should be jobs waiting for all you fellas, not the dole queue. You're still nice and brown though, and you've filled out a bit.'

'That's digging up potatoes for you,' Jack said with a weak grin.

'You were like a string-bag when you joined up,' Eileen said archly. 'I saw you stripped off, swimming in the brook. Remember? Forty-three?'

Jack gave Terry a playful cuff and mumbled something about getting this lad home to bed. Eileen started walking with them, though Terry knew she lived the other way, on Hovingham Street.

'Ever go to the Carlton?'

'Er, no ... not recently.'

'Me and Ivy go every Saturday. It's a good night. Full dance band with vocalist. They have spot prizes.'

'Sounds grand.'

'I won a compact. Real mother-of-pearl. Fancy going?'

'To be honest,' Jack said, the weak grin coming back again, 'I never learned to dance.'

Eileen blew out a gust of air. 'Oh don't let that put you off! You just smooch around the floor, three steps forward, three steps back. You might really enjoy it.'

'I'll have to have a think. I'm a bit tied up at the moment, looking for a job and what-have-you.'

'Well, he can't be short of brass, sitting in the one-and-threes eating choc ices, can he? Eh, Terry?' Eileen said brightly.

'Are you coming to our bommie, Eileen? Your Phil's collecting wood with us.'

'Bonfire?' Eileen might have been saying Plague or Dog Muck. 'Not my cup of tea. I've got better fish to fry.' She held out her hand for Jack to shake, which Terry thought was slightly odd, and then moved off in the other direction. 'You know where I live, Jack, don't you? Same house. No. 23.'

'Next to the snicket …'

'Next but one. Pop round some time. We'll have a proper chat.'

Eileen clip-clopped off down the street, a slim figure, not much taller than Terry, with fair hair that gleamed in waves under the sodium lamps. He'd never thought of her as a woman before, someone with friends and a job, just Phil Kershaw's elder sister.

Jack took a deep breath and thumped himself on the chest.

'You know what?'

'What, Uncle Jack?'

'I'm hungry. How about you, Corporal Webb?'

'Starving. I could eat a horse.'

'How about fish, chips and mushy peas instead, plenty of salt and swimmin' in vinegar. The corner chippy's still open. I'll race you. Last one there's a daft pie-can!'

C-in-C

*

'OFF UP TO THE DALE, JOE?' JACK ASKED, SITTING down at the kitchen table. Barbara was ladling out plates of mince in gravy with dumplings, mashed potatoes and cauliflower. They had the same every Saturday dinner-time.

Joe was still in his overalls, having done a morning shift at Riley's spring works.

'Aye. Bradford City. We'll get murdered.'

'Why don't you go up as well, Jack?' Barbara said. 'Be a break for you, and it's a grand day.'

It was. Terry had been out in the backyard all morning, releasing his piddies and watching them doing circuits against a backdrop of huge tumbling clouds and vivid blue sky. It was a perfect late October day.

'Wouldn't mind but I've got an interview,' Jack said, tucking in.

'Saturday afternoon?' Barbara said.

'This fella I met in the Cloverdale, thought there might be a vacancy at the Rope Works on Acker Street, packing crates. It's a mate of his as owns it, so he's taking me down there.'

'What happened to that job at Croft mill you went for?' Joe asked. 'They had half-a-dozen vacancies.'

'Aye, that's true, but they wanted experienced carders. I never served me time in't mill.'

'Beggars can't be choosers. If you don't start somewhere you'll never get taken on full time.'

'Come on, Joe, be fair, Jack's doing the best he can.' Barbara tapped Terry on the shoulder and pointed to the untouched cauliflower on his plate. 'There's a lot of young blokes in Jack's position, all of them looking for work.'

'Some of 'em even manage to find it.'

Barbara sat down heavily and picked up her knife and fork like weapons, tiny spots of colour in her pale cheeks. Jack wiped gravy off his chin and grinned at Terry.

'How do you fancy coming with me to the Rope Works? It's a fair walk, take us half-an-hour at least, but we've got all afternoon.'

'I can't, Uncle Jack. I'm off collecting bommie with the gang. Then we're having a meeting.'

'A meeting?' his mam said, frowning. 'About what?'

Terry's stock had never been so high. Word had got round that he had an uncle living in his house, handsome as a film star and a war hero to boot who'd fought with the Desert Rats. Together Jack and Monty had kicked Rommel's arse clear across Africa.

'It's like a war council. We're sorting out our tactics and stradge-ity. Or summat.'

'Tactics and strategy,' Jack said. 'Good for you, Terry lad. Got to stop the other gangs pinching your bommie. Give 'em what's what. Chase 'em all the way back to South Street!'

Joe said, 'What you doing, Jack, putting such daft ideas in their heads? They're a bunch of kids, not the 8th Army.'

'Not that daft if it stops their bommie getting nicked.' Jack winked at Terry. 'You can't have a bonfire without any wood. We're all looking forward to it, aren't we? Roasted spuds, black peas. treacle toffee, parkin ...'

'I do enjoy bonfire night, I must admit,' Barbara said. 'Apart from the bangers. Joe isn't all that keen. I don't think he's been to one of their bonfires yet.'

'Well, it's simple – no bommie wood, no bonfire, sis. These lads have put a lot of effort in. Can't let it get nicked after all that hard work.' Jack pushed his plate away and stood up. 'Mustn't allow the enemy to step in at the eleventh hour, Terry, can we?' He raised his fists in a boxer's pose and jabbed the air. 'Biff 'em, that's what I say.'

Joe looked at the ceiling. 'Enemy,' he muttered. 'Must have spent too long in the desert.'

'I wish you wouldn't fill their heads with all this war stuff, Jack. For goodness' sake, we had six years of it. I want to forget all that and settle down to some peace and quiet. Some normality for a change.'

'So you'd rather they give in to the South Street bully boys?' Jack's face had clouded over and his eyes had gone hard. 'Don't you get it, sis? You've got to stand up to them, not cave in like a bunch of cissies.' He opened the stairs door. 'That's what some of us were fighting for overseas while certain other people had a cushy number back in Blighty.'

'What other people?' Joe looked up.

'No names, no pack drill.'

'And some of us have full-time jobs instead of sponging on other folk,' Joe said thickly as Jack's footsteps thudded up the stairs.

Barbara gathered the plates up and dropped them into the enamel bowl in the sink with such an almighty clatter that Terry grabbed his windjammer from behind the back door and was outside in two shakes of a donkey's tail.

'You need a plan, everything worked out in advance, down to the last detail. The first priority is to secure your flanks and seal off the perimeter. Control everything coming in and going out of Denby. That means checkpoints and guardposts. Where's the map?'

Terry unfolded the map and spread it out.

'Where's that come from?' Kevin Hartley asked.

'I asked Terry to do it,' Jack said. 'I could remember most of the terrain, the general lay of the land, but Terry's good at drawing with his coloured pencils. We need a checkpoint here, at the end of Hovingham Street adjoining the main road. Stop anyone entering without proper authority. Another one here, to block off the Common.'

'What about the pens?' Spenner said. 'They can come through there dead easy, it's pitch-black.' Terry studied Spenner's face in the glow of candlelight for any signs of jealousy or reluctance; he had worried that being the oldest and the leader up to now, Spenner might resent Jack taking over like this, but no, he seemed as keen as the rest of them. Terry claimed the idea to ask Uncle Jack for help was his, though if he was being honest, it might have been Roy or Dougie. As it turned out, Jack hadn't needed asking twice. He said yes, straight off, and accompanied his nephew down to the shelter to give the gang what he called 'a briefing'.

'That's just a narrow ginnel, isn't it?' Jack bent over the map, frowning. 'Less than three feet wide as I recall. We need to seal it off somehow.'

'Barbed-wire?' Kevin said. 'Me dad's got some on his allotment. It's a bit rusty.'

'Good thinking, Kevin. Barbed-wire emplacement. Just the job.' Jack traced the map with his finger. 'That's three possible danger points covered. Your HQ is in a good position really, with the river securing your rear.'

'Couldn't they get across?' Alec said. 'I've seen Brian Creegan on a raft near Nile Street, oil drums and planks lashed together.'

'Not likely if you think about it. They'd have to cart the wood the length of Gower Street and up Oswald Street – stretch their lines of supply to the limit. Now then, Spenner, let's get the ranks sorted.'

'Ranks?' Spenner said, puzzled.

'You're the CO, Commading Officer. Who's your Communications Officer?'

'Um ... er ...' Spenner looked round the circle. 'Dougie.'

'Right, Dougie, it's your job to alert HQ in the event of an attack. How are you going to do it? By what means?'

'Wave a flag?'

'Are you in direct line-of-sight with Kellett Street and the Common? Can you see 'em both from here?'

'Yeh.'

'What about at night?'

There was a silence. 'Carrier pigeons?' a voice said.

'Who said that?' Jack asked.

'Mitch,' Spenner said. 'Sir.'

'Use your loaf, Mitch. We're sending messages two hundred yards, not from here to Timbuktu. And it'll be dark.'

Terry said, 'What about candles in jam-jars? We could work out signals. Up and down means all clear. Side to side means enemy approaching.'

'Not bad, not bad,' Jack said. 'What about friend approaching?'

'Big letter F for "Friend",' Malc suggested.

'That's daft that is,' Dougie said. 'Do a circle. Round and round—'

'That's stupid. Circle dun't stand for owt.'

'Not as stupid as a big letter F.'

'Your idea's even more stupid—'

'Not as stupid as yours—'

'All right, you two, put a sock in it,' Jack said sharply. 'Can't have this, Captain Spenner. To be an effective fighting force we need discipline, not argy-bargy.'

'Very good, sir. Dougie, Malc – cut it out. Or else.'

'Am I still Communications Officer, sir?' Dougie asked anxiously.

'Yes. It's up to you to get organised. What do you need?'

'Flags, candles and jam-jars.'

'Good man,' Jack said, giving him a quick salute. Dougie stiffened with pride. 'Now let's see, who's next? Terry?'

'Yes Uncle ... sir.'

'You're the Liaison Officer. When Dougie receives a signal from the checkpoints he passes the message on to you and you report to the CO. Then if necessary Captain Spenner reports to me, as C-in-C. Commander-in-Chief. Is that clear?'

'Yes sir.'

'Kevin, as you have access to the barbed-wire we'll make you Supplies Officer. It's your task to supply whatever the troops need to defend our position and repulse invaders.'

'Where do I get the stuff ... supplies from?'

'Do what everybody else in the army does. Scrounge it.'

'Okay.' Kevin raised his eyebrows. 'Where from though?'

Jack said, 'A good officer uses his initiative. Now who's left?'

'Phil's not here,' Spenner said. 'That leaves Roy, Alec, Malc and Mitch, sir.'

Jack addressed the circle. 'Roy, you're the officer in command of Kellett Street – Checkpoint K. Alec, you're officer in charge of the Common – Checkpoint C. Malc can watch the pens – Checkpoint P. Dougie, see to it that these officers are issued with flags, candles and jam-jars, signalling, for the use of.'

'Very good, sir.'

'Right, that's that,' Jack said, beaming all round. 'Everybody happy?'

'What about me?'

'What about Mitch, sir?' asked Spenner.

'How old is he?'

'Eleven next Tuesday,' Mitch piped up.

'You be a soldier then.'

Mitch's face fell. 'Is that all?'

'You can't have an army without soldiers,' Jack pointed out.

'Yeh but – I'm the only one!'

'Somebody has to take orders,' Jack said, folding the map.

Mitch carried on grumbling that it wasn't fair, just because he was the youngest, and everyone was an officer bar him, until Spenner barked out: 'Quiet! No talking in the ranks!'

'One other thing,' Jack said. 'IDs.'

Everyone looked blank but no one wanted to betray their ignorance by asking the question.

'Passes,' Jack said. 'Identification. Can't have civilians traipsing back and forth without proper papers. They could be enemy agents, fifth columnists, saboteurs even. Liaison Officer, see that identity cards are issued to all relevant personnel.'

'Right, sir,' Terry said. 'Who are them exactly … rel-ev-ant persons?'

'Everybody living within the sealed zone.'

'You mean all of Denby?'

'Correct. Kellett Street, Hovingham Street and Cayley Street.'

'That's hundreds,' Terry said. 'How do I do all them?'

'I've seen a John Bull printing kit on the shelf next to your bed. Should be a doddle printing ID cards. Couple of hours at most. Take one of the men and distribute them to every house.'

'Who should I take?'

'Who should he take, Captain Spenner?'

'I suggest Private Mitch, sir.'

'Good thinking. You and Private Mitch get it organised between you.'

The meeting was over. They filed outside into the encroaching twilight. The gaslamps were just coming on. Mitch had found something else to grumble about – 'being stuck with a kid's John Bull printing kit' – until Spenner jabbed a finger. 'That man there. Pipe down!'

Jack rubbed his hands. 'Right, we've all plenty to do, let's get on with it. Everybody assemble here for reports and debriefing at nineteen hundred hours tomorrow. Any questions?'

There was an awkward silence until Roy plucked up the courage to ask what time nineteen hundred hours was.

'Seven o'clock after tea. And one last thing.' Jack touched a finger to his lips. 'Keep this buttoned. What's been said here goes no further. Careless talk and so on. Anyone caught blabbing to *anybody* will be severely reprimanded. Dismiss them, Captain Spenner.'

'Very good, sir!'

The Gang stood and watched in silence as Jack strode off along the Bottom Track. Somebody said under their breath, 'Steaming Nora, Terry... your Uncle Jack. He's teriff!'

'Fan-bloody-tastic!'

'As good as Monty.'

'Bugger Monty. The C-in-C beats him any day.'

Terry didn't say a word. He imagined if he did he might burst with pride.

Wearing only vest and trousers, feet bare to the kitchen fire, Joe leaned back in the rocking-chair. 'What you rooting for?'

'I've lost me comic.'

'Which comic?'

'*Rover*. I was halfway through a story before tea.'

'You'll ruin your eyes with all that reading. Have you fed your pigeons?'

'Here it is,' Barbara said, finding the comic under a cushion. 'What do you expect it to do, our Terry, jump up and wave its arms around and shout, "Here I am, here I am!"'

'Thanks, mam.' If Terry had a tanner for every time his mother had said those exact same words he'd have had enough for a brand-new bike. He looked up as footsteps thumped down the stairs and Jack came into the kitchen. To Terry's dismay he was dressed to go out.

'What's that yer reading, Terry?'

'Alf Tupper.'

'Tough of the Track still scoffing his fish and chips and living under the viaduct.' Jack pushed back his glossy black hair with his fingertips. 'I'm sure I've got a pile of old *Rovers, Hotspurs* and *Wizards* somewhere from before the war. Wilson. Morgyn the Mighty. Baldy Hogan. I bet I've got some Dinkies as well somewhere. I'll root 'em out for you.'

'Thanks, Uncle Jack.'

'Shouldn't you be down at the shelter?' Jack lowered his voice. 'Who's on guard?'

'Kevin, Roy and Private Mitch. The rest are coming down later for that thing ... what do you call it?'

'De-briefing.' Jack pulled a face. 'We'll have to cancel that, sorry. You're on half-term, aren't you? Tell 'em tomorrow afternoon instead.'

Terry became aware that his dad had taken an interest in the conversation, and using his initiative as officers were supposed to do, burst out: 'Hey, guess what – Spenner found an air-raid siren with a wooden handle down in his cellar! You want to hear it!'

Barbara looked up from her *Woman's Friend*. 'I have damn well heard it. What a racket! You'll have the bobbies round, investigating. Them daft cards you've printed out's bad enough, like being back in wartime. Milkman's got to have one, window-cleaner. The fella from Stead's coal merchant was having a fit. He said two kids stopped him at a "checkpoint" and asked for his "ID papers" or summat. He couldn't get his wagon through because there was barbed-wire blocking half the street.'

'Don't trust nobody, that's my motto,' Jack said, stooping to straighten his tie in the small cloudy mirror next to the geyser. 'He could've been a spy for all you know.' He pulled on his overcoat. 'Ta-ra then, see you later.'

'Where you off to?' Joe asked him.

'A bloke I was demobbed with works for a haulage firm on Rugby Road. Maybe he can put a word in for me. I'm meeting him in Yates's Wine Lodge.'

'Can you drive a wagon?' Terry asked.

'That's what I did in the Forces. Driver-mechanic, four-tonners. Drove all the way to Benghazi and back.'

'Jack – why don't you take Eileen to the pictures for a change?' Barbara suggested. 'Or the Carlton.'

'Who?'

'Eileen Kershaw! Who do you think?'

Jack shrugged and gave a sheepish grin. 'What with, brass washers? I'm hard up as it is.'

'Good job Yates's have started taking brass washers then,' Joe said, raising his voice as the door scraped over the lino and banged shut. Joe Webb never set foot inside a pub except at weddings and funerals. Even in his younger days, a pint of shandy was his tipple.

'Terry,' his mam said, pointing to the yard. 'Pigeons.'

'Let me just finish this last bit. Alf's beating a toff on the final lap.'

Barbara turned several pages of her magazine like whipcracks, her eyes not focused. 'I don't know why you have to keep harping on at him,' she said half under her breath. 'Jack's doing his best.'

'Aye, doing his best drinking,' Joe said. 'Why does he have to meet up with blokes in the pub?'

'Where's he supposed to meet them, in the cemetery?'

'In his case it'd be the Cemetery Hotel on Bury Road. If he was really trying to find a job he'd have got fixed up by now.'

Barabara was tight-lipped. 'You know bugger-all, Joe, about anything Jack's trying to do.'

Terry held the *Rover* close to his face, hardly daring to breathe. It was rare to hear his mother swear; maybe plates and dishes would start flying soon.

'I'll tell you what I do know,' Joe said, tempting fate. 'Your kid brother shows more interest playing at soldiers with the Denby gang than he does finding paid work. Wouldn't surprise me if he started swapping tabcards and Dinkies with Dougie Milne and building skyscrapers with Terry's Meccano set. He's twenty-five and he acts like he's twelve. About time he settled down with that lass who's supposed to be keen on him.'

'You forget, you – Jack wasn't even eighteen when he got called up. He's moved about all over since he was demobbed, never had the chance of a steady girlfriend.'

Joe yawned and scratched his armpit. 'Not likely to get one, either, the way he's shaping.'

'Do you think he's not trying to get a job?' Barbara demanded, homing right in on the nub of the matter. 'Deliberately on purpose?'

'What I'm saying, woman, if you'll just listen, is we can't keep feeding him and providing a roof over his head for ever and always and . . .' Joe waved his hand in the air, trying to find a way to express the far-distant future or eternity or till the cows came home, whichever was longest.

Barbara's face had closed up like a clenched fist.

She glared at him, biting her lips white. From the corner of her eye she caught sight of Terry lurking behind the *Rover* and the next moment he got a right belter on the back of his head, bringing tears to his eyes. 'How many *more* times do I have to tell you? Get them pigeons fed. Now! Go on! Out!'

Raid on South Street

*

'**K**EEP IT DOWN,' SPENNER SAID. 'LET'S HAVE A bit of hush. The C-in-C has summat to say.'

'Thank you, Captain Spenner. Right then, listen carefully. I've decided to set up a Long-Range Bonfire Raiding Party. Its first task is to strike behind enemy lines.'

Water dripped from somewhere in slow plops. Somebody cleared his throat and somebody else's shoe scraped on the concrete floor. Otherwise there was complete rapt silence from the circle of lads in the candlelight.

'I'm going to hand-pick the team,' Jack said, 'but first you need to know what the mission is before you become a member of the L R B R P. It'll be dangerous, you'll need strong nerves, and you'll have to stay out after ten or even later. So have a careful think first if you're selected.'

'Sir, sir – I want to go. Pick me, sir!'

'Pipe down, Private Mitch,' Spenner said.

Jack held up his hand and they all leaned forward to catch every word.

'Our objective is to raid the South Street gang.'

There was an audible intake of breath.

'Strike at the heart of the enemy. If we carry out the mission according to plan and keep our nerve, we can be in and out before they even know it.'

'How the bleedin' hell do we manage that?' Kevin muttered in Terry's ear.

'Spenner, who's their leader?' Jack asked.

'Brian Creegan.'

'Aye, I remember now, yes. The lad with a big gob on him. Another loud-mouth bully who needs sorting out.' Jack lit up a Park Drive. 'I have a request. I need some of you to stay behind at HQ. We don't want to leave ourselves open to a sneak attack while we're away. Dougie, I'll put you in charge. That okay with you?'

'Count on me, sir.'

'That's the spirit. I want Spenner, Roy, Kevin, Malc and Terry as members of the LRBRP. You lot can stay out up till ten o'clock, can you?'

'You would get picked,' Mitch hissed in Terry's ear. 'Just 'cos he's your uncle.'

'Nowt to do with it —'

'I bet you asked him —'

'I didn't!'

'Oi, you two!' Spenner drew his hand like a knife-blade across his throat. 'Carry on, sir.'

'Assemble back here at twenty-one hundred hours, nine o'clock on the dot, wearing windjammers, balaclavas and black socks.'

'Sir?'

'Yes Kevin?'

'I haven't got any black socks.'

'Dark blue or brown then. I'll supply the boot blacking.'

Malc gave a whine of anguish. 'We don't have to polish our shoes, do we?'

'It's not *for* your shoes, it's for your face. This night op is going to be run by the book.'

They crossed Entwisle Road under the Arches and walked up Oswald Street as far as Selby Street. After a few moments to make sure the coast was clear they moved into the shadows of the back-entry behind the terraced row that ran parallel with the railway embankment. From here there were two ways to South Street: up the hill to the main road, left under the bridge, then turn back on yourself, or the short way over the embankment and down the other side – which was quicker but also riskier because they would be exposed crossing the railway lines. Anyone posted to keep a look-out couldn't fail to spot them. Jack had already made his mind up. He climbed over the fence made of railway sleepers and started up the embankment, the rest following in a straggling file. As they neared the top, Roy said between gasps: 'I don't get it. We haven't brought our bogies with us. How do we carry the wood back?'

This hadn't occurred to Terry. 'Not a clue.'

'He's *your* uncle.'

'So what? I'm not a bleeding mind-reader. Why don't you ask him?'

Kevin came up behind them, mumbling and cursing. 'This boot polish is running down me neck. If it gets on me shirt collar me mam'll kill me.'

Terry had the same fear. The stuff was awful. His forehead and cheeks felt stiff where the blacking had dried to a crust, though the edges were sticky with sweat.

One by one they crossed the lines, taking extreme care not make a noise stepping on the loose chunks of granite ballast between the sleepers. If anyone was watching it was a dead cert they would be seen, clearly visible under the dull yellow illumination from at least three gaslamps. Soon they were safely across, with no shout or alarm given, and descending the embankment to where Jack crouched in the shelter of some bushes and gathered them round. From up here they could see the compound where the South Street gang stored their wood. At one time, just after the war, it had been a dump for old army trucks and vans being broken up for spare parts, and was well protected by an eight-feet high perimeter fence of steel mesh. A pair of double gates reinforced with corrugated metal sheets was the only entrance.

Jack produced a torch from the bulging pockets of the battle-dress tunic he was wearing, which had faint patches on the sleeves where the badges had been removed.

'I'm going on a recce. When it's okay to move, I'll give you the signal. Three long flashes means it's all clear.'

'What if it's not?' Kevin said. 'You know, danger.'

'Two quick flashes, pause, two more quick flashes.'

'Two quick flashes, bugger off,' Spenner said. 'Roger.'

Jack moved down the slope leaving the rest of them in a huddle. Terry found he was shivering and it wasn't a particularly cold night. This game of raiding another gang to steal their bonfire wood was turning into something else, and he didn't know what to call it, except it felt more serious and far more dangerous than any game. The fact that it was Brian Creegan and his gang they were raiding made his balls shrivel. Without Jack as leader of course, none of them, not even Spenner, would have dared anything so mad and reckless.

'There it is!' Kevin said. 'Three flashes.'

Jack was waiting in the shadow of a gable end, where the dirt banking and muddy grass met the cobbled street, his breath pluming into the air.

'The wood's been stacked up to make a den.' The five lads had to lean in to catch his whisper. 'I counted three sitting inside it with a lamp. Could be a few more.' Three and maybe a few more; Terry felt his bowels rumbling. 'The gate's not padlocked,' Jack said, 'but it could be barred on the inside. We need to create a diversion.'

'A what?' Spenner said.

'Make a row – a racket. Malc, see that end garage. Bang on the side with a brick. Make as much noise as you can.'

'On me own?'

'It's just to get 'em to open the gate. As soon as they do, the rest of us'll be waiting, ready to pounce.'

'Pounce on what?' Kevin said.

'The prisoner.'

There was a silence that stretched out for ages.

'This is a raiding party,' Jack said, looking at each of them in turn. 'Raiding parties take prisoners. That's what we're going to do. Come on.'

'Wait ... no, wait,' Roy said in a frantic whisper. 'You mean capture somebody?'

'That's what I said.'

'One of the South Street gang?'

'That's our mission.'

'What do we do with him?'

'Take him back to HQ for interrogation. Now, all ready?' Jack pointed to the dark silhouette of the garage. 'When you get there, Malc, count to fifty and start your racket. Kevin, you keep watch. If you see anybody coming down the street, give a whistle. Once we've snatched him, you and Malc do a quick scarper. If anybody gets separated we'll rendezvous back at base. Right, off you go!'

They waited until they saw Malc reach the garage, then moved in single file towards the mesh fence, stepping lightly over the stony ground. There was no one on guard. Inside the compound, as Jack said, the long lengths of timber and some doors had been stacked into a makeshift den. Through the gaps filtered the steady beam of a lantern, partly obscured by seated figures, and at this closer distance they could hear fragments of voices and laughter.

Following Jack's signal, Spenner and Roy flattened themselves against one of the corrugated iron gates. Jack pulled Terry to the other side and whispered in his ear, 'I need your windjammer. Empty the pockets.' When Terry had taken it off Jack zipped it up again. He took a piece of washing-up line from the side pocket of his tunic and wound it loosely round the windjammer. Terry was so intrigued by this that he jumped out of his skin when Malc's diversion shattered the peaceful night. Dogs started barking furiously in nearby backyards. A minute later, footsteps thudded across the compound and there was the sound of a bolt sliding back.

'Who is it, Bri?' a voice called from the den.

'Somebody playing silly buggers down at the end garage,' Brian Creegan said, poking his head round the gate. He shouted back, 'You stay here, Hoggy, I'll go and sort the pillock out.'

As he pulled the gate shut Jack stepped up behind Creegan and slotted the windjammer like a bag over his head, criss-crossing the flapping arms and knotting them together at the back of his neck. He looped the clothes-line round and round and drew it tight so that Brian Creegan was trussed up like a chicken. The big lad started cursing and swinging his arms through the air in futile punches. Spenner grabbed one arm and Roy the other, and with Jack's arm round his neck the three of them frogmarched him towards the back-entry.

Hoggy's voice floated over the fence: 'Did you get him, Bri? Smack 'im one for me. Bring him here and I'll smack 'im one meself.' Evidently under the illusion that his mate was leathering some poor kid.

Brian Creegan was still raging and struggling but the words were too muffled to make sense. Half-dragging, half-pushing, feet slithering in the dirt, they got him into the darkness of the gable end before any of them realised there was a problem. Going back the way they had come, over the embankment, was out of the question. But if they took the prisoner the usual way into Denby, which was across the main road and along Hovingham Street, it would take the South Street gang less than five minutes to track them down.

While they dithered over this, they could hear Hoggy opening the gate to find out what was happening, and Terry had a brainwave. 'Take him down the Ginnel! I bet they won't think of going through the pens.'

Spenner was losing his rag. He said, 'Right – come on. If we're gonna do this, let's do it!'

Part way down the back-entry they found reinforcements, Kevin and Malc, but even with the six of them it was a comedy performance, sliding in the dirt and tripping over flagstones, all done in almost total darkness. The trickiest bit was crossing the steep cobbled slope of Brunswick Street (from the top they could have been easily seen) and then they were safely past the telephone box on the corner of Trafalgar Street (which still held creepy memories for Terry) and at last down into the pitch blackness of the Ginnel, which they all knew like the backs of their hands, and into Denby, home and dry.

His head still wrapped in Terry's windjammer, Brian Creegan was lying motionless on the floor of the shelter, which was thick with dust and littered with dimps. He'd given up cursing and struggling several minutes ago. Terry wasn't sure he was even breathing. A terrible thought struck him. What if Creegan had suffocated to death? Or been strangled with the clothes-line? Terry was almost too scared to look at his Uncle Jack in the beams of several candles propped in wall niches. Under the wavering light, his uncle's face with its coating of boot polish streaked with runnels of sweat reminded Terry of something like a witch-doctor's mask. Seeing it, Terry felt a spasm of terror as he recalled sleeping in the back bedroom with his mam, the night they'd been to the Ceylon, and the Man in the Iron Mask was creeping up the stairs to get them. That had been terrifying, but it was a film, it was all in the imagination; this was happening.

Some of the other lads glanced at Jack, Terry noticed, and looked away, as if the vision was too disturbing.

Jack took out a packet of Park Drive and lit up. He tossed the packet to Spenner, with a gesture of help yourself. Spenner took one and passed them on.

With so many bodies in such a confined space the shelter had a fetid air, like the smell of dried cold sweat. This wasn't due to just their recent exertions – carrying Creegan's dead weight after he'd gone limp and slumped to the ground. There was also the odour of danger, of fear, and the shocking unknown. All the gang could sense it, as if reality had been pushed out of shape, and they were explorers on an alien planet. The unimaginable might happen any second.

'Roy, take the windjammer off his head. Get him up and sat on that box.'

Brian Creegan blinked his eyes open. He looked round, his head wobbling slightly, two wet trails from his nostrils caused by his restricted breathing. Gradually his gaze swam back into focus. His head jerked back in fright at the sight of the faces all around him streaked with black and white stripes where the sweat had run down. He said, 'Jesus Mary Joseph.'

'Not much the big man now, are we, Creegan?'

Brian Creegan frowned at Jack, shaking his head. 'Who the hell are you?'

'The Bogie Man.'

'You're a bloke, you,' Creegan said, realising the others were lads of roughly his own age. He looked at them more closely and recognised Terry. 'Christ, it's the Denby lot.' He bared his teeth and croaked a laugh with no humour in it. 'You bunch of twats must be crackers. Soon as my gang find out, they'll come down on you like a ton of bricks and paste the hides off the lot of you. They'll have your guts for garters—'

'Watch it,' Spenner spat at him. 'That's our C-in-C you're talking to.'

'Your what?'

Jack stood with the cigarette dangling from his lips. 'I know your type, met 'em all over, the loud-mouth bully, big talk and no balls.'

'What you on about?'

'I'm on about you, Creegan. Picking on kids half your size.'

'Wrong fella. Not me, chum.'

'You're forgetting – chum – I was here when you were thump-ing my nephew, Terry Webb. Dead easy when you're a big lump and they're a lot smaller than you. Oh yeh, you're strong and they're weak so you think you can trample all over 'em —'

'Are you puddled or what?'

Spenner barked, 'Don't interrupt the C-in-C.'

'I don't like bullies, Creegan. And I don't bloodywell like the look of you. You're nothing but a fat tub of yellow lard.'

'I'm not scared of you.'

'You better be, chum.'

'Who says?'

'A tough guy,' Jack said, wiping his chin, leaving a dark smear. 'I think we've got a tough guy,' nodding to himself. 'Another George Raft.' Jack put his hand in his side pocket and pulled out the Luger. His face and eyes had gone the same, clouded and hard, as in the kitchen in Cayley Street when he'd spoken of what he'd been fighting for. 'How tough are you really, George?'

'My name's Brian.'

'Shitehawks and corruption,' a voice whispered. 'Is that a real gun?'

'Yeh,' Terry said under his breath. 'It is real.' His lips felt numb.

Jack pulled back the bolt with two hooked fingers, released it and let the oiled mechanism snap forward on its powerful spring. The sound was satisfyingly solid.

'That's one in the chamber.'

Brian Creegan wasn't convinced. 'Ton of crap. It's not even loaded. You've got no slugs.'

Jack sighted down the barrel at him. 'I hear you like sticking kids in dustbins and setting a fire going underneath. That's the kind of bastard you are. I bet you'd even do it to a puppy, would-n't you, George? You're just the fucking type, I can tell. Would you do it to a puppy, George, I think you would. I bet you'd even enjoy it, roasting a little puppy in a dustbin.' A muscle twitched in Jack's cheek. His eyes were large, the whites showing. 'Terry, go and get Champ, bring him here, let's see what George would do to him. If he's got the nerve.'

'I don't kill puppies,' Brian Creegan said. 'My name's not George.'

Terry was half-prepared to go and fetch Champ. His Uncle Jack had told him to. Should he go and get him? So Brian Creegan could kill him? That didn't make sense.

Jack aimed down the barrel. 'If I pull the trigger, nothing will happen. Is that what you're saying, George? Is that your guess?'

'You don't have any bullets, it's against the law. You'd get arrested.'

Jack fired. The explosion was like a bomb going off. It reverberated inside the concrete walls, back and forth, deafening them. There was the sound of tinkling glass, which was the jam-jar with a candle in it that Jack had been aiming at.

'Jesus Mary Joseph,' Brian Creegan said from the floor, where he'd gone sprawling on his back. 'You could fucking kill somebody with that thing.'

Jack stood over him, pointing the Luger. 'What do you say now, George?'

'I don't know, honest I don't. What do you want me to say?'

Jack pulled the bolt back and reloaded, moving the barrel to within a few inches of Creegan's forehead. 'I asked you a question. Tell me.'

'Tell you about what?'

'I want to know.'

'What about?'

'You'd murder Champ, wouldn't you? I think you would, you bastard.'

'Who's Champ?'

'I want to know about George Raft.'

'What about him?'

'What about him? *What about him?*' The gun barrel was touching Creegan's forehead. 'You are fucking about him! You fucking evil swine. You'd kill my Champ just for the fun of it, wouldn't you? Say it! Admit it!'

'I don't know any Champ,' Brian Creegan said. The sweat was pouring off him. 'Is he your puppy?' He screwed his eyes shut. 'Jesus Mary Joesph. Don't, please. I wouldn't harm a puppy, ask anybody.' The circle around him drew back as the smell wafted up in waves, the lad having pissed and crapped himself.

During the Holidays

*

ON WEDNESDAY AFTERNOON DURING THE HALF-term holiday Terry cycled over to Gowers Street. The day was dry and cold, with a sharpness in the air that made the rims of his ears tingle. He was hoping that Margaret would invite him inside the house. Both her parents were at work, so it seemed a golden opportunity. The fly in the ointment was Margaret's younger sister Lyn, a precocious eight-year old brat who understood all Terry's dirty jokes and double meanings even when he took the trouble to make them unintelligible to her.

The jokes led quite naturally to smutty talk and Terry started to boast about what had happened (or supposedly happened) with Laura Parfitt and Sandra Weeks down the Figure 7. He was hoping it would get Margaret going, but all that it aroused was her sister Lyn's voracious curiosity, so that she asked endless questions about the meaning of such words as 'having a bit', 'dropping them', 'groping' and 'finger-pie'.

For an eight-year old kid she was intolerable, and Terry had the sneaking suspicion that she already knew what these expressions meant and was just having him on for a giggle. He said to Margaret, 'Does she always have to hang round? Can't she stay with her auntie or something?'

'I'm not going,' Lyn said defiantly, clenched fists by her side. 'It's my house. I'm staying here with Margaret. She's got to look after me.'

'What about your own friends?' Terry said truculently. 'Why don't you go and play with kids your own age?'

'Don't want to.'

'What if I give you a penny for some toffees?'

'Still not going. It's my house. Can't make me.' She smirked at him and stuck her tongue out, knowing he was beaten.

'She's a pain in the ...' Terry said under his breath.

'Arse,' Lyn said. She turned to Margaret. 'Arse is your bum, isn't it? Me dad's always saying that.'

Even worse, Margaret seemed to find the situation amusing, apparently not a bit bothered whether Lyn stayed or went. This vexed and disappointed Terry, who had coldly planned his campaign to get Margaret in her house during the holidays. He'd had enough of girls thinking him mard and nice, it never got you anywhere, and he'd vowed to become a dirty sod like Shap and Colin Purvis.

The afternoon wore on, kids playing on the pavement with whips and tops and chalking the flags for hopscotch. Housewives came to their front steps to beat doormats against the wall or empty tea leaves down the drain. The life of the street went on around the three of them and they were part of it, and yet separate, in a little closed world of their own. Terry racked his brains for a way to get Margaret inside, away from the interference of Lyn, but the answer to his prayer (if there was an answer) eluded him. At one point a police car followed by a cream-coloured ambulance with a clanking bell shot past on the main road, raising Terry's hopes that Lyn would run to the end of the street to see what was happening, but no such luck. He even prayed for a thunderstorm, which would drive all of them indoors, but for once the weather let him down.

'When are you having your bonfire?' Margaret asked.

'This Saturday.' That was three days away. Terry was filled with anticipation and yet he felt sad. It would be his last bonfire in Denby: they were moving after Christmas to Kirkholt Estate.

But this one at least was still his to look forward to and enjoy.

'Do you always follow your big sister?' he said, a rankling irritability making his voice thin and peevish.

'She's *my* sister,' Lyn said, sticking her chin out and adopting a pose, hands on hips and head lifted haughtily, a regular little madam. 'I know what you want.'

'Do you?'

'Want to kiss her.'

'I don't.'

'You do.'

'*Don't*,' he said, digging his thumbs into the rubber handlebar grips.

'You've gone all red.'

'I haven't.'

'You have.'

'*Haven't*,' Terry said, an even deeper shade of beetroot.

'She wants to kiss you as well,' Lyn said.

'I do not,' Margaret said, confused, her green eyes shifting.

'You do, 'cos you wrote it in your diary!' Lyn said triumphantly. She was the complete mistress of the art of manipulation, wallowing in her power as arch torturer.

Terry gathered up all his patience and even managed a smile. 'You're a right little tearaway, aren't you?' he said not unkindly.

Lyn kicked the spokes in his front wheel. 'That's a swear word,' she said accusingly.

'Is it heck,' Terry said. 'And stop kicking me spokes, you'll buckle 'em.'

She kicked them again out of sheer defiance.

'I said quit it.'

'What if I don't, what if I don't?' she chanted.

'*Lyn!*' Margaret said, for the first time becoming annoyed. She glanced at Terry, sensing that his patience was wearing thin. 'I've got to do the washing-up. Do you want to come in?'

Terry propped his bike against the window sill.

'Me too, I'm coming as well——' Lyn said.

'No you're not,' Margaret said, and locked the front door behind them. Terry followed her through to the kitchen. There was a pile of dirty dishes in the sink. Margaret reached out to turn the geyser on and Terry spun her round and clamped his mouth against hers. She kissed him with tremendous passion: he could feel her sharp fingers through his pullover and shirt. The kiss lasted forever.

'We'll have to be quick,' Margaret said in the breath of a whisper.

'All right.'

'Let's go upstairs.'

Terry nodded.

They went halfway up the narrow staircase and had to stop to kiss again. He got his hand up her jumper and felt her bare back. They stood hard against one another on the worn stair-carpet in the semi-darkness, compressing the blood out of their lips. She moved up a step during the kiss and they broke away. She led him into the sepulchral stillness and quiet of the front bedroom, her parents' bedroom, with the embroidered pink eiderdown floating like a cloud under the grey light from the leaded window. The sight of that neat embroidered pink eiderdown generated within him such terror that he stopped dead inside the door, avoiding it with his eyes.

'What's up?' Margaret said.

They were strangers to each other now, as awkward and uncomfortable as two people alone together in a railway compartment.

Terry said, 'What time do they get home from work?'

'Ages,' Margaret said. 'Half-past five at the earliest.'

She looked at him, waiting for him to make the first move. Terry examined the wallpaper, the carving on the handles of the wardrobe, the objects on the dressing-table with unusual interest. He had somehow to take those three steps towards her and push her onto the neat embroidered pink cloud hovering in the corner of his vision. Strategy was everything; passion had fled.

'We'd better take our shoes off,' Margaret said.

Thankfully it was something to do. He took his shoes off, unfastening and loosening the laces before removing them. He put his shoes carefully side by side near the wardrobe. Then looking through the window and moving with discrete sideways steps towards her he said: 'You can see the Arches from here.'

Terry shut his eyes, turned his body blindly, trod on her foot, and kissed her on the chin. They fell onto the bed. The shock of it jarred his gums. He adjusted his lips to hers, simulating an intensity of feeling that in reality had flown away through the grey air and got lost somewhere beyond the Arches.

But her saliva tasted sweet. It brought him back solidly into the here and now to realise that he was on a bed with Margaret Parry in her house. What would Shap and Colin Purvis have to say about that?

He put his hands under her jumper and moved them upwards until his fingers touched what must have been, though he could hardly believe it, a brassiere. He had never unfastened a brassiere in his life. He tried manfully to perform the task.

Margaret said, 'What are you fidgeting with?'

'Don't worry, I've done it before,' he said airily.

'Well you won't get it off by breaking it.'

Terry kissed her again to stop her talking. During the kiss he wondered if he could get it off by gnawing through the strap. The bloody trouble was, there didn't appear to be a catch or a press-stud. And she was lying on his left hand, which meant that his fingers were inoperative; and he was getting pins and needles as well. He tried with his other hand to slide stealthily under the shallow cotton cup, but it was a tight squeeze. Margaret winced and said, 'Ouch.'

'What's up?'

'You can't do it like that. It's cutting me in half.'

The options were disappearing one by one.

Margaret sat up. She reached behind her and unfastened the strap.

'Haven't you undone one before?'

'Course,' Terry said. 'Loads.' He conjured up his laziest, most confident smile, lying back on the pink eiderdown; only the smile, when it came, was defective, sitting clumsily on his face.

Margaret lay back, the brassiere loose and ruckled under her jumper, making her chest lumpy and unattractive. She said: 'We'll have to be quick, I've got the washing-up to do.'

Terry kissed her again, gladly shutting his eyes to the drab daylight, moving his hand very slowly, pretending (both of them pretending) that he wasn't really moving it at all. It wasn't really moving, his hand, he wasn't moving it, and so it moved of its own accord, as it were, by default – not really moving (but moving all the same).

When it encountered the warm shallow rise both of them pressed their lips tighter together. His fingers touched the soft peak, as soft as a deflated marshmallow, and paused; partly in silent reverence and partly because his fingers didn't know what to do next.

They had to discontinue the kiss in order to breathe.

'Aren't they soft,' Terry said in a reverential murmur.

'It makes me want to wee when you touch the tip,' Margaret said.

He pushed the jumper and brassiere out of the way and looked at the first young girl's nipples he had ever seen in daylight. They were surrounded by goosepimples. He looked at them for a while. His own feelings were dormant. He felt nothing physical.

Margaret lay with her eyes closed, black curls on pink eiderdown, her lips dry and slightly parted so that he could see the shiny whiteness of her teeth inside. She breathed as if asleep.

A terrible thought had come to Terry. He could go no further. He had a disfigurement, unlike Taylor. He was prevented from pushing it inside because of the offending flap of skin. He was physically disbarred from proceeding any further. He was finished for life.

Margaret opened her eyes and he quaked.

'Why do you like looking at them?' she asked.

'Dunno.'

'Aren't boys funny?'

The bedroom lay around them, quiet, very still, attentive.

Terry wondered what he ought to do next, what he was capable of doing next. He couldn't remain forever in this state of paralysis. Did she expect him (was it necessary) to proceed further? His scheme for getting Margaret Parry into the house, up the stairs, on the bed, had worked, but he had made no provision for anything further. It had worked, he had done it, now what?

He was conscious of her two nipples staring up at him with inquisitive frankness, supported like two bulging eyes on their small white mounds.

His hand, when he touched them, had the quality of strangeness, as if it were newly created, as though he had never looked at his hand properly before. Touching her breast with his alien hand, he wondered what came next.

'We'll have to be quick,' Margaret said.

'All right.'

But he was far from all right. He was weary and faintly sick.

'They'll be home in an hour.'

An hour. What had he to do in that hour?

'Shall I take me knickers off?'

'If you want.'

She took them off and smoothed her skirt back into place. The next move was up to him. At least he could kiss her, which he did.

Aware that the furniture, the wallpaper, the objects on the dressing-table were watching and waiting in silent anticipation, he put his hand on her leg. This move, he was sure, hadn't escaped the attention of her vigilant nipples – which might have even swivelled downwards to observe the manoeuvre.

'Why do you keep stopping?' Margaret asked.

'It's better when you do it slow.'

'Why?'

'It just is.'

'Who says?'

When he seemed stuck for an answer she said, 'Touch it, Terry. Go on.'

He touched it, this warm fatty purse, without a nerve in his body. It was devoid of blemish, until his fingers, by misadventure, stumbled upon the mouth of the purse, so slyly hidden and secretive; he put the tips of two fingers inside, thinking: This is where she wees. I've got my fingers up Margaret Parry's fanny.

With this thought in mind at last there was a gentle uplifting of excitement and the kiss between them became imperative. At last he was able to feel something, a dormouse stirring from its winter sleep, uncurling from its snug little nest. Margaret said close to his ear:

'I've never let anybody touch it before.'

'Nobody at all?' Terry said, keeping his voice low so that the objects on the dressing-table wouldn't overhear.

(Yes he could feel a response, something was definitely moving, he wasn't dead or a robot after all. But the knowledge of his shameful deformity wouldn't go away. He knew what to do, but what good was that to him? He might just as well not have had one.)

'It tickles,' Margaret said drowsily.

'Is it nice?'

'Mmm.'

He could feel her heart beating against his chest. Perhaps she wasn't disappointed in him after all. Perhaps he was even capable of —

'Margaret!' Lyn's voice piped from the street. She was hammering on the front door with her fists. 'It's starting to rain! Let me in or I'll tell me mam!'

Margaret brushed his hands out of the way and stood up. She pulled on her navy-blue knickers and wriggled into them. She did this quite unashamedly, as though he wasn't there, and said, 'You won't brag to anyone, will you?'

Terry said seriously, 'We're going together; I won't say nothing to nobody.'

'I'll have to let her in,' Margaret said, putting on her shoes. 'Hurry up or she'll tell me mam on us.'

Terry put his shoes on and followed her down the stairs as if returning from the mountain-top, lord and master of all he surveyed, and offered to help with the washing-up.

Terry left the house with twenty minutes to spare before Margaret's mum and dad got home from work. He rode back whistling along the main road, wondering what there was for tea, bouncing over the cobbles into Cayley Street, where he stopped and got off his bike, thinking he'd ridden into a street party like the one they'd had just after the war, with trestle-tables and balloons and bunting and flags.

There weren't any tables or flags today, though all the doors were open. Dozens of people were standing on their front steps or on the pavement, even in the street itself. Terry wheeled his bike through them, mystified by all the commotion. He heard someone say, 'nervous breakdown I heard' just as he saw the ambulance standing outside No. 77 with its doors open. His heart constricted painfully in his chest, as if someone had squeezed it. His first thought was that his mam had collapsed. There was only so much the human mind could take. The strain of living with

Joe had finally snapped her sanity, as it was bound to do in the end.

Terry tried to urge himself forward but his guts felt hollow. His hands were welded to his bike and he might have fallen over without it. Then he saw the police car in front of the ambulance, a black Wolseley with a radio aerial. This altered the story in his head to the possibilty that Joe had throttled Barbara. They'd had another of their flaming rows, his mam had gone for the bread-knife and Joe had gone for her throat with his square workman's hands.

A policeman in a peaked cap on duty outside the front door moved aside to let a stretcher out with a body under a grey blanket, fastened down with leather straps. People in the street shuffled forward, craning to see, as the attendants struggled to lift the stretcher into the ambulance, needing the policeman's help. Terry heard a woman say, 'Apparently there was blood every-where, all over the bedspread and headboard.' The man with her said, 'Funny, I didn't hear a dickey-bird, did you? No bang or anything.' Another voice said, 'Blew his brains out, poor bugger. What a way to go.' A woman turned to her companion: 'What was he doing with a gun in the house? It's illegal,' and her com-panion said, 'He was one of Monty's lads, so I've heard. They say he couldn't settle — ' before a woman noticed Terry nearby and shushed her friend with a nudge, mouthing *Shurrup this is their lad.*

Cayley Street being a dead end, the cream-coloured ambulance had to reverse all the way down to Hovingham Street. The police car reversed after it. They backed onto the cobbled street and waited several moments, blue exhausts chugging, while one of the policeman went to talk to the driver of the ambulance. The policeman did some pointing and got back in the black Wolseley.

In just a few minutes it had become dark, as if a curtain had abruptly fallen. The gaslamp on the corner of Cayley Street splut-tered into its orange glow, and as the police car and the ambu-lance went slowly by and disappeared in the direction of Entwisle

Road, the gaslamp on the corner brought a memory to life, as vivid in Terry's eyes as a picture on a cinema screen. What he sees is a dark-haired broad-shouldered man in a khaki uniform striding past the gaslamp into the street carrying a kit-bag on his shoulder. And he sees a snotty-nosed urchin in short trousers pelting over the ruts and potholes towards the handsome brown-eyed soldier, feet barely touching the ground, yelling at the top of his lungs Uncle Jack, Uncle Jack, yelling over and over again, 'Uncle Jack! Uncle Jack!'

Trevor Hoyle was born in Lancashire, where he still lives. In his youth he was an actor in repertory and an advertising copy-writer; people with long memories will recall a weekly arts programme he wrote and presented for Granada TV.

Since the mid-seventies he has published fiction with John Calder, including *Vail*, a dystopian vision of Britain as a police state, and *Blind Needle*, a chase thriller set in the Lake District. *The Last Gasp*, an environmental disaster story, is currently under option in Hollywood. In 2003 Pomona reissued *Rule of Night*, a novel about skinheads in a northern town (originally published in 1975) which was *Time Out*'s Book of the Week and critically acclaimed in the *Guardian* and *City Life*.

More recently Trevor Hoyle has written for BBC Radio 4. His first play, GIGO, won the Radio Times Drama Award, and the actor in his play Randle's Scandals won the Sony award for his portrayal of rude Wigan comedian Frank Randle. As well as drama, he wrote and presented "The Lighthouse Invites the Storm" for Radio 4, in memory of the writer Malcolm Lowry. At the moment he is working on a novel, *Kingdom of Darkness*, about the takeover of Britain by a secret ultra right-wing group. www.trevorhoyle.com

Pomona Backlist

*

Pomona is a wholly independent publisher dedicated to
bringing before the public the work of prodigiously
talented writers. Tell your friends.
Our books can be purchased on-line at:

www.pomonauk.com

FOOTNOTE*

Boff Whalley

ISBN 1-904590-00-4

*Footnote** is clever, funny and irreverent – a story about a boy from the redbrick clichés of smalltown England reconciling Mormonism and punk rock, industrial courtesy and political insurrection.

He finds a guitar, anarchism and art terrorism and, after years (and years and years) of earnest, determined, honest-to-goodness slogging, his pop group† makes it big; that's BIG with a megaphone actually. They write a song that has the whole world singing and, funnily enough, it's an admirable summary of a life well lived – about getting knocked down and getting back up again.

Meanwhile, there's a whole world still happening: authentic lives carefully drawn, emotional but not sentimental and always with a writer's eye for detail. *Footnote* is not another plodding rock memoir but a compassionate, critical and sometimes cynical account of a life steeped in pop culture, lower division football and putting the world to rights.

---

* See page 293 of Boff Whalley's book.

† Boff Whalley is a member of Chumbawamba.

*

RULE OF NIGHT

Trevor Hoyle

ISBN 1-904590-01-2

If the Sixties were swinging, the Seventies were the hangover – darker, nastier, uglier – especially if you lived on a council estate in the north of England.

Rule of Night was first published in 1975 and has since become a cult classic. It pre-dates the current vogue for 'hard men' and 'football hoolie' books by 25 years.

It is, however, much more than this. Trevor Hoyle creates a chillingly detailed world, where teenagers prowl rainy fluorescent-lit streets dressed as their *Clockwork Orange* anti-heroes. The backdrop is provided by Ford Cortinas, Players No.6, the factory, the relentless struggle to maintain hope.

Hoyle, who has since been published by John Calder (home to Samuel Beckett and William S. Burroughs), has added a fascinating afterword to his original book which has been out of print and highly sought-after for many years.

THE FAN

Hunter Davies ISBN 1-904590-02-0

Hunter Davies is one of Britain's most acclaimed writers and journalists. He has written over 30 books, among them modern classics, *The Beatles* and *A Walk Around The Lakes*. *The Glory Game*, published in 1972, is a benchmark work on football and is still in print today.

The Fan is a collection of very personal, unusual pieces about his life as a supporter. He observes football in its sovereignty of the late 1900s and early 2000s and tackles the big topics of the day: Beckham's haircuts, high finance, the price of pies, the size of match day programmes, the enormous wages, the influence of Sky TV, England's numerous managers.

Along the way, he also lets us into his home life, in London and the Lake District, his family, his work, his tortoise, his poorly knee (caused by too much Sunday football).

Originally published in the *New Statesman* magazine, *The Fan* catches Davies at his very best and most amusing. It will appeal to supporters of any age, sex and loyalties.

*

LOVE SONGS

Crass ISBN 1-904590-03-9

> *Our love of life is total,*
> *everything we do is an expression of that.*
> *Everything that we write is a love song.*
> – Penny Rimbaud, *Yes, Sir, I Will*

CRASS: a rural collective based in Essex, formed in 1977 of a diverse and eclectic group of individuals who operated for several years using music, art, literature and film as vehicles to share information and ideas. They also wanted to change the world.

This is a collection of words spanning those seven short years; a book of shock slogans and mindless token tantrums. An anthology of passionate love songs that sought to inspire a generation, and succeeded.

SUM TOTAL

Ray Gosling ISBN 1-904590-05-5

Sum Total is a lost masterpiece of British literature, a restless, hungry riposte to America's finest Beat writers.

Written in 1961 when he was just 21, Gosling's itchy 'sort of' autobiography is a startlingly original take on the England of the early Sixties: rock 'n' roll, trains, dead-end jobs, drizzle, hitchhiking, jukebox cafés, trudging through hometown streets.

All the time he remains gloriously indulgent, disillusioned yet hopeful, tired but desperate for every new day.

Although now famous for hundreds of television and radio documentaries, in *Sum Total* Gosling reveals himself as a writer years ahead of his time, presenting a skew-whiff, arch and droll view of the world, both inside and out.

He has added a typically idiosyncratic and lengthy preface to the original text.

*

DIARY OF A HYPERDREAMER

Bill Nelson ISBN 1-904590-06-3

Bill Nelson is one of Britain's most respected creative forces. He came to prominence in the Seventies with Be Bop Deluxe and later Red Noise. He has collaborated with like-minds such as Yellow Magic Orchestra, David Sylvian, Harold Budd and Roger Eno and still releases a prolific amount of new music.

Diary of a Hyperdreamer is his day-by-day journal in which he ponders on life, art and the nation. His unique perspective is fed by a career creating and producing music, photography, painting and video.

Written from his home in a hamlet in north Yorkshire, he also includes engaging details of his family life, regular musings on mortality, along with reflections on his childhood and former life as a globe-trotting 'pop star.'

THE PRICE OF COAL

Barry Hines

ISBN 1-904590-08-X

Barry Hines is a master craftsman. While he is rightly celebrated for his classic, *A Kestrel for a Knave* (later filmed as *Kes*), his other work is equally powerful.

The Price of Coal is an uncompromising depiction of life at a colliery where beer, snooker, cricket and time spent on the allotment is the only respite from clawing coal from the earth.

A royal visit prompts the introduction of soft soap to the toilets, grass seeds scattered on the slag heap, and lashings of white paint across the site.

But when disaster strikes the superficial is forgotten as men fight for their lives in the darkness underneath collapsing seams of coal.

As ever, Hines proves himself an exemplary storyteller with a discerning eye for detail and when bolder, gaudier writing is long forgotten, his stays in the mind and nourishes it.

He has written a new foreword to the original text which was first published in 1979 and later adapted for television as two linked plays, directed by Ken Loach in the acclaimed *Play for Today* series.

*

LOOKS & SMILES

Barry Hines

ISBN 1-904590-09-8

Looks and Smiles is a lost bulletin from the early-Eighties when the sun felt to have set permanently on hope and optimism. Unemployment was rampant, especially in the north where traditional industries were laid waste by Margaret Thatcher and her government.

Set amid this gloom, *Looks and Smiles* is an under-stated love affair between unemployed school-leaver Mick and Karen who works in a town centre shoe shop. They both want little more from life than a decent chance.

Hines never resorts to sentimentality, and hope, however slender, flickers always.

The book was originally published in 1981 and later made into a film by Ken Loach.

ZONE OF THE INTERIOR
Clancy Sigal

ISBN 1-904590-10-1

'The book they dared not print', *Zone of the Interior* is a lost classic of zonked-out, high-as-a-kite Sixties literature. It tells the story of Sid Bell, an American political fugitive in London, who falls under the spell of Dr. Willie Last (partly modelled on the radical 'anti-psychiatrist' R D Laing). This unlikely duo feast on LSD, mescaline, psilocybin and psycho-babble, believing that only by self-injecting themselves with schizophrenia will they become true existentialist guerrillas. Their 'purple haze' odyssey takes them into the eye of the hurricane – mental hospitals, secure units for the violent, the Harley Street cabal of the 'Sacred 7' and semi-derelict churches that come complete with an underground tank for the woman convinced she's a fish. Sigal's approach is richly sardonic and anti-establishment, of both right and left, in a jazz-influenced free-form prose, comic and serious, myth-puncturing and elegiac. Along the way Sigal, now an established Hollywood screen-writer, makes the case for a revolutionary period of mental health nursing whose task is as yet undone.

*

KICKED INTO TOUCH (PLUS EXTRA-TIME)
Fred Eyre

ISBN 1-904590-12-8

Fred Eyre's sporting life began full of promise when he became Manchester City's first ever apprentice. He never made their first team. In fact, he seldom made anyone's first team. Injuries played a part but limited talent was the greater curse. As he plummeted down the leagues he had something few footballers possess: a stud-sharp memory and an ability to write humorously about the sport he loves.

Originally published in 1981, *Kicked Into Touch* has become an enigma – selling more than a million copies yet still retaining cult status within the sport and among fans. This new version has been completely revised, extended and updated with a new set of photographs included.

It is set to reach a new generation of football fans looking for an antidote to the glib reportage of a sport lost to show business.

MEAN WITH MONEY

Hunter Davies   ISBN 1-904590-13-6

At last, a book about money that tells it straight: put it under the bed. All of
it. Sure, it makes for easy access to burglars but better them than the felons
passing themselves off as financial advisors or acting as foot-soldiers for
organisations with words like union, mutual, trust, alliance, equitable or as-
surance in their name.

Mean With Money, inspired by Hunter Davies' well-loved column in *The
Sunday Times*, is wilfully short on practical advice but offers instead good humour and much-needed empathy as we face the corporate horror of high-
handed and indifferent financial institutions.

Davies, one of Britain's most celebrated writers, also looks at ingenious
ways to save money (cut your own hair, for starters) and what to do with it
when it arrives. Along the way, he reveals details of his regular visits to
McDonald's (it's free to use their toilets), the eccentric old ladies who staff his
local Oxfam shop and the swim that cost him £333.

Famous for seminal works on The Beatles, football, and subjects as diverse
as lottery winners and walking disused railway tracks, Davies is, once more,
on top form. Go get 'em Hunt.

*

THE ARMS OF THE INFINITE

Christopher Barker   ISBN 1-904590-04-7

Christopher Barker is the son of the cult writer Elizabeth Smart (*By Grand
Central Station I Sat Down and Wept*) and the notorious poet, George Barker.
The Arms of the Infinite takes the reader inside the minds of both parents and,
from their first fateful meeting and subsequent elopement, Barker candidly
reveals their obsessive, passionate and volatile love affair.

He writes evocatively of his unconventional upbringing with his siblings
in a shack in Ireland and, later, a rambling, falling-down house in Essex.
Interesting and charismatic figures from the literary and art worlds are
regular visitors and the book is full of fascinating cameos and anecdotes.

Barker is himself a gifted writer. An early draft of his memoir formed a
cover story for the literary magazine, *Granta*.

THE SECOND HALF

Hunter Davies ISBN 1-904590-14-4

The Second Half is another collection of personal pieces from the *New Statesman* covering three domestic seasons; the Euro Championship of 2004; and the 2006 World Cup when he unexpectedly became Wayne Rooney's top buddy.

'When a player gets sent off shouldn't we fans get some of our money back?' ponders Davies in one piece. 'I just wish he'd shave his stupid face,' he berates José Mourhino in another. And, goooaaal!, Hunt rumbles Sven early doors: 'He's a spare swede at a veggie gathering. What is the point of him?' he writes two years before England's World Cup debacle.

As ever, his outlook is fiercely that of the fan – disgruntled, bewildered and passionate – wondering what the players do with all that money, all those girls, and why match programmes are 'full of adverts or arse-licks for sponsors.'

And, finally, why did Peter Crouch? Because he saw Darren Bent, of course.

*

BELIEVE IN THE SIGN

Mark Hodkinson ISBN 1-904590-17-9

Believe in the Sign is about a damp corner of England where nothing much but everything happens. It is a 'sort of' memoir of a normal, average boy who would have grown up happily average and normal but for a dark and perverse passion: the seductive lure of masochistic devotion to a no-hope, near-derelict football club.

But it isn't all joyously uplifting. Swimming through the murk is a swarm of snapshots that bring growing up in the 1970s and 1980s into startling focus. Mad kids and sad kids and good kids from broken homes; teenage wrecking parties; pub brawls; long existential marches along the motorway banking; the baiting of Elton John and a club chairman caught playing 'away from home.'

Then Death bumps into Life. A girl is abducted and the town becomes a cave, the light sucked out. Meanwhile in the sunny shine outside, the future is afoot: cotton mills close down and supermarkets invade; school-leavers evolve into YOP-fodder and everyone's mum is holding Tupperware parties to get the down-payment on a colour telly.

Variously serious and funny, steely-eyed and tender, Hodkinson plumbs the depths but isn't afraid of the shallows. Dip a toe.

THE NOT DEAD

Simon Armitage ISBN 978-1-904-59018-7

"*The Not Dead* is uniquely impressive. In transmuting the stories of particular soldiers into the lyrical music of Simon Armitage's poems, something exceptional is achieved: the painful truth of lives damaged beyond help is made meaningful for the rest of us. We can only catch our breath and read them again and again."

– Joan Bakewell

*

THE RICHARD MATTHEWMAN STORIES

Ian McMillan & Martyn Wiley ISBN 978-1-904590-21-7

For a Yorkshireman who has spent half a lifetime in his native pit village, moving south is a mixed blessing and it is where Richard Matthewman's memories begin as he looks back with affection, humour, and no small measure of exasperation at 42 summers – and bitter winters. From boyhood through adolescence to marriage and a family, his stories are filled with a rich gallery of characters – the relations, friends and village notables of a vital community filled with life and incident but as brittle and unmistakably northern as the coal seams on which it was built.

Ian McMillan is a highly regarded poet, writer and performer from Barnsley. His work has led to extensive writing for Radio 1, 2, 3, 4 and Five Live as well as Yorkshire Television and BBC's *Newsnight Late Review*. He has been profiled on the *South Bank Show*.

The Richard Matthewman Stories were originally aired as a popular series on Radio 4. Co-author Martyn Wiley died in 1994.

THIS ARTISTIC LIFE
Barry Hines   ISBN 978-1-904590-22-4

An anthology of essays and stories by Barry Hines. Many of the pieces were written at the same time as *A Kestrel for a Knave* and have never been published before.

They cover Hines' love of sport along with his reflections on his home town of Hoyland Common, near Barnsley, both its landscape and the colourful characters that people it.

*

THE LAST MAD SURGE OF YOUTH
Mark Hodkinson   ISBN 978-1-904590-20-0

"A good group isn't about everyone being able to play well. You need people to shape it, give it heart. The best bands, the ones that matter, are a group of people singing about their lives, their mams and dads, the streets they came from, the crap jobs they've had, everything. And serving it all up pure to the public, saying, 'This is what we are – do you recognise any of it?' All the better if you were dragged up because punters see a kind of glamour in squalor. Ideally they'd like you to have been brought up by wolves, living half wild on the streets. That's what rock'n'roll is, why bands from these shitty estates get to be massive. And do you know why people like all this? It's because they're envious but rooting for you at the same time. Their own gang – the kids they grew up with – didn't stick together. They see you as someone who made it through and they want to be part of it. That's why they buy the records. It reminds them of what could have been."

The Last Mad Surge of Youth is an intelligent, literate work that sidesteps the usual clichés of rock novels. Its authenticity and authority is never compromised, a viewpoint held dear by punk and newwave. It is also about growing up, friendship, fame, addiction, love. And hope.

Forthcoming Titles

*

My Improper Mother and Me,
a biography of Lotte Berk
Esther Fairfax

ISBN: 978-1-904590-26-2

The Celestial Cafe
Stuart Murdoch

ISBN: 978-1-904590-24-8

J.D. Salinger: A Life Raised High
Kenneth Slawenski

ISBN: 987-1-904590-23-1

POMONA BOOKS

Pomona is a wholly independent publisher dedicated to bringing
before the public the work of prodigiously talented writers.
Our books can be purchased on-line at:

www.pomonauk.com

Pomona backlist